NIGHT MEDICINE

The Hotel Dick

"The plot is as devious as any of Donald Westlake's and hard-boiled enough to please Bill Pronzini fans. The end result is pure entertainment." –*Library Journal*

The Dead Genius

"With a narrative voice reminiscent of Dragnet's Joe Friday, and a spot-on style that subtly slips modernism into the smooth, often humorous telling, Brand has written a sound period piece featuring Lt. Joe Sonntag. ... The end result is pure entertainment." –*Library Journal*

"Sonntag is an appealingly laconic sleuth."
–*Kirkus Reviews*

NIGHT MEDICINE

A JOE SONNTAG MYSTERY

AXEL BRAND

Book design by Get It Together Productions
(www.awritersaide.com)
Printed in The United States of America
Cover design by Kae Cheatham

To Margot

Chapter One

The body was near the lions. That's what they told Lieutenant Joe Sonntag when they woke him up early. A young woman had been found dead at the Washington Park Zoo, a few blocks from Sonntag's house, so the dispatcher had called him. Another death. Sonntag had seen his share of death as chief of investigations for the Milwaukee police department.

He spotted half a dozen uniforms and one man in white ahead in some shrubbery. Some patrol cars and an ambulance were nearby; they had been driven along asphalt walkways to get there. He drove his ancient coupe past the cop who was blocking off the area, and parked on the grass.

The cops were knotted around a body, which lay in a beautiful bed of ferns, neatly manicured by the keeper of this most famous of Milwaukee parks. She lay on the ferns as if in a casket: her legs straight, her arms folded, her sightless eyes staring at the overarching elms above her. Someone had placed her there in that state of repose.

Sonntag studied her a moment, taking in all the oddities. She was terribly white, her flesh waxen. She was young, maybe just out of high school and a pretty, brunette, nicely dressed. She wore a white blouse, a pleated woolen skirt in a soft gray and blue and

brown plaid, a thick black belt, bobby sox, and brown penny
loafers. She also wore a sky-blue cashmere cardigan.

"Tell me," he said to Bulwer, the nearest cop.

"A guy found her half an hour ago."

"Anyone questioning him?"

"Yeah, he's over there with Musgrove and Bark."

"Any ID?"

"Nothing we could find."

The man in white knelt over her, a stethoscope hung from his
neck, looking at causes before allowing her to be moved. The doc
was unfamiliar to Sonntag.

"I'm Sonntag, investigations. You are?"

"Stoppl," the man said.

"The dispatcher sent you over here?"

"My office is nearby, sir. I came at once. Have them back
off, would you?"

Sonntag waved the uniforms to back away.

Doctor Stoppl waited until the area was cleared, and then
tugged the woman's pleated skirt upward. A pair of clean white
underpants came into view. He tugged the skirt down.

"Didn't expect that," he said.

"How long dead?"

"Body temperature same as ambient air. Sixty-two. So, early
last night."

"She was brought here?"

"She didn't arrange herself on the grass and expire, sir."

"You have any cause of death?"

Stoppl peered up and sighed. "Hemorrhage. There's not much
blood in her. Mostly in her torso."

"Where did the blood go?"

"Whoever brought her here can answer that, Lieutenant." The
doc was sounding testy.

"What caused the bleeding?"

"I have a pretty good idea but it'll have to wait. I'll have to
do the examination at the morgue."

"Want to take a guess?"

The rotund man stood slowly, lifting his Gladstone as he

struggled to his feet. "No. It might start you off on the wrong foot. I'll have something within the hour."

"You done here?"

"I am, but your people may not be." It was a chill September morning, but the doc was wreathed in sweat.

"I'll head for the morgue," Sonntag said.

He discovered Tech Corporal Gorilla Meyers hovering nearby with his 35-millimeter Leica.

"You shoot this yet?"

"I did, Lieutenant. Every angle. It was strange, her lying like that, surrounded by the ferns, like someone wanted her to be honored. Like whoever put her there wanted her respected. Like going to a funeral home, ferns all around her."

"Accident? Homicide?"

"Maybe both, Lieutenant."

"No ID?"

"Bulwer told me there was nothing. They checked her and the shrubbery and the paths."

"Any laundry marks on the clothing?"

"We didn't get that far. When we got here she was dead. There were a few people waiting for us. We moved them back and got the doc in, and you."

"Does she look like maybe there's some money?"

"Those are nice clothes, yeah."

The strengthening sun was liberating zoo smells. There was always that strange animal odor around zoos, especially this one. This location was not far from the big cats, yawning behind bars fifty yards distant.

"I'll want photos, okay? And a couple of reference shots. Where the lion cages are, where we are."

"Sure," Meyers said.

Sonntag found Bulwer near the cruisers.

"Call about missing persons," he said.

Bulwer nodded, slipped into the black and white, where he spun some knobs and pulled a mike to his lips. Sonntag heard some scratching and squealing and staccato voices. In a moment, Bulwer emerged.

"No female missing yet."

"Tell them to get an artist busy. Meyer's driving to the station with some photos."

There would soon be a sketch of the girl, with her eyes open and maybe a slight smile on her lips. It would be shown to people. That worked better than a photo of a dead woman.

Sonntag headed for Musgrove and Bark, who were sitting on a park bench with an old guy.

"I'm Lieutenant Sonntag, sir. I understand you found her."

"I did. It was exactly six-twenty-seven."

"Your name, sir?"

"Oh, of course. Launcelot Wills. Wills with an S. I'm a retired music teacher, and a poet."

"Where do you live, sir?"

"West of here. These gents have the address. I'm up at five each morning and begin the day with a bracing hike. And this is my favored route."

"You hike the park each morning?"

"Even in bad weather, Lieutenant."

"What happened?"

"Why, let me see. Out and about at ten after six, with good hiking shoes, leather soles, and there she was, obscured in the dawn light. I thought that's odd, and started past, and stopped, and headed back there, and she lay there banked by ferns, as in the Smith Brothers Mortuary—that's their custom, you know. Lots of ferns. There she lay, and I said, young lady, it's not proper to lie there like that. You might be accosted by unsavory souls. She didn't reply, so I warned her she was taking her life in her hands, lying there like that, but she ignored me. So I approached, careful to say I meant her no harm, that I was quite safe, and she didn't respond, so I leaned over and touched her cheek, and it was cold. Goodness, cold indeed. Then the horror of it began to infiltrate, and I touched her nose, and it was cold, and her cold hand, and then I knew, sir, that on this day some mother, some father, some brother or sister, would weep. And you know, sir, I hadn't the faintest idea where to go, there being no pay phones anywhere, and I finally struck out for Vliet street, and found a dry cleaning establishment that was open early, and made the call. Then of course I headed back here to direct officers to the site of the tragedy. I simply waited for what seemed forever before any of you gents appeared, and I led them to her at once."

"That's very complete, Mr. Wills. Do you have any idea who she is? Have you met her?"

"No idea, sir, but she comes from a good family."

"Why do you say that?"

"I wasn't a music teacher for a lifetime without knowing what I am looking at."

"By good family what do you mean?"

"Look at those tasteful clothes, bobby sox apart, sir. One can't hope for everything."

"Did you ever see her during your morning walks? Some people see other people regularly."

"Never, Lieutenant. I walk this park at about dawn most every day, and I've never seen that young lady before."

"Do you do your walk alone?"

"Always. My wife's unwell, sir."

"When she seemed to be dead, what did you think?"

"Think? Surrounded by beautiful ferns. I think she may have composed herself and died, as happens from heartache. I thought of Romeo and Juliet."

"Was she just like the way she is now? Laid out, legs together, arms folded over her?"

"Exactly. Some loving soul stretched her out for eternity."

"Why do you think it was loving?"

Wills pondered that a moment, and smiled wryly. "I guess I wanted it to be."

"How do you think she got here, Mr. Wills?"

"Someone must have carried her, I suppose. The walk's rather narrow for a car, isn't it?"

"Yes, and there are barriers," Sonntag said.

"Then it was someone for whom this child was light as a feather."

"Did you see anyone at all before you found her?"

"Not a soul. I usually don't."

"There are people who lurk where they've done something bad."

"Oh, I don't doubt it. But the joy of my morning walking is that I can hike through the mists of dawn quite alone, even in the heart of the city."

There wasn't much more to be gotten from the elderly gent, so Sonntag turned him loose. He directed the remaining cops to begin a search in any direction that led to a parking area, and to look for anything, anything at all.

He watched the ambulance men load the unknown young woman into the vehicle, which they did gently, because there was a terrible sadness lingering here, and in her composed pale face and the way she rested in the beauty of the ferns. It was as if her killer had been an artist. If indeed she had been killed. There were questions crowding Sonntag's thoughts just then. Might it have been a suicide? And if so, how and why?

He corralled Dr. Stoppl as the man was brushing grit off the knees of his trousers.

"You're a pathologist?"

"An underappreciated branch of medical science, Lieutenant."

"I sure appreciate it. What you fellows discover has helped us time and time again. You ready to say anything a bout it?"

Stoppl wiped his brow. "That's our calling. We rarely see patients. Until they're dead, I should say. Then we see patients." He smiled. "I am absolutely devoid of a bedside manner."

"You're heading for the morgue?"

He looked annoyed. "I will report to you, sir, the very moment I have come to valid conclusions."

"But you already know?"

"I'm afraid I do," Stoppl said.

Chapter Two

Sonntag guided the old Hudson coupe toward the station house, his mind chewing on the strange death. How did a beautiful girl come to the end of her life surrounded by ferns? Or was that merely a coincidence? Was it even a homicide? He'd get a report from the pathologist soon, and he hoped there would be something in it that would steer him somewhere, toward someone.

Lizbeth would have to hitch a ride from one of her friends this day. It was women's Mending Club day. Joe had the car for a change. And this one day he would escape the ordeal of riding the Wells streetcar to work.

Maybe there would be a missing person report awaiting him at the station. That would help. She sure was a sweet girl, ready to explore life, beautiful except for that waxy paleness in her face and limbs. Someone would call to report a missing young woman, and then it would all fall together. She was so young. A high school senior, perhaps, or someone not far along at a college. But that was just guesswork.

He steered the coupe eastward past dowdy neighborhoods of flats and bungalows, with shops and services at most every corner. Dry cleaners, grocers, laundries, ice cream parlors, taverns, bowling alleys, photographers, a hobby shop for model airplane and model railroad enthusiasts. He pulled into a private parking lot near the station, annoyed that the few hours he would store the coupe there would cost him thirty-five cents, a big chunk out of a day's income. With a monthly streetcar pass, he could get to work and back for a dime.

Captain Ackerman was waiting behind his naked desk.

"So, tell me," he said.

"We'll know pretty quick," Sonntag said.

"The radio's already calling it the Zoo murder," Ackerman said.

"We don't know that."

"Sure we know it. You're being a little cautious, right?" the captain said, reaching for one of those dogturd yellow five-cent stogies in his shirt pocket.

"We'll see," Sonntag replied, stubbornly.

"Some fiend got her."

"And settled her in a grotto of ferns, every limb carefully arranged?"

"That makes him all the more fiendish."

"I'm thinking this may be more a tragedy than something depraved."

"No evidence? No stab wounds, no nothing, eh?"

"Yes, there's evidence. No blood in her."

"A vampire then."

Ackerman was enjoying himself. He stripped away cellophane and fired up his yellow torpedo. Sonntag wasn't enjoying himself. The sight of that girl, so serene in the ferns, and so dead, wasn't the way to boost his spirits.

"Did you start any missing person search?" Sonntag asked.

For once Ackerman seemed nonplused. "All I hear is complaints," he said.

Sonntag headed into the bullpen and found young Frank Silva reading memos.

"Start calling schools, Frank."

"About the girl? You have a description?"

"Five-eight, upper teens or low twenties, brunette, pretty, dressed in, well, nice clothing."

Silva was grinning. Nice clothing was a class issue.

"White blouse, light blue cashmere cardigan, pleated woolen skirt, soft-colored plaid in blues and tans and browns. Bobby sox. Brown penny loafers."

"Schoolgirl, right?"

Silva dug up a list of area schools. Sometimes you could ID someone without waiting for a missing person report to drift in.

"Gorilla should have some photos by now," Sonntag said. "I'll get some to you."

"So what's that pathologist going to say?"

"He's going to say there's a lot of her blood somewhere, because it's not in her body, Frank."

"Oh oh," Frank said.

"Stick to high schools for now," Joe said. "Colleges later."

"What about preppie schools like Milwaukee Downer?"

"Especially those."

>> | <<

The pathologist didn't take long. Sonntag took a call from the morgue.

"Stoppl here. The girl died of a hemorrhage probably induced by an illegal procedure."

"Abortion?"

"Yes, sir. She bled to death."

"Any other possibilities? Violence? Rape?"

"None. I examined with great care. Not the slightest exterior abrasion or laceration elsewhere."

"How did she end up dressed like that and at the zoo?"

"That's for you to discover, sir. She was carefully washed, and that included a douche. There was no visible sign of blood anywhere. It was as if someone wanted it to look like it never happened."

"Are you saying an abortionist thought he could fool you?"

"I'm not hazarding any such guess."

"There's a lot of blood somewhere."

"Indeed there is, if it hasn't been thoroughly hidden or burned. Have you any clue about her identity?"

"That's my next question. What about her dental chart?"

"She did not have a single filling. She must have had fine hard teeth."

"Well, that's a help. There aren't many people her age who lack a filling. What about wisdom teeth?"

"None as yet, Lieutenant."

"An overbite? Underbite?"

"That's a little outside of my field, sir."

"We'll pick up the clothes. The labels might help us," Sonntag said.

"They're ready for you, sir."

"Can you think of anything else that might help?"

"If you have a photo of her, you might start with every general practice physician in town."

Sonntag went to Mike Lammers, the dispatcher. "Would you have someone stop at the morgue and pick up some clothing for me?"

"I'll put someone right on it, Lieutenant. It's that girl's stuff. What was the deal?"

"Looks like an abortion."

"Christ," Lammers said. "Those guys are butchers."

"Maybe not," Sonntag said.

He wondered what to tackle next. Some good clothing, some school attendance records, an unusual dental record. And then there was the mystery. Why had the girl been carried to that place, that bed of ferns, near the lion cages? And why had she been cleaned of every last bit of blood, dressed neatly, as if nothing deadly had touched her life? And who had done that? The abortionist or someone else?

There were so many angles to this that Joe Sonntag couldn't even make any sense of any of it. He needed to talk. That's how he evolved his ideas, and in recent times he had done more and more of that with the youngest and maybe the best investigator on the force, Frank Silva.

He waited by Silva's desk while the young man talked to the principal at Pulaski High, and apparently striking out.

"Nothing, no one not showing? All right, sir. Thanks." Silva, not yet thirty, with dark and sad eyes, shook his head. "Nothing so far," he said to Sonntag.

"Well, we need to talk. I'm striking out."

"Yeah, let me load up," Silva said. He headed for the coffee pot that rested on a hotplate, poured a cup, and grabbed two fat glazed doughnuts and a napkin. "I think better with food in between my teeth," he said.

"I prefer to think with my brain," Sonntag said.

Sonntag pulled up a swivel chair from the next carrel. "We've got an unknown girl, upper teens likely, dead near the zoo. We've got a cause of death—hemorrhage. We've got a medical opinion there's likely been an abortion. Stoppl seemed a little hesitant about that. But this girl's cleaned up and dressed nicely and laid out nicely, like someone cares. We've got clothing that looks like some money. We've got an old guy finding her early this morning on an asphalt walkway blocked to vehicles. The nearest parking's a block away. We don't know how she got there. We don't know whether the abortionist is alone. We don't even know if the girl's family is involved. We've got time of death late yesterday. We've got teeth without any fillings. We've got zero ID, no ring, no jewelry. So where are we, Frank?"

"Maybe we have a very caring abortionist, cleaning her up and carrying her to the ferns, like a grotto," Frank said.

"Abortionists care about three things: money, not getting caught, and some of them probably do care about doing it right."

"Yeah, like who?" Silva asked.

Sonntag leaned forward over his desk. "Here's something to look into. If this girl got an abortion, she had to learn it was available. Maybe a friend had one. She's desperate. She maybe has some cash, or some way of getting some money. She's heard of a place, and a way to get one, someone to contact. So, where are we?"

Silva smiled wryly. "We could ask all the high school seniors around here if they ever had one."

"What schools have girls who wear nice stuff like that?" Sonntag asked.

"Suburbs," Silva said. "Or northeast side."

"Ah, yes, and the blood. Somewhere there's a lot of blood."

"Was. That stuff gets burned."

"Maybe not. Might be in the garbage."

"What? Towels? Sheets? Rags? Can that stuff be washed and bleached?"

"Not so it'd get by us."

"Maybe we shouldn't jump to conclusions. Maybe she bled to death straight into the ground. Or sitting on a toilet. Or into a metal pan."

"Who knows?" Sonntag said. "We need to find out who she is, first. And who she talked to. And where she got the name of the abortionist."

"Hey, let's slow down. Could she have done it to herself? You know, coat hanger?"

"She could. Maybe there's no abortionist at all."

"Maybe her family carried her there, in the fern grotto." Silva's disbelief in his own theory spread into a wan smile, but then he continued. "May be she tried a coat hanger. Maybe her parents found her dead. Maybe they didn't want a scandal. Maybe they found the courage to clean her up and carry her away from their house. Maybe they thought it would all go away, and that none of it would be found out."

"Maybe," Sonntag said, thinking of a few reasons it didn't make much sense.

"Do rich families get that desperate?" Silva asked. "Now if it was a girl from my neighborhood, her parents would likely kick her out, and she'd either have the baby in one of those shelters, or head for Mexico to get it done."

"Frank, there's no telling. Each girl, each family, they deal differently with it."

"Yeah, and we're forgetting something, Joe. The father. That little blob in there was started by some guy. And some guys might go into a panic if a girl says she's knocked up. And other guys might kill a girl."

"That's good, Frank. We've got to put the future father high on the list."

"We gonna set up some priorities here?" Silva asked.

"Find out who she is. Everything flows out of that."

"Can the press help?"

"You know, I'll talk to Dugan at the *Journal*. With the right kind of story, we might get some tips."

"It'll be back with the classified ads, if they run it at all," Silva said.

Sonntag nodded. Neither of the Milwaukee dailies ever used the word "abortion," and neither of them used the word "rape." The usual journalistic phrases were "illicit procedure" and "illegal assault," and the story was invariably buried deep in the second section, behind the sports pages and in front of the classified ads. The unvarnished words, and what they signified, would shock the sensibilities of the city. It would be a tough task to get anything published in a town that pretended that certain crimes didn't exist.

Chapter Three

Joe Sonntag pushed aside the package of the girl's clothing and dialed the *Milwaukee Journal*. He asked for Matt Dugan, who was the crime and courts reporter, and a very good one.

"I've got a favor to ask," Sonntag told him.

"That's a switch."

"We've got an unidentified body."

"The girl you picked up this morning in the ferns at the zoo."

"That's the one. No ID, no one reported missing. She's probably out of high school, but we're checking the schools. Her clothing isn't telling us much. The labels are brands, not stores. She's got no dental history that would help us much. Matt, here's what we need. I've a good drawing of her. We're looking for a tip. Would you run it?"

"What did she die of?"

"That's under investigation."

"I think you know. I called Stoppl in his office after he returned from the morgue, and he's not talking. So why are you being quiet?"

"You'll have that soon enough. We need to find out who she is first."

"Hey, Lieutenant, you telling me you're hiding what she died of?"

"After we find out who she is we'll tell you. Hey, Matt, I'll take it to the *Sentinel*. They'll run that drawing on the front page."

"I got ya. If you gave me the cause of death, the story would appear somewhere behind the sports pages."

Dugan was sharp. And there was no way around him. "That's right, Matt."

"That poor girl," Dugan said. "That poor miserable girl."

"Can we get the drawing on the front of the second section?"

"I think so. Now what did she die of, off the record?"

"Hemorrhage following an abortion."

"How come she was laid out like that, like in the ferns?"

"We don't know. But first things first, Matt. A drawing might give us a tip. Maybe even positive ID."

"There's time to make the city edition. I'll send a boy for the drawing."

The city edition was the last of the afternoon daily's editions. The state was the first one out the door. "Thanks, Matt. I'll look for him."

Sonntag hung up. Dugan was the sort of reporter he liked. Smart as hell. He understood the world. He was tough and relentless, and yet there was room for some give and take. Like now. There'd be a story of the body found in Washington Park, and a drawing of the girl, and a request for tips. There would be nothing about the cause of death this time around.

Sonntag waited for Silva to get off his phone.

"Nothing?"

Silva shook his head. "We've got one girl at Milwaukee Downer who's out for two weeks with her parents in New Mexico. Took the Super Chief."

"Is there a school picture of her?"

"Damn, I didn't ask. I'll call."

"Nothing in the public schools?"

"Some girls out sick, got cramps, stuff. I've called a few parents. Nothing."

"You tried colleges, or secretarial schools?"

"That's next."

"If they've got a photo at Downer, and if she's a brunette, better drive up there. Take the sketch. I've got a couple of copies that Gorilla made. Also, take a photo that Gorilla took of the girl, but don't show it to anyone there."

"Yeah. Have you checked the record? Have we got a convicted abortionist who's at it again?"

"That's next. That and the labels in the clothing. I need to find out what stores sell what brands."

Silva grinned. "Leave me out," he said.

Sonntag tried Chapman's first, figuring that was an upscale department store. He eventually found himself connected to the buyer for women's wear, an Ethel Barbour.

"You're calling about that girl on the radio this morning, aren't you?" the buyer asked.

"Guess I am."

"Well, word is, she was assaulted."

"Where did you hear that?"

"I dunno. Word gets around. Now was she?"

"We have no evidence of it."

"That's how you guys talk. You won't say she wasn't; you just say we have no evidence."

"That's the only response I can offer you, Mrs. Barbour. Now, we don't know who she is, and we're looking at labels. Do you stock Tweeters sweaters?"

"I wouldn't touch them with a ten foot pole," she said.

"Why not?"

"Their sales rep, that's why."

"What did she do?"

"It's he. He wants to show his line of Tweeters in his hotel room after a drink and a dinner. I wouldn't mind, but he's a hairy ape."

"I didn't know that went on."

"Lieutenant, take me to lunch some time and I'll tell you how the fashion business works."

It turned out that Chapman's didn't sell Tweeters, but did sell Missy, the label in the skirt.

"Any chance you can find out who bought any Missy skirt from you? Like on a charge account?"

"I always knew detectives were nuts," she said. "But I'll look, if you'll buy me lunch. I love gossip."

Silva returned to the bullpen around three, shaking his head.

"That gal on the trip with her folks wasn't even close. So they invited me to study their yearbooks. I went through the last four, nice glossy photos of the graduating class in each, which I checked one by one, and there may have been one or two. You've no idea how hard it is. I borrowed the yearbooks, and you can back me. You saw her; I didn't."

"I'll look, Frank. Now see what you can find on abortion cases around here."

"Ah, some history. Is our local abortionist out of the slammer and on the loose?"

"Yeah, find that out."

"Who'd know something?"

"Try the gynecologists."

"Anyone else?"

"There's a convent out on Bluemound Road that shelters girls in trouble. I forget the name."

Silva smiled. "That's why you head investigations. Thanks."

>> | <<

The city edition of the *Journal* landed on Sonntag's desk, and true to his word, Dugan managed to get his story on the front of the second section. It was short but good. The police artist's sketch seemed close to the mark. The headline said Young Woman Found Dead Near Zoo, and the subhead said she remained unidentified. It was a good story. Joe thought the phone would start ringing pretty quick, and he had better stay late and take the calls.

And it did ring. Casey Tiffen, the afternoon dispatcher, put it through.

"Say, I saw the picture," said a lady.

"I'm Lieutenant Sonntag. And you?"

"Oh, is it important? Can't I just leave an anonymous tip?"

"I'd like any information that can help us identify the girl in that drawing, ma'am."

"I think it was my niece. The picture looked just like her."

"What's your niece's name, ma'am?"

"Linnea Dietrick."

"And you are?"

"Oh, you don't need to know my name, officer. I just want to help."

"Sorry. Where does she live?"

"Lived, sir. She's no longer there."

"I'd sure like an address, ma'am. We'll check it out right away. And of course we're grateful to hear from you."

"The family moved, you know. That was in forty-three. After she ran away."

"Linnea Dietrick ran away?"

"With a soldier."

"Who was the soldier?"

"Maybe it was a sailor at Great Lakes. I don't remember. You know how the war was."

"How old would she be now, ma'am?"

"She was born in nineteen twenty-one."

"And when was the last time you or your family saw her?"

"In forty-three."

"And that's a drawing of her?"

"Linnea was blonde, you know, but the rest looks just like her."

"Where did her parents move to?"

"Arizona, officer."

"Could I have an address and phone number?"

"Oh, I don't have my address book."

"Their name is Dietrick?"

"No, there was a divorce. Her mother's in Arizona."

"How do I get in touch with her?"

"I think her new name is Easton. She was on my husband's side."

"Do you a first name?"

"Her mother was named Eulalie."

"And what city in Arizona."

"One of those big ones."

"We'll check it out. Why do you think the girl in the drawing is Linnea?"

"It just struck me."

"What color eyes did Linnea have?"

"Lavender. Like Elizabeth Taylor. Like in *National Velvet.* Did you see that? Linnea looked like that."

"I think that film was black and white, ma'am."

"Yes, but she has lavender eyes."

The dead girl's eyes were brown. "We'll look into it, ma'am, and thanks for the tip."

"You'll let me know, won't you?"

"We'll publish who it is as soon as it's found out, ma'am."

"You'll have to find me, because I'm anonymous," she said.

Sonntag sighed, thought he was in the wrong vocation, replaced the black receiver on its cradle, and made a few notes. He wondered whether the rest of the afternoon would be so unproductive.

Cigar odor assaulted Sonntag from the rear. Captain Ackerman had been eavesdropping behind him.

"No luck," Sonntag said.

"You'll get twenty duds for every call worth something," Ackerman said.

"We sure haven't got anything else going for us."

"Ah, go on home. Silva's working this eve. If anything comes up, we'll patch the call to you."

Sonntag stared. Getting sent home on time was unheard of. "Are you feeling sick?"

"That girl. It could have been my daughter," Ackerman said.

Sonntag was half inclined to stay. The new case was eating at him. He wanted a name; he wanted the abortionist. But he'd get a call if anything big came up.

He threw away the remains of a half-eaten peanut butter and jelly sandwich from his lunch bucket. He never did touch the coffee or the Jonathan apple. Then he clamped the fedora on his graying hair, struggled into the trench coat, and headed toward the Wells Street stop.

Only then did he remember he had driven the Hudson coupe

to work this day, and he wouldn't have to face the mortal danger of crossing the Menomonee River Viaduct on the streetcar. He could drive underneath, on State Street, and hope no orange streetcar would land on his head.

Chapter Four

Lizbeth pounced the moment he entered the back door of their modest bungalow. "Okay, who is she?" she asked.

"We don't know," he said, supplying the obligatory peck on her cheek.

"And what happened?"

"How about a Manhattan?"

"It's already made. Here's your bourbon."

He laughed. She was so eager for the scoop that she had begun building their evening cocktails when he pulled into the driveway.

She steered him into the living room, intent on the Third Degree.

"She was lying in a bed of ferns near the lion cage," he said. "She had been arranged there, legs straight, arms folded, by someone who plainly cared."

"Yes, but what?"

He sipped. The Jim Beam was cold and fine.

"There was a pathologist handy, and he said she died of a hemorrhage."

She went silent. She probably had it figured out.

"No blood there?"

"Not a drop. Nothing visible on her, either."

"I knew it. That's what we were saying at Mending Club."

"Who was saying what?"

"Marge Carlson was saying it was, you know, an abortion."

"How did she know that?"

"She said she'd heard it."

That's what she and her galfriends did at Mending Club. Each week eight or ten of Lizbeth's friends met at one home or another, each armed with a sewing basket. They darned socks, turned collars and cuffs, replaced buttons, patched pants, lowered hems, adjusted skirts or pants for expanding waistlines—and gossiped, which was the real business of the Mending Club.

"That's what the pathologist reported."

"Just that?"

"Nothing more. The girl had not been abused in any way the pathologist could see."

"How'd she get there?"

"Carried. It's a good distance from a parking area."

"And someone arranged her there, like that? It must be a family thing. Maybe a sister or mother did it, got into trouble, and tried to remove the evidence."

"Or a boyfriend," Sonntag said. "But you don't just remove the evidence. When we get a name, we'll find out who she was seeing. And who her family is. You don't escape by taking her somewhere and leaving her beside some ferns."

"So, who?"

"Maybe Kilroy. Like in, Kilroy was here."

"Ha, ha," she said.

"You sure got me there, babe. She was well dressed; probably out of high school."

"That's what Marge Carlson said. She said it wasn't a local girl."

"How'd she know that?"

"She's got pipelines," Lizbeth said. "Or thinks she does."

"I'd like to know."

"Okay, that picture in the paper. Is that drawing any good?"

"I thought so."

"Agnes Willow said she'd heard the girl was naked."

"White blouse, plaid pleated skirt, blue cardigan, bobby sox, loafers."

"Well, she sure must have been naked sometime or other," Lizbeth said.

It was odd. Joe Sonntag didn't like that. He didn't like gossip.

"I guess a young woman can love a man," he said.

Lizbeth went silent.

This death had all the earmarks of deepest tragedy, and those were the saddest cases to deal with. If there were crimes here, and there were, they were crimes of desperation and shame and sorrow. These were the hardest cases for Joe Sonntag. He could go after someone who was vicious, cruel, sadistic, rapacious, barbaric. But this was simply a desperate thing that went bad, that unraveled, and left a girl dead when she should have been up and back in the world.

"Anyone phone in?"

"We always get a few. You can guess."

"You just don't know who she is, right?"

Sonntag nodded and sipped.

"That's because girls in trouble go somewhere else. The first thing they do is disappear from where they are."

That was interesting. "I've got people checking the shelters. Some nuns run a big one out on the west side. So far, nothing."

"She's from somewhere else. Madison, Chicago, somewhere far away."

"Why here, then?"

"I wouldn't know. I'm not up on that stuff," she said. "But girls from here go to Chicago or some place like that. You always hear of them going to Mexico, or Nevada, or someplace, but Chicago's what you hear most. They get themselves out of trouble there."

"How do they learn that?"

"Mostly from their boyfriends. Guys seem to know where to go."

"Where do they get the word?"

"I haven't the faintest idea. But you want me to shock you? I think parents tell them. It's mom and dad who hear about some doctor somewhere, running a mill out of his back door. Some mom and dad who hear it in clubs and bars and keep it in mind, just in case."

"We've started looking at old Milwaukee cases, and there's almost nothing, babe."

"Well, now there is," she said brightly. She sipped. "And this time he got himself into a fix."

"Or she?"

"I hate to agree with you," Lizbeth said.

"Or none? Just a mother or sister or boyfriend with a coat hanger?"

"That is so bad," she said.

"Or maybe a midwife or nurse, with some training? Some woman full of pity, who got into it thinking she could help a desperate girl, and soon discovered there's a lot of desperate girls, and they knew her name?"

"Why would she carry the body to the ferns near the zoo, then?"

"Because she loved that girl; loved and pitied each girl she thought she was helping."

"Where would you find anyone like that?" she asked.

"Maybe in a doctor's office after hours."

"Pretty risky, don't you think?"

"There are ways to stop a hemorrhage. Clamps, a speculum, stitches," he said. "It would be the least risky place. And if there's blood, that's not unusual in a doctor's office. Anywhere there's medicine, there's a lot of blood being mopped up."

"If you were doing that—illegal stuff, where would you do it?" she asked.

"Where it would blend in. I don't think I'd do it in some room at the end of some alley. But then, I'm a cop, not a doc."

"I don't think a doctor would take a girl out to a fern bed, dressed so nicely," she said.

"Yeah," he said. "Nothing makes sense."

Almost by some hidden consensus, they quit talking about it. He couldn't say why, but there had been an invisible wall between himself and Lizbeth when they talked about it; something so deep and obscure it might have been merely his imagination at work. He wasn't sure what it was. Maybe it was something she didn't want investigated. Maybe the girl should be buried and forgotten, and whoever did it forgotten too.

That was an odd feeling. He had never felt the subtle wall before, and he couldn't really fathom it. He wondered how women like her really felt about it. Everything about her was traditional, from her faith to her belief in the sanctity of life, to her belief in the sacredness of marriage and bringing children into the world. They'd raised two boys, and that was different. This time there was something veiled. In the morning she slept in, so he made himself a peanut-butter sandwich for lunch and added a Macintosh apple and two Oreos, and headed out the door. She didn't sleep in very often, and he thought it had something to do with the nameless girl.

The Wells streetcar scraped to a stop, the door flapped, and he let the conductor punch his pass. He was going to work a little early. The girl haunted him. He remembered how he had stared into her ghastly pale beautiful face, somehow knowing before the doctors confirmed it, what had happened. Now he wanted a name, the way that girl was christened, they way she was known to her mom and dad and all the others in her life.

The Wells car ground over the terrible trestle that spanned the Menomonee Valley that was his nemesis, always reminding him of his own cowardice, but it was the girl who occupied him this time. He wore his trench coat this day, against an autumnal chill.

At his desk he found a stack of notes, all from Frank Silva, who had worked the case into the evening. He settled in his swivel chair and began reading them. There had been five more calls from informants who thought they could identify the girl. None amounted to anything. Silva had carefully handwritten a report on each call, and also a conclusion. Hair color or eye color had eliminated some of them. Age had been a factor in one call. The drawing in the paper wasn't striking any bells.

Sonntag hung his hat on a hook and his coat beside it, loaded up a doughnut and coffee from a table at the wall, and settled into his chair. As usual, he was stymied. Maybe something would show up. He remembered Lizbeth's remark that girls in trouble head somewhere else. That was as good as anything. He'd get permission to run missing person ads, using that drawing, in the *Capitol Times* in Madison, and the *Tribune* in Chicago, and maybe Ackerman would let him try some ads in Janesville, Beloit, and Green Bay, for starters. Maybe Milwaukee was the somewhere else for some poor girl.

Today he'd put one of his men, maybe Eddy Walsh, on the shelters. He two-finger typed a directive to Walsh, and left it on Walsh's desk. Eddy Walsh had a gift. He could put women at ease. Maybe even put a suspicious girl or two at ease. Maybe they would know a thing or two about an abortionist operating in town—if he was allowed to talk with them.

Sonntag checked into old cases involving abortionists in Wisconsin. One was prewar, and that man had died. Another was 1943, and that one had served five years in Waupun and had gone somewhere out of state. There were a couple more. There weren't any behind bars in the state now. And none of them had been women. One was a rogue doctor.

Matt Dugan from the *Journal* called.

"You get anything from the drawing?" he asked.

"A lot of nothing," Sonntag said. "Silva took most of the calls last night. He heard a lot of crazy stories. A mother who complained that their blonde thirty-year-old daughter had skipped town. A woman who said she had given her twelve-year-old girl to her grandmother in Watertown to raise, and the girl looked just like the drawing—except she was too young and had red hair. Frank called; the girl was listening to Amos and Andy on the radio. So, no much yet, Matt. But thanks for running the story."

"I've got to run another giving the cause of death. You want to make it official?"

The story would be ascribed to Detective Joseph Sonntag.

"Yeah, you've got to report it," Sonntag said. "You gave me a fair shake yesterday, and it really helped."

"Hemorrhage as a consequence of an illegal operation?"

"You can say it. And I'll look for it behind the sports pages."

"If it was the *Sentinel* it'd be front page," Dugan said. "And I've got to tell you something. My editor's gonna get a mess of calls complaining that we ran the story at all. Those things shouldn't be made public. Especially in Milwaukee."

"Especially here," Sonntag said. "Where there is no crime."

"And dead girls are laid to rest in a bank of ferns," Dugan said.

Chapter Five

Eddy Walsh had done an impressive job over at the two homes for wayward girls. He'd talked to the administrative ladies and nuns, who had talked to some of the sequestered girls, a few of whom agreed to talk, some of them from behind a screen that ensured their privacy.

Leave it to Eddy, Sonntag thought. Eddy sat in the swivel chair across from the lieutenant, working from notes.

"There might be a ring at work here," Walsh said. "Two of these girls discovered cards tucked into women's room mirrors at schools. They simply said Need Help, and had a number."

"You get one?"

"Nope. The girls got rid of them fast."

"What happened when they called?"

"Nice lady, asking how her society, with some name or another that sounded like a legit group, could be of service."

"Legit up front, eh?"

"Yeah, laying out options, talking about how to break the news to parents, listing places to go, including the county home. But there'd always be some drift toward money, and a request for an interview in some out of the way place, like a park bench somewhere. And eventually, the abortion option would be offered, but remember, the girl still didn't know who she was talking to. Just a friendly lady. Never a guy. And the lady would make it sound easy. A quick ride, an hour somewhere, and then head home."

"And bring cash."

"Yeah, thousand bucks."

"Which few girls have."

"Pick up any descriptions of the women doing the interviewing?"

"Yeah, motherly. They all looked motherly to these gals. But not all these gals are teen-agers, Joe. Some are up as high as their thirties."

"What do you think, Eddy?"

"We've got a big abortion ring going. They're careful, elusive, and almost impossible to track."

"Until a girl died. That wasn't in their business plan. So what about these girls, the ones who called that number?"

"I talked to three. The people running these shelters didn't push, but three volunteered. I have no names. Two were religious and knew in their gut that what they were doing would be real bad, and hurt them, and maybe keep them from having children later. They backed away. They said nothing to their parents about looking for a way out; just went through the tears and get themselves put into the shelter for a while."

"And the other?"

"She would have been okay with it, an abortion I mean, but she came from a real poor family. A thousand bucks was like a million to her. One day she just knocked on the door at the county shelter."

"No names, no phone number, and meeting middle-aged motherly types on park benches."

"You know what? I had the feeling I was invading something so private, so female, so veiled, so filled with tears, that I was an intruder, a male rat."

"I never had a daughter," Sonntag said. "I guess I just wouldn't know."

"You know, it's not like what we think. We think a girl talks to her boyfriend, and he talks to shadowy people in bars or night clubs, and the boyfriend lays out cash, and the girl takes a quick trip somewhere, for a weekend, and comes back, and it's the guys who arrange the whole deal. But that's not what I was hearing. Not like that at all."

"Do we have any solid leads?"

"Yeah, we need to find one of them calling cards. We need to talk to janitors in the schools. We need a card with a phone number, and then we can maybe get somewhere."

"We can ask school officials if they've seen any of the cards. Maybe someone's got one in a drawer."

"I'll do it," Eddy said.

"An abortion ring needs customers, and that's where we start looking." Sonntag said. "Eddy, what do you think happens? From start to finish?"

"Girl gets knocked up, and in a couple of months she knows, and she's desperate, and she finds a card and a number and calls, and talks, and an operation isn't even mentioned. Lots of talk about having the baby, being a mom, getting prenatal care, hiding it all from everyone in the whole world, and what it costs to have a baby in a hospital, and so on, and then they are given another option. They think about it. They break their piggy bank. They get cash from their boyfriend. They take a streetcar somewhere and get it done by some cheerful person dressed like a doc, and rest an hour and take a streetcar home."

"Okay, Eddy. One last question. Are there other channels? Other contacts?"

"I'd bet my boots on it."

"Like what?"

"Beats me."

"Talk to the girls in the homes some more, if you can. Keep asking. Maybe it's just something they heard, but keep asking."

"Got it," Walsh said.

"And we still have a girl with no name," Sonntag said.

"That's part of it. The moment a girl finds out, she enters a world without names. The girls in the shelters, they don't even know each other's last name. It's just Mary and Joan and Beth in there. They were all behind screens, didn't want a cop to see them. I haven't the faintest idea what they look like."

"So both the girls in trouble and the abortion ring operate without names?"

"Yeah, the girls who called the number met someone who called herself Mom, wearing glasses and a flowery hat, or the Traveling Nurse, or maybe a made-up name. All those motherly types, they're just as nameless as the girls."

"Payment by check?"

"Cash."

"Maybe we can go where we're going with some marked bills."

Walsh smiled. "Maybe," he said, sounding like he didn't believe it.

"Eddy, something else. Parents. You know what? There are plenty of parents around who'd like to run their daughter through an abortion mill, quick and easy. So when you go back there, see about that. Did any of those girls have parents who were pushing them for an abortion?"

Eddy grinned. "Well now, there's a question worth asking."

A big question, Joe Sonntag thought. Maybe the real pressure came from the daddies and mommies, not the girls in trouble. Daddies and mommies have ways of asking the right question to the right people. Some daddies and mommies can pay the bucks and hardly notice it. Daddies and mommies may have tried to force the issue, and some of the girls in the shelters may be runaways.

"If anyone can do it, you can, Eddy."

"Yeah, I'm a ladies man," he said.

"And Eddy, there will be lots of those girls who don't feel troubled at all. They are looking forward to being a mom with pure happiness. Even a single mom."

"Bring on the diaper pail, right?"

Sonntag laughed.

Walsh clapped his porkpie on his salty locks and abandoned the station. He had gotten valuable stuff out of the shelters.

Sonntag dialed the coroner, Harry Bledsoe.

"Harry, do me a favor. I want a second opinion about that girl. The one we haven't IDed."

"Doctor Stoppl won't be happy, Joe. He's a topnotch man."

"I just want two opinions from two good pathologists."

"I guess I ought to bill your department," Bledsoe said. "Okay, I'll get back to you tomorrow some time. Truth to tell, I've been wondering about it."

Bledsoe was a good man, a born skeptic.

The smell of yellow five-cent stogies reached Sonntag, along with the blue wall of Captain Ackerman.

"*Journal* buried it," the captain said.

"That's what happens in a town without crime."

"No, it's a town without sex," Ackerman said. "She died of complications arising from unlawful surgery."

"I'm having Bledsoe give me a second opinion."

"Why don't you trust the first? You just trying to throw money around?"

"I don't know. I think I want to see of there was anything else. I mean, other than the hemorrhage."

"Like a bullet hole?"

"Like a beating. Whether she was forced into the abortion by someone."

"What else you got?"

"Eddy's sniffing an abortion ring, big time."

"In Milwaukee, Wisconsin? Who runs it? The Mafia?"

"At the moment, I'm more interested in who signs up."

He apprised the captain of what Eddy Walsh had found out, after talking to some expectant mothers at the County Home for Wayward Girls. And what Eddy would try to do with another round of interviews.

"Maybe it's a rich people's abortion ring," Ackerman said. "Save a lot of debutantes heading for old Mexico."

"That's a thought," Sonntag said.

"What is?"

"Debutantes. That girl was neatly dressed. Who publishes stuff about debutantes?"

"Beats me. *Sentinel*, I guess."

"Well, go find someone," Ackerman said, and went sailing off in cigar fog.

Sonntag knew nothing about debutantes. He didn't know any rich people. They all lived mysterious lives up in Whitefish Bay or Fox Point. He didn't know what made a girl a debutante. He wasn't even sure what a debut was. Or where debuts were held, or why, or how. Or what rich girls did, or anything else.

But he knew who would. He found Frank Silva still working schools to come up with missing brunette girls, and waited for him to get off the line.

"Frank, what exactly is a debutante? Like in the *Sentinel*?

"A girl being introduced to society, I think."

"What's society?"

"Damned if I know, except it takes money."

"Where do they do this?"

"Ballrooms, or country clubs. Sometimes there's a charity veneer, but the deal is to present the girls in order to marry them off."

"Ackerman thinks the girl might be a debutante."

"We'd have found out by now," Frank said. "But you know, the captain's still on to something."

"Abortions. Rich girls, I mean rich families, they think getting knocked up is just a minor inconvenience. Go to the right place and get it fixed, real fast. It's even fun; a little vacation, and it's all over."

"Don't they care? I mean, about scraping life out of themselves?"

"You're thinking middle class, Joe. The middle class gets itself into a moral snit about abortions. All full of rights and wrongs, and if a girl is so wicked as to get herself PG, she should have the baby and maybe go live in Peru the rest of her life."

"Yeah? All I hear is how bad it is, real evil."

"That's your world, Joe. Church says one thing, everyone agrees. All the girls you see out there on the west side, they sing in church choirs, they are real nice, and they're virgins, more or less, until they get hitched. They're good girls. I mean good, good girls."

"What about the rest? I mean the poor?"

"That's where I'm from. That's a different world. Girls, they get pregnant, they get desperate. They can't afford a kid. Their boyfriends bug out. They want help. They don't care if it's right or wrong, they want to get taken care of, and can't find anyone, and end up being moms because there isn't any help, and this thing in them becomes a child, and that means they're stuck."

"Don't they have a moral sense about it? I mean, doesn't it offend them?"

"Of course they do. But they're desperate. They're the ones that try coat hangers and spoons, and end up dying in hospitals. They're scared and guilty, because they think God's against them, and they'll get punished for trying. The government's gonna hit them, God's gonna hit them. And they can't find a guy who wants to marry a single mom, so they're stuck."

"Yeah, you're right," Sonntag said. "I know nothing about it. I guess I'd better learn."

Chapter Six

For reasons he couldn't fathom, Joe Sonntag dreaded this foray into high society. He dragged Frank Silva with him as they headed into the *Sentinel's* newsroom for a visit with Dorothea Blue, the paper's society editor, and a most formidable lady, by all accounts.

She received them coolly, at a desk with a bouquet of yellow roses on it. She wore a rather dowdy gray dress over her ample figure and peered at them through half-glasses.

"We're here to find out about the way upper crust people live," Frank said.

"When you say upper crust, I am sure I don't know what you mean," she said. "And if you're intending to talk about the young lady who was found the other day, I have nothing to say at all."

"Well, yes, we think she might be someone you've met," Sonntag said, bravely.

"I have met several thousand young ladies," she replied, "but not that one."

"She was dressed real fine," Sonntag said.

Madame Blue arched an eyebrow.

"I mean, she wore a blue cashmere sweater, And she had a pleated wool skirt, with a plaid, sort of soft greens and blues and tans. And almost new loafers. We checked. These don't come cheap."

"Any suburban girl could afford them. And most of the ladies I write about wouldn't be caught dead in an outfit like that."

"What would they wear?"

"Slacks are in. Right now, blue jeans. I'll tell you one thing: any girl who wears pleated wool, well, it's almost cruel."

"Well, ah, it appears this girl at the zoo was in trouble, and we were sort of wondering what you might know about how, ah, young ladies deal with that," Frank Silva said. He was sinking into his shoes as fast as Sonntag was.

That elicited an icy stare. "If I knew, I wouldn't tell you," she said. "I utterly respect the privacy of my sources. They are fine people."

"Well, someone's doing dangerous and illegal things here, and if you have anything that would help us, we'd sure appreciate it." Sonntag felt the thin ice snapping under him with every step.

Madame Blue smiled suddenly. It was an oddly electric smile. "This girl. Why do you come to me? Bobby sox? Loafers? Cashmere? Goodness sakes. You are silly men. You might prefer to bark up the right tree."

"Which is?"

"I don't think the young ladies of my acquaintance would devote their time to the Washington Park Zoo. Saddle horses, yes, hunters, jumpers, polo horses. But not lions."

"Ah, Mrs. Blue, we don't think she went there voluntarily. She was left there."

"Certainly she was left there. By someone who knew her social standing."

In an odd way, Sonntag thought, she had a point.

"Mrs. Blue, there's someone in town who's doing illegal operations," Sonntag said. "And now we have a death. That's a homicide. We want to put a stop to it. This person is endangering lives. Maybe lives of people you know."

"And why have you come to me?"

"The girls most likely to get one of these, ah, operations, are girls who can afford it. People you write about."

"That's very interesting, gentlemen. I'm afraid I have nothing that might support your novel ideas." She rose, dismissively.

"You might be asked about this when you're under oath," Silva said. "Are you ready?"

"For what?"

"Whether the people you regularly write about have ever talked about these things, or gossiped, or sought your advice about what to do. Under oath."

"Well, if you do, I will be forced to answer. But until then, sirs, I will protect my sources. I'm sure you understand. I cannot possibly report society news if I have no access to these fine people."

"I would remind you, ma'am, that if you have any knowledge of these crimes, and fail to report them, you become an accessory. Think about it. Maybe your memory will be stirred. It beats facing an indictment, doesn't it?" Sonntag said.

She stared. "I don't know a thing," she said. "Good day."

Sonntag smiled. "You've been very helpful, ma'am. We'll be back in touch."

"If I was, I didn't mean to be," she said.

Sonntag and Silva made their way through a warren of oak desks, scalloped with cigarette burns, past reporters banging on ancient typewriters, down gloomy marble stairs, and into the light of day.

"She knows a few things. Like who had a little surgery here and there," Silva said.

"Yeah, and pulling that out of her is going to require a little heat. We may have to put the district attorney on it."

"What do you make of her?"

"She knows plenty. She might even know the name of our friendly abortionist. And she might know a bunch of girls who've had their little procedure. And she didn't like our visit one bit. In fact, I think she's probably going to take a leave of absence and disappear for a while."

"She's one of them, I mean money. I can smell it," Silva said. "Grow up poor like me, you get a good sniffer for those people. The way they dress. What's in, what's out."

"I guess girls who wear plaid skirts and bobby sox aren't part of the group she covers," Sonntag said. "I wouldn't know who wears what, and why. But maybe we're shooting too high. Maybe this is a nicely dressed daughter of an accountant or a dentist."

"Dentists are rich," Silva said.

Sonntag laughed. It was a fine chill hike back to the station. A message on his desk, left by the dispatcher, asked him to call a Mrs. Barbie of the Ranger Girls of America, as soon as possible. It was a Shorewood number.

"Lieutenant Sonntag here. You called?"

"Why, yes, Lieutenant. I fear something dreadful has happened."

"Well, I'll do what I can."

"We run a summer camp, you know, near Mequon. The Ranger Girls do. Girls come all summer, but we keep it open for weekend camps in the fall, you know."

"And you are?"

"I'm the regional director, sir. We're missing our young camp director. She's usually the only person there in the fall, after the girls are back in school, and she takes care of everything, and oversees the weekend camps. And now we can't find her."

"Have you contacted officers up there?"

"Oh, no, she lives here, you know. Her parents do. But they're traveling. We just discovered she's not on duty there. We drove there this morning and looked around, and she's simply gone, and from the looks of things, she's been gone a week or so. I mean, like moldy bread, and sour milk. And there was that girl in the paper. I heard about it."

"Her name?"

"Sandy. Sandra Millbank."

"And she's from Shorewood?"

"Yes, and she's not there, either. I mean, the phone doesn't ring."

"And how old is she?"

"Twenty-one, sir. She's a lovely girl. We need to find her."

"And what color is her hair?"

"A rich brown with a glint of red."

"And her eyes?"

"You know, I'm not sure. Isn't that odd? I'm not sure."

"And when did you discover this?"

"We've been calling the camp for two days, thinking we just missed her. I mean, she isn't there all the time. She has to get food for the weekends, and all. And she administers the camp in the fall. During the summer, a more senior lady administers."

"And you drove there this morning?"

"Yes, two of us, Ethel Mays and I, we drove to find out what was going on, and she wasn't there. So we thought she was here, Shorewood, and she's not. Then Ethel told me she had heard about a girl in the newspapers, and we're just worried sick."

"What did you do at the camp?"

"She has a cottage she lives in. There are dorms for the visiting girls. There are other cottages. We checked them all, walked around, opened doors—I have keys—and she wasn't there and the mail hadn't been opened or picked up, and it was just awful."

"By awful you mean her not being there? Or something else?"

"No, just not being there. She was gone."

"Where are her family?"

"Overseas, sir."

"We may have you come her and identify her, ma'am. If you can manage it."

"Identify? You mean, look at her, I mean, dead?"

"Yes, ma'am."

"Could I send Ethel?"

"We need someone as fast as possible. It won't be easy for you. Maybe you're talking about a different girl, maybe not. But we need to know, just as fast as possible. We'll send a car there for you—twenty minutes, okay?"

"Oh, heavens, this is awful."

"I'm going to need more info, ma'am. Where are her parents?"

"Lima, Peru. He's setting up something."

"Any brothers or sisters?"

"She talked of a brother—somewhere. And a married sister—somewhere."

"Relatives here?"

"I wouldn't know, officer. They've been here only two or three years."

"Did Sandy have a boyfriend? Fiancé?"

"She was seeing someone. But I wouldn't know his name. It's a Ranger Girl camp, you know."

"Did she talk of leaving? Being in trouble? Anything at all like that?"

"Well, when the summer ended, and school started, she wasn't sure she'd stay. She seemed uncertain. That's all I can say."

"Her father's business?"

"He's a very gifted man, sir. She introduced me once, very distinguished."

He got the names of other counselors, who could identify the girl. He'd fall back on those if Mrs. Barbie couldn't handle it.

There wasn't much else. He sent a car for her and another for Ethel Mays. He have a Shorewood cop check the house to see if anyone was there, and report anything unusual. They might need a warrant to break in. He put Silva on the travel agents. Maybe there would be a complete booking for the parents. A hotel, a ship, at least an itinerary.

He told Captain Ackerman he was heading for the morgue; the girl was probably a Sandra Millbank, and she ran a girls' camp out of town. Family scattered to hell and back.

"Tell me," Ackerman said. That was his shorthand for letting him know about two seconds of a positive identification.

This was going to be hard on these Ranger Girl leaders. Hard on everyone, the family, the girl's friends.

The morgue was grim gray concrete block walls and zinc tables and zinc sinks and a cruel antiseptic odor. Sonntag headed for a refrigeration chamber containing wide drawers, a little larger than a human body.

The coroner, Harry Bledsoe was at hand and the unidentified body had been withdrawn from its cabinet in the wall.

Mrs. Barbie arrived, plainly distraught.

"Ma'am, this won't be easy. It's just something we have to do. If you'd like to wait a few minutes we'll wait with you."

"No, I'm not a Ranger for nothing," she said.

He took her into the icy room, where the girl lay, covered with a sheet. It was very cold. He slid the sheet back from her head. Mrs. Barbie stared for only a moment.

"That's her," she said.

"Name her please."

"Sandy. Sandy Millbank."

"Any room for doubt?"

"She looks so gray. Oh, dear child, what ever happened to you?"

Chapter Seven

Then things moved fast. Eddy Walsh located the brother, Darren, in Santa Barbara. From him he got the name of the sister, Marge Wald, in Spring Valley, New York. And from them both they got a hotel address in Lima for the parents, and cabled them, with a copy to the U. S. Embassy. The father, John, was a consulting engineer who custom-designed heavy equipment, which was built by various Milwaukee companies. His wife, Linda, was there for the sightseeing. There is no more beautiful city than Lima in South America, or so the son believed.

The bad news traveled fast. The brother, Darren just kept muttering My god, My god, My god. The sister, Marge, wept and finally abandoned the phone.

From Darren, Detective Walsh got the name of a neighbor, Walt Gillis, who looked after the Shorewood house and had a key. Darren gave permission to look at Sandy's possessions.

So Joe Sonntag dialed.

"Mr. Gillis, Detective Sonntag here, Milwaukee police. You're taking care of the Millbank place, right?"

"Yes, sir. Is something wrong?"

"Yes there is. We've identified the young lady found in Washington Park as Sandy Millbank."

"Oh, no, oh, no."

"And we need to look in her room there. We have permission from Sandy's brother Darren. Could you meet a Shorewood policeman there in a few minutes?"

"Oh, no, not Sandy. I'm next door, to the south. Oh, how did this happen?"

"She was a counselor at a camp, right?"

"Yes, but here a lot, too."

"Did she have any boyfriends?"

"I couldn't say, sir. Have you notified her family?"

"Just did; that's how we found you."

"Is there any way I can help?"

"Let the Shorewood officer in, and help him."

Sonntag called Carl Marconi up there with the Shorewood PD and laid it out. Any scrap of paper with an address or phone number. Anything in Sandy's pockets. Anything that might point to a contact with an abortionist, or someone fronting for one.

Marconi, the senior man up there, listened carefully. "You want to join me, Joe?"

"I think so. I'll need an okay from the captain. How about a half hour?"

"I'll be waiting for you at the Millbank house."

Sonntag left his own people with plenty to do. He corralled Frank Silva and Eddy Walsh to run down some things. Who was the boyfriend? What did he know? Did he give her an address to go to?

"And see if you can get out to that camp," he told them. "We need to look at everything there. Mrs. Barbie's got keys and might help. We want addresses, phone numbers, camp logs if there are any, any regional phone calls in and out of there."

"The boyfriend, that's gonna be the best lead," Silva said. "Some boyfriends specialize in getting girls out of trouble."

"We'll see," Sonntag said shortly.

He told Ackerman where he was heading. "Nail that sonofabitch that got her pregnant," he said. "Loose peckers lead to trouble."

Carl Marconi was there when Sonntag found the place. It was a handsome brown brick home on an elm-shaded boulevard, with a manicured lawn flanked by beds of marigolds. Just the sort of place a young woman dressed in a pleated wool skirt would come from.

Marconi's claim to fame was that his great-uncle Guglielmo had invented the radio. And even now, the Shorewood cops had the best radio equipment of any force in the Midwest. They could even carry portable units on their belts, as Marconi now did.

"So this is the girl, eh?"

"'Fraid so, Carl. We got a positive ID this morning from a Ranger Girl lady."

"It just makes me sick, a girl getting life cut out of her like that. She should've just had the baby. Another innocent lost. Another life taken."

He was talking about the fetus, not the girl. Sonntag saw it differently. The girl's death was the tragedy.

Marconi unlocked, and they entered a cool, shadowed home with the curtains drawn tight against late summer heat.

"What are we looking for?" Marconi asked. "You sure we got permission?"

"The brother told me it's okay. Sandra's room, first of all. We're looking for anything that might lead us to the abortion mill that killed her. Like an address or phone number."

"Well, I hope we find what we're looking for. I'd like to close down that shop and throw the killer in jail for a few lifetimes."

"Let's just start downstairs. Anything, especially around the phone, or the kitchen."

But there wasn't anything. The place was spotless. Perhaps a cleaning lady kept it so. At least the phone did have a notepad beside it, and it was worth a look because there were indentations on the paper.

"I'll have our tech guys try to read it," Sonntag said.

They headed up a stairway with a runner on the polished stairs, held in place with brass rods. This was a four-bedroom home, with a master bedroom across the entire front of the house. Another room was obviously for guests or company. Now it was there for Darren or Marge. Sandra's room was easy to spot. It was well lived in. Its closet and dressers were stuffed; she had never lacked clothing. And what hung in the closets fit nicely with what she was wearing at the time she was found. There were photos of the parents and siblings and some children, all on her bedside table. The room was filled with her things, but intensively dusted and clean and kept in perfect order. Even the boxy gray bedspread lay flawlessly over her bed, the piping on it marching in arrow-straight lines down the sides.

"Carl, I'll start in on the pockets of everything in her closet; maybe you can tackle the dressers and anything else."

"I want a phone number or address so bad I can taste it," Marconi said.

"It'll probably be out at the camp," Sonntag said.

He examined Sandra's clothing a bunch at a time, and found no scrap of anything in any pocket. But Marconi did better. In a drawer of the bedside table, he found a gilded address book, gold fleurs-de-lis on brown leather. One got a sense from it that the numbers it contained were far more important than the numbers caught in an ordinary address book.

"Here," Marconi said.

He sat on the bed and began thumbing through. "What are we looking for?"

"Everything in there is what we're looking for," Sonntag said.

They studied the names and numbers. Lots of names and numbers. Sandra Millbank was a social young woman.

"We want names with addresses that aren't around here," Sonntag said. "Could be wrong, of course. Our abortion ring might be right down the boulevard. But I'm thinking we'd have better luck looking for the odd address."

They paged through, looking at each entry, neatly written in blue ink. Shorewood people, Whitefish Bay, north side Milwaukee. Also, the newer ones would be more interesting than the early ones high on the pages. There weren't any that stood out, until they got to the last pages, and one Arnold Wenzel, the last entry in the W pages, caught his eye. Arnold Wenzel lived on Lisbon Avenue, east of the zoo.

"Mind if I take this?" Sonntag asked.

"It's all yours. Your case, not mine, so far."

"While we're here, we'd better do a complete search," Sonntag said.

They pawed through the room, trying pockets, poking through drawers, looking for whatever. Sonntag felt he was intruding. He didn't always feel that way, digging into someone's life.

There was nothing else of interest.

"I guess we did some good," Marconi said. "If there's anything else, let me know. This is a Shorewood girl got killed, and I'm going to keep this deal open even if it didn't happen here, far as we know."

"That's good, and maybe it'll end up in your lap," Sonntag said.

They locked up, and Marconi headed next door to return the key.

Sonntag knew what he would do next. He'd find out who Wenzel was. And he'd have one of his detectives call Darren Millbank and have him identify all those people in the address book.

"Frank, you want to go with me?" Sonntag said. "We might have the guy. He lives a few blocks from the zoo."

Silva nodded. "I think I'm going to carry," he said.

"That's a very good idea. I'll carry too."

Usually, they didn't. And sometimes it was best not to. But this time, busting in on an abortionist, maybe there'd be some trouble, along with some arrests. Sonntag made sure he had a pair of cuffs as well, and then they were set.

Silva's cheap suit barely concealed the forty-five automatic in his shoulder holster. Silva would travel without a coat this day; you never knew about him. Sometimes he would bundle up on a warm day, and other times he would ignore cold and wander around as if it didn't exist. Sonntag always marveled at it.

"We got anything on this Wenzel?" Silva asked, as they headed for an unmarked car.

"I checked. Nothing. Unknown."

"Well, that's how an abortionist would want it. How long's he been at this address?"

"I didn't check that."

"It must be a lower flat. Thirty-seven fourteen-A. B will be upstairs."

Sonntag fired up the cruiser, a venerable Ford with the police decals painted over. Captain Ackerman thought that way. Cops didn't look like cops, and cop cars didn't look like cop cars, so plainclothes cops could wander around unnoticed.

Only Ackerman wasn't living in the real world.

"This looks like an easy one," Silva said. "Catch Wenzel and nail his associates and it's over."

"There's no such thing as an easy one," Sonntag said.

Silva grinned at him. Sonntag was famously the pessimist.

They pushed out Walnut to Lisbon Avenue, brick paving making the tires rumble. This was seedy Milwaukee, struggling little shops, walk-ups, bungalows, corner bars, peeling paint. This is where working folks with lunch buckets caught streetcars to the factories. It sure wasn't where well-off people collected. Not a place where the likes of Sandra Millbank would come—unless she felt she had to.

The building turned out to be a white frame duplex, the paint stained yellow and gray by weather and the toxic chemicals pouring from Milwaukee's smokestacks.

Sonntag cruised past, for a good look, and studied the rest of the street. Rust-bucket cars, rotting from salt on the wintry streets. A Chinese laundry. He cut north and turned again at the alley, and crawled down it. Garbage cans, junk, a bedspring, a small garden plot, carefully tended. Scruffy back yards, utility poles. No rear door, but a side door opening onto a concrete walk that would take people to the alley. Probably a stair well inside, so the tenants upstairs could use that door. No parking area back there. No place to stash a car for the duration of an abortion. Also, no rear apartment or separate building back there. Just a scruffy lawn and what looked like a rabbit hutch, or maybe it was for something else, birds or something.

Sonntag crawled past, eyeing the neighborhood. Not Sandra Millbank's neighborhood.

He swung around the block and parked on Lisbon, directly in

front of the place.

"The abortionist isn't making much money," Silva said. "Or at least not spending any around here."

They headed for the front door. There were two, and one said 3714A.

Sonntag knocked.

It took a while, but eventually the door creaked open, and he beheld a cleanly dressed and bespectacled young man, who looked puzzled. The guy used a single crutch, and a glance at his leg explained why. Wenzel had a severe clubfoot, wore a brace clamped over his trouser leg, and needed the crutch because his right leg was inches shorter than the other one.

"You Mister Wenzel?"

"I am, sir."

"I'm Lieutenant Sonntag, Milwaukee police, and this is Detective Silva. You mind if we talk?"

"I knew it, I just knew it," he said. "It's about Sandy."

Chapter Eight

Wenzel invited them in. The room was sparsely furnished, and the furnishings were decrepit.

"Have a seat," Wenzel said. "I'm Arnold Wenzel. I suppose you've figured it out."

"Figured what out?"

"How I got to know her."

"Know who?" Silva asked.

"Sandy Millbank."

"Okay, tell us," Sonntag said, sinking into a lumpy couch with springs jabbing his rear.

"Are we talking about the same thing? Are you here for some other reason?"

"What reason is there, Mr. Wenzel?"

The young man sagged into a horsehair chair. "It's Sandy, then. I knew we'd be found out some day."

Sonntag wasn't making a lot of sense of it. "Okay, tell us how you met her."

"Are you sure this is private?"

"No, it's not private. We're cops. Public servants."

"But it might hurt her reputation. Have you given no thought to that? Isn't it best just to keep quiet about hurtful things?"

"What would hurt her reputation?"

"Look, I'm embarrassed. I thought you were here for some other reason."

"What was your relationship to her?" Silva asked.

Sonntag interrupted. "Yes, we'd like to protect Miss Millbank, as much as we can," he said.

Wenzel blinked, and Sonntag swore there were tears rising in the young man's eyes.

"We were more than friends," he said. "I don't know what we were. I owe it to my bad leg. Maybe it was charity. Maybe she was just a rich girl who wanted to be kind."

Sonntag stayed quiet, and Silva did too.

"She was an impossible dream for me, you know. When you face what I face every hour of my life, you know there's no chance of romance. A girl, a marriage, children, home, family, love, tenderness. You live here, as I do, half-starved, unable to go out much. It's all I can manage just to get on a streetcar, and I can't afford a taxi. Or ride a bike. I mean, this is my home and my jail. I do have a little work, mostly seasonal, because I'm an accountant. They bring files here for me to work on. If it weren't for that, I'd be in the county home."

Sonntag eyed Silva, willing him not to say anything, not one word. Silva nodded slightly. Wenzel was getting around to it his own way, and that was good enough.

"Do you want some coffee?" Wenzel asked.

"We're fine, sir, but if you'd like to make some for yourself, we'll wait," Sonntag said.

"No, it'd be for you," Wenzel said. "She was the only woman I ever knew. I mean, as a friend."

Silva was getting itchy, so Sonntag gave him a stern stare.

"The Millbanks, they haven't been here long," Wenzel said. "But she got right into the thick of it. She joined everything there was to join. She'd always been in the Ranger Girls, so that was easy. But she got into other stuff, like the Milwaukee Friends Society. That's where rich people try to help handicapped people like me. She joined that, you know. They try to get shut-ins outside and give them a good time, brighten their lives some. Well, that's how I met her. They arranged to have a big party at a nice place, the Eagles Club, and sent drivers for all the people like me, so I went. I'd hardly ever gotten out in my life. It's too hard. But they took people like me there, to the ballroom, and it was all decorated with balloons and crepe, and there was even a band., like Jimmy Dorsey's but it wasn't him. I'd never even seen a band live, like that. And all those society people, they were trying to make us all happy, good time, and all. So that's how I met her."

"She sounds like she was a sweet gal," Silva said.

"Oh, officer, you don't know the half of it. That night, well, I'll never forget it. She came over to where I was sitting and said she wanted to dance. You can guess how I felt. I just shied away and wanted to tell her to go away, but she just smiled. She said, You don't have to hold me; I'll hold you. And I was real angry at her for ignoring my leg, but she held out a hand and I couldn't resist. I'd hardly held a girl's hand in my life, not like that, and she helped me up and I got this crutch under me, and just like she said, she led me out to the floor, it was so shiny and waxed, and then she held me. My one hand was holding my crutch, so I couldn't dance, but she took my other hand with hers, and we just sort of rocked back and forth. The band was playing "I'll Be Seeing You," and then it was playing "Perfidia," and then it was playing "Someone to Watch Over Me," and there she was, just sort of holding me up, because I was worthless to dance, and there she was, her face looking across at me, and she was smiling like that, and she was pretty, and the fox trots were playing, and the waltzes, and then the band played "All of Me," and she smiled, and she let me dance with her for a long time, until I couldn't lean on my crutch any more, and then she helped me to my seat and got me stuff from the buffet ..."

Wenzel was fighting back the wetness welling from his eyes.

Sonntag just sat there, dumb in the head.

Silva kept quiet too.

"A man doesn't kiss and tell," Wenzel said.

"I guess not," Sonntag said.

"It was charity, you know. She just wanted someone out of luck, with a bad leg, to know—to know what it was like. Just to know. Just once in his miserable life. It just was a kindness, that's all. She just was being kind to me. I mean, it would never go anywhere. It was just her thinking she'd make that poor guy happy for a little while."

"She was like that, I guess," Silva said.

"She just had a big heart. She was trying to make the whole world happy. I just was lucky. She spotted me, and she thought she could give this guy a break, and that's how it happened. I shouldn't even be telling you this. It's private. It's none of your business. But you came here, and so I tried to help you, and now you know."

"Ah, know what?"

"What I saw in the *Journal*. I saw the picture and it was her and couldn't bring myself to call you. Then it said she died of a hemorrhage from an unlawful procedure. I may be stuck in this dump, but I try to know what the rest of the world knows."

"Your child?"

Wenzel's face clouded. "Maybe she had six charity cases going." The tears rose again. "No, that's not fair. Sandy wasn't like that. It was the first time for both of us. I didn't want to, but she just sort of led me. She'd never been with a man. I shouldn't be talking like this, like it's anything for strangers to know about."

"First time for her?"

"We were both pretty dumb," Wenzel said. "But we laughed. She's the only person on earth who could make me laugh."

"For a few days, a few weeks?"

"A few weeks, Mr. Silva. She came back from her camp sometimes, just to see me."

"And she kept coming?"

Wenzel sighed. "She told me she couldn't come here any more, and my whole world turned dark again."

"Was that recent?"

"It was a month or so ago. I don't think I'll ever forget it, the way she tried to say it kindly but it still was goodbye, and then I never heard again."

"Then what happened, sir?"

"Nothing. My whole world went back to what it was."

"She didn't ask you for help?" Silva asked.

Sonntag wished he hadn't asked that.

Wenzel stared. "I get it now. You want to put me in handcuffs and haul me off."

"Mr. Wenzel, it's okay. That's not what we're here for," Sonntag said. "Somebody did something to her, and we'd like to know who. She died. We'd like to keep other girls from dying."

"And that's what boyfriends do, find out where to get the little problem fixed." Wenzel's face had turned dark, and if anything, even more bleak. "So you came calling."

"I'm sorry," Sonntag said. "Sometimes it's hard to get at what we need to know."

"So, here are my wrists," Wenzel said. "Snap on the cuffs."

"Actually, you've helped us a great deal," Sonntag said. "We share your grief. You cared a lot."

"If I could make an altar, I'd have her picture on it," Wenzel said. "But she was a temporary god, you know. And it wasn't love; it was pity."

"I think it was more than that," Sonntag said. "She met a fellow named Arnold Wenzel and she cared a whole lot."

"Are you done?" Wenzel said, struggling to his feet.

Sonntag thought he'd only made it worse.

"We're done. Thank you for your help."

"What help?"

"Part of finding who did what is simply a process of elimination," Sonntag said.

Wenzel, crutch in hand, herded them to the door. "I've got to get back to my accounting," he said.

"If you think of anything, call us," Silva said. "Here's a card."

They found themselves on the shabby porch, smelling the exhaust of cars rattling along Lisbon Avenue. At least the day was bright.

"I'm sorry," Silva said. "I keep learning from you about talking to people."

"You're better at it than I am," Sonntag said.

They clambered into the unmarked car, rolled down windows to let some air in, and Sonntag drove toward the station. They both were oddly silent.

But then Sonntag broke the ice. "It took an able man to carry her body to that spot in the ferns. Someone who could drive to the parking lot, and then carry her."

"You never know," Silva said. "Did you see his shoulders?"

"I'm a sucker for a few tears," Sonntag said. "But let's put it this way: we've got better leads."

"I think we should check out his story. The Eagles dance, all that," Silva said.

"You just volunteered," Sonntag said.

"I want to do it. I'm curious about it. That Milwaukee Friends Society, her membership, all that. And what the band was playing."

"Like I say, I'm a sucker when it comes to tears," Sonntag said. "Give it a whirl."

Back at the station, they found Eddy Walsh waiting for them.

He waved that gilded leather address book, and plunged in. "I called the brother, Darren, and read him these names. He said he'd never heard of any of these people. They weren't family names or old family friends. But he said he'd never lived in Milwaukee; settled in California before his parents moved here. So he wouldn't know these people."

"No relatives?"

"Not a one. He thought Sandy must have some other address book, with family in it."

"Who are these people, then?" Sonntag asked.

"Well, I called the sister, Marge, and tried the same deal, and got the same result. She hadn't spent much time in Milwaukee either, and didn't know anyone listed here. Just Sandra's friends, that's all, she said. So she wasn't helping any. I tried Mrs. Barbie next, you know, the regional Ranger Girl director, or whatever office it is. I read her the same names from this address book, and she hardly knew many. She did know a few. North side people, mostly. I asked if these were names from camp, and she didn't think so."

"So we have a book of contacts, and we don't know who or what?"

"Yeah, that's it."

"What do you make of it, Eddy?"

"Sandra Millbank was living one hell of a life, if you ask me," Walsh said.

Chapter Nine

Some of the trees were starting to show fall color, capping the surrounding hills with crowns of gold. Sonntag and Silva drove the two-lane ribbon of concrete north and west, toward Mequon, where the summer camp nestled in gentle hills covered with oak and walnut. This was dairy country, with herds of black and white cattle clustered in the bottoms. The unmarked cruiser was behaving itself.

They would meet Mrs. Barbie at the girls' camp. The brother, Darren, had given them permission to go through Sandy Millbank's stuff. Sonntag badly wanted a number. One little phone number written somewhere, but he knew the chances would be slim. The scattered family had requested that the girl be buried as soon as possible; there would be a memorial service when the parents could get back from Peru. The second autopsy revealed nothing new; it ratified the first, without the slightest deviation. She had died of a hemorrhage. That ended the police department's interest in the remains, and the family had been in touch with a mortician.

"Open country is scary," Frank Silva said.

"This? What's scary about it?"

"There's no people, and lots of cows."

"Cows are scary?"

"Anything with four feet larger than a dog is dangerous."

"Lizbeth and I drive out here all the time, and visit cheese factories."

"Well, cheese is scary. I mean, that's rotted leftovers from making butter, isn't it?"

Sonntag laughed. Frank Silva got uneasy whenever his feet left pavement.

"I don't know what it is, but it tastes good."

"Are there snakes out here?"

"Probably some garter snakes."

"I'm staying in the car."

"Everything you eat comes from farms," Sonntag said. "Farms like these."

"Well, I'm almost a vegetarian. Can you imagine killing a chicken? Can you imagine slitting the throat of a hog? I can't even eat a hamburger without thinking of some cow in its last mortal agony."

"You should be glad wheat and corn don't die in pain."

"I'm not so sure about that. Plants have feelings. I feel guilty whenever I bite into a carrot. Or lettuce. I eat murdered lettuce. I eat potatoes whose life ended violently. I live in guilt."

"Well, do you like bouquets?" Sonntag ventured. "They're nothing but murdered flowers."

Silva pondered that. "I'll never look at a bouquet in the same way again."

They reached a long rise, and the engine began to labor, so Sonntag shifted to second gear, and the car recovered and crawled upward. When they topped the hill, they found a broad valley flanked by bluffs ahead. The camp was along there somewhere. Sonntag restored first gear, and they rumbled down the hill, the noisy tires protesting.

A birch-bark-framed sign announced Camp Ravenswood, and Sonntag turned off on a sandy two-rut lane that was flanked by towering forest.

"We're crazy to come here," Silva said. "A tree could fall on us."

But Sonntag shifted to second gear to help the tires plow

through sand, and eventually the lane opened out on a meadow dotted with structures. There were rows of wall tents in military array, some board and batten cabins, and what appeared to be a dining and administration center. Off a way were tennis and badminton courts, horseshoe courts, and a volleyball area.

A blue Buick was parked at the administrative building, so Sonntag headed there and parked beside it.

"There's gonna be snakes," Silva said.

"Maybe even saber-toothed tigers," Sonntag said.

"You're making fun of me, but I mean it."

"I'll dispatch any snake," Sonntag said.

Silva slowly emerged from the black cruiser and studied the immediate surroundings until he was satisfied that no man-eating armadillo would crash through the trees.

Mrs. Barbie was awaiting them.

"Welcome, gentlemen," she said. "This is our summer camp. This is where Sandy Millbank lived, and kept the camp operating on weekends for various groups of girls."

"Is it entirely safe?" Silva asked.

"Why, certainly it is. And we teach safety and first aid to the girls who come here. We even have a small infirmary where we can patch up girls who scrape a knee or cut a finger. In fact, all our counselors and guides are trained in first aid. And we have a visiting nurse during the season. The girls are always catching something or other. Once in a while we need to call parents and ask them to take a girl back home. Especially when it's measles or something like that. And of course, polio. . . oh, how we worry during the polio season."

"I mean, like snakes."

"I haven't seen one here in years, detective."

"Ah, Mrs. Barbie, this is Detective Silva. He's one of our finest."

"Well, we welcome you, then," she said. "May I give you the tour, or do you want to go straight to Sandy's cabin? As a camp administrator she rated a cabin of her own, you know."

"Let's see the camp first," Sonntag said.

"I'll stay here," Silva said.

"Detectives, I'd love to show you the place," Mrs. Barbie said.

Silva surrendered.

She led them along well graveled paths, past the tennis and badminton courts, and playing fields.

"The courts are always busy," she said, "but we spend far more time and energy on our nature walks. We have trails that run several miles, going through woods and meadows where there's abundant wildlife and plants. Some walks are discovery trips, to teach about nature, but some walks are for safety and health and emergency survival in nature. That's where the girls learn to forage for food, stay warm, avoid things like poison ivy, and build emergency shelters."

"Where's the poison ivy?"

"Why, it isn't common, but it's lurking around."

"I knew I should've stayed in the car."

She led them along another graveled pathway to the wall tents, a sea of sun-bleached canvas with a small commons in the middle, and a fire pit in the commons.

"The girls stay here, about a hundred at a time, usually for two weeks through the summers," she said.

"There are four cots per tent. The tents have wooden floors, and there are two washroom facilities over there."

"The girls have to walk over there at night?"

"It's well lit, detective."

"What's to keep bears out?"

"I don't think we've ever seen a bear, sir. We're only a few miles from Milwaukee."

Sonntag peered in. The cots were narrow metal bedsteads with bare springs that would support a mattress. The bedding had all been removed. The tents actually looked quite comfortable. The girls were well cared for.

"We usually have a bonfire in the commons here, and the girls sing and sometimes hear speakers," she said. "The girls make friends here, and just love these bonfires. But it's too late for that now. We do keep weekend camps going into late fall, but they're indoors for the most part."

"Doesn't the rain come through the canvas?" Silva asked.

"Oh, sometimes, when the canvas is worn. But mostly it runs off."

She led them past horse shoe courts, and eventually back to the dining hall, kitchen and administration.

"Here's where they're fed," she said, ushering them into a hall with trestle tables and benches. "All the girls get some kitchen duty. This isn't a camp for rich children. The girls clean up, wash dishes, sweep the floor, wipe down the tables. All of that. It's good for them."

"Do snakes get in here?" Silva asked.

She laughed.

They peered into the kitchen, with its black ranges and banked refrigerators and zinc-topped work surfaces, and then the rest of the building: an office, a medical room with an examination table and various sorts of bandaging. Sonntag thought a doc or nurse could stitch a wound and bandage it, but not do much more.

"We rarely need this, but it's good to have," she said.

There were six administrative cabins in a row, behind the administrative area, and Mrs. Barbie led them that way, while Silva dodged gophers.

"Well, here we are," she said. "This is where Sandy stayed. It hasn't been touched."

She unlocked the door. The cabin was simple: a rectangle with a bed and a living area. The bathroom facilities were in the administration building.

"Shall I wait for you?" she asked.

"I guess that would be best, Mrs. Barbie." Sonntag said. "Thanks."

"Are we cleaning out the room? I really need to move these things to storage. We have a storage room in the office area."

"You know, that might be helpful. But I can't guarantee that we'll release any of this. It may be evidence," Sonntag said.

Mrs. Barbie headed into the sunlight. The detectives eyed the room, which was clean, neat, orderly, and plainly temporary. There was only a small electric wall heater that would not suffice in serious cold. Sandy Millbank lived quietly. The bed was made.

There was no spread; simply a blanket drawn tight, folded well at the corners, with a pillow at the head. The bedside table had no drawer. Her skirts and dresses and jackets hung neatly in an alcove. Another alcove had a counter and a mirror and some pine shelves. There was a bottle of aspirin on the shelf. A small bag on the counter contained toothbrush and paste, a small razor, some soap, and shampoo. The three drawers of the dresser held neatly folded blouses, Bermuda shorts, sweaters, stockings, underwear, and pajamas. A row of canvas and leather outdoor shoes lined the floor of the alcove. On a hook were several belts and a cotton nightgown. On another hook was a terrycloth bathrobe. Below it, some blue slippers. There was no phone. No loose papers with addresses or phone numbers or appointments written on them.

"We'll need to look at the bathroom in the other building, and also the office," Silva said.

"We're going to have to check pockets here," Sonntag replied.

They worked systematically through the skirts and dresses, finding nothing. They tried the blouses and sweaters, finding nothing.

Silva pulled the two suitcases at the back of the alcove out and opened them. He searched the pockets, finding some band-aids, an emergency sewing kit, a pair of sunglasses, and a fever thermometer in its case.

"We ain't finding any royal highway into the offices of any abortionist," Silva said.

"We shouldn't make assumptions," Sonntag said. "We don't even know whether she found an abortionist. We don't know whether she was pregnant. If there was an abortion, we don't know who did it. We can't rule out a little home intervention."

"Wenzel?"

"I'd hate for that to be the case."

"Yeah, who knows?"

"Still, if a lady's going to get the procedure, she would need to plan it; know where to go and when; know what to do if she bleeds. And we're not seeing any of that here," Sonntag said.

They finally gave up. Sandy Millbank's home away from home revealed nothing more than her bedroom had in Shorewood. All it told Sonntag was that she was an orderly young woman.

They drifted to the bathrooms in the administrative building, knocked, and found a room with two showers, some shelves with neatly stacked towels and wash cloths, two partitioned johns, two sinks, and some small mirrors. She had not left anything there, unless some shampoo was hers.

Silva intuitively steered toward the laundry, which had two wringer-type machines. Here were some used sheets unwashed and soaking in water.

"I guess she had changed her sheets," he said. He stirred the soaking sheets.

"Why do you soak sheets?" he asked.

"Good question. I'll ask Lizbeth," Sonntag said.

They poked around the office, looking for something, anything, in her handwriting. Mrs. Barbie sat at a desk there, staring at them.

"I thought you were looking for information about Sandy," she said. "This is our camp office."

"We thought she might have left an address or phone number," Sonntag said. They did not have permission to look there and really had little reason to do so.

"Well, should we move her stuff?" she asked.

"I think you can go ahead. We're through here," Sonntag said.

"Well, I'll take care of it. We'll have to find another woman to stay here. Either that or cancel our fall program."

"What do you do in the fall, ma'am?"

"It's less focused on nature, and more upon womanhood and the responsibilities we assume as we reach adulthood," she said.

"You have teachers?"

"Yes, and Sandy was one."

"What did she teach?"

"Good behavior," Mrs. Barbie said.

"Do you have a personnel list?" Silva asked. "I mean, the people who run the place? Employees? Pay ledgers?"

"Certainly," she said. "But I don't see what business it is of yours."

"I'd like to talk to them," Silva said. "Maybe get some more ideas about Sandy."

"Yes, that's good, Frank," Sonntag said. "A ledger, ma'am?"

"Well, it's mostly volunteers, you know. We had only a few paid people. The camp director, Amanda Winthrop, paid of course. She's a teacher; this is her summer occupation. And our visiting nurse, Mrs. Boetticher, of course. And our cook, a lovely nutritionist, Sylvia Purdy. But really, our instructors and counselors, all volunteers. Lovely women, dedicated to the Rangers."

"Sandy was paid?"

"Yes, for her off-season time. During the regular season, she was a volunteer."

"We'd like to borrow the ledgers, ma'am," Sonntag said.

"But we need them. I have a camp to run."

"Just for a day or two. We can make photocopies."

"Why do you need them?"

"The people who knew Sandy best are in that ledger, ma'am. And we'll be talking to them all."

"That's awful. Please don't. It's invasive. They'll be so distressed."

"If we have to get a court order for those personnel documents, we'll do it, ma'am."

She stared, and surrendered. "I'll want a receipt,' she said.

There were two ledgers, neatly maintained with pen and ink entries. One for all personnel, and another for paid personnel. Sonntag and Silva collected them both and left a receipt.

Chapter Ten

It had come to nothing. Somehow, Sonntag had guessed how it would end. They now had worked through everything Sandra Millbank possessed, and had found no numbers, no appointment, no clue. Somewhere, she had probably gotten an abortion and it had turned fatal. But several days of investigation had not yielded a lead.

"That ended about the way I thought it would," he said to Silva as they drove back to the city. "I'm wondering now if we're looking for the wrong thing. Maybe there's no abortion ring, no back-alley joint operating somewhere. No one out pimping the place, slipping phone numbers to school girls."

"Yeah, I'm thinking the same thing."

They drove east, into a fading afternoon, along a little-used two-lane highway. Pretty soon the northwestern reaches of the city would begin to show up in the split-glass windshield. The ranger camp was just far enough out to give city girls a country session in Wisconsin's rolling hills and introduce them to Burma Shave signs.

"We've got that phone book full of upper east side people. And the camp personnel ledgers. I suppose we could start by asking questions. Do they know her, and how did they meet, and why are they in her address book? Who knows where that might go?" Sonntag asked.

A box turtle was crawling across the lane ahead, so Sonntag braked.

"What are you stopping for?"

"Why should I kill the turtle?"

"Jaysas," said Silva.

Sonntag stopped on the shoulder, got out, lifted the turtle and carried it to the other side of the highway. The turtle pulled inside of its shell and didn't move after Sonntag said it down. Sonntag climbed in and shifted to low gear.

"We're going after an abortionist and you're saving turtles," Silva said.

"When you've seen as much death as I have, maybe you'd care about turtles," Sonntag replied.

"That rings a bell," Silva said.

"I'm for life."

"Tell that to your hamburger."

"Sandy should have had her child. She'd be alive today. And she'd either be blessed with a baby, or she'd bless some family that adopted it."

"Yeah, if the baby was a good one. But if it had two heads or no brain or someone raped her, or she had a bad heart and couldn't carry a child without killing herself, maybe it'd be another story."

"That wouldn't have made it any less wrong," Sonntag said.

"Yes it would. I don't see it the way you do."

"Or the way the law does?"

"Yeah, that's right. I don't like that law. I'm sworn on my badge to enforce it, but I don't always like it."

"There's a lot of those laws," Sonntag said.

"I don't know why government has to stick its neck into everyone's business," Silva said. "If a girl needs an abortion, she should have the right."

"Theology," Sonntag said.

"Well, me and theology don't mix."

"I'm caught in the middle," Sonntag said. "I always figured that life begins at birth. You know, if it can't live outside the womb, it's not life. It's proto-life. Live cells developing into human life but not there yet. Not actual life, not a baby breathing on its own. So it seems sort of minor if someone chooses to get rid of it. Maybe still wrong, just because we need to respect our nature, but not a big deal."

"Then why are we chasing down a phantom abortionist?"

"Accidental death in the commission of a crime. Manslaughter. We do what the law requires us to do."

"You mind telling me what Lizbeth thinks about that?"

"She's sort of secretive. Like it's not men's business. She's a good church lady, and sort of goes along with everything coming from the pulpit, but you know what? She wants a little wiggle room in there, but doesn't want me to see it. I don't think she believes that a soul magically settles upon a few cells the moment of conception. She leaves that stuff to the doctors of religion. There's something more practical in her. Like she thinks it's wrong, but maybe sometimes it's okay, and sometimes it's necessary, and it's not the business of any man. I think she'd like to see a women's hospital where women make those decisions and to hell with men and a mess of law enacted by men. But she's sort of squirrelly about telling me what she thinks. It's like, stay out of here."

"Molly, she just laughs and tells me to mind my own business," Silva said.

"Maybe that's how it should be," Sonntag said. "If women were in legislatures making laws, things would be different."

Silva mulled that a moment. "Hell, if Molly were making laws, rich people and capitalists wouldn't be allowed to have children."

"If I could write that law, Frank. I'd make some exemptions. No woman should bear the child of her rapist. Or any child that's incestuous. Or any child that's deformed or not viable when born. I mean, look at nature itself. Miscarriages. When do they happen? When the mother's ill or so weak she can't carry. When the genetic material's bad or the embryo can't live. That's what happens with incest or rape. That's basically my belief. Whatever the medical reasons for a miscarriage, that should be a valid reason for an abortion. I'm saying, a woman should have the right to abort if it is what happens in nature anyway, sort of haphazardly."

"So you'd like a few loopholes?"

"I've seen too much hurt, Frank. Yeah, for any good medical reason. That's where I am."

"Only we're sworn to arrest people for doing some of that stuff."

"And that's not going to change, Frank."

"Yeah, me against theology again."

Sonntag was hooked into traffic now, and on the tail of a Packard working down Fond du Lac Avenue. "It doesn't matter what we think. We've got an abortionist around here, doing illegal operations, cleaning girls out of every dime they can raise, sometimes ruining them, destroying their chance to have children, lead a regular life. He's got contacts out, luring girls, pulling them into a shadow world. And killing a few because he's not very good at it. Sandra Millbank was murdered, one way or another. And we're going to stop that. Here's one thing I'm going to do when we get back. I'm going to have a look at hospital and death records. I'm going to look at every case where a woman of child-bearing age either dies, or has some sort of female surgery. Sandra Millbank isn't very likely to be the only one. That can be a dangerous operation in the hands of someone who's not skilled and doesn't have a lot of medical equipment right there. And that means maybe there are others who've slid past; a hospital repair that got listed as something else. And that's likely to lead us somewhere, even if we didn't find anything out there."

"Yeah, there's the predator, and the pimps and the guys who want a cut of the dough, and that makes it worth while, even if the rest of it bothers me." Silva paused to watch a mother wheeling a pram along the sidewalk. "I just wish there was a safe place for those girls to go. A legal place. I wish some state would offer it. Maybe not here, but somewhere."

"Maybe Nevada," Sonntag said. "They're the only state with quickie everything."

He steered into the lot where the cruisers were parked. It had been full day's trip, but they'd gotten a little farther along. Sandy Millbank's life was a little clearer now. And one by one, they were eliminating possibilities.

"You start in on death records for, say, the last two years?"

"Yeah, and hospital records. Women of child-bearing age in for female operations, right?"

"You sound like Lizbeth," Sonntag said. "But yeah. Let's try some history. And I'll be working on those people in that address book."

He found a message from Charles Bauer, the mortician up in Shorewood, asking him to call.

Sonntag dialed at once, and was swiftly connected to Bauer.

"Ah, yes, detective. It's about the remains of Miss Millbank. Am I correct in believing we may gather these at the morgue?"

"Yes, sir, the coroner's done, and we're done, and a release is waiting for you there."

"Good. We'll be along, then. Mr. Millbank, the brother, is making arrangements. He's on his way here."

"On his way?"

"Yes, sir, on the Super Chief. Be here tomorrow. His parents will have to get here from Peru. His sister is, I believe, incapacitated for the time being, so the memorial service won't be too soon."

"Incapacitated?"

"Almost nine months along, sir."

"Will the brother, Darren, be arranging any immediate service?"

"That's something we'll discuss, sir. All we know at the moment is that the remains will be buried promptly and a service will follow when the bereaved can gather."

"I'm going to butt in here, sir. Is there any hope for a viewing? A visitation?"

"We haven't discussed it, but I will bring it up."

"If there is, Mr. Bauer, please let us know."

"I understand, sir. You will want to know things."

"Yes, and it would be best if none of this reaches the brother."

"I understand, sir."

Sonntag hung up, thinking it was a break. Anyone who would arrange the girl's body beside a bed of ferns, and fold her arms over her breast, and line up her legs, might well be among those who signed the guest book.

He wondered who he could send over there who didn't look like a cop. He knew full well that anyone on the force looked like he belonged on the force, whether he was in blues or wearing street clothes. That's just the way it was. He wondered what it was about cops.

It occurred to him to send Lizbeth. She was sharp. She wouldn't miss a thing. Maybe Ackerman would let him. She had x-ray vision. She could see inside a turnip. She could read minds across a room. And she could linger there, in a chair, and watch the strangers drift in and out, and no one would pay her any heed.

Chapter Eleven

Amanda Winthrop turned out to be a silver-haired, slim woman with hawkish features. She met Sonntag and Silva in the teachers lounge at Shorewood High School, where she taught social studies. If she found the interview disagreeable, she was not revealing it, Sonntag thought.

"Poor dear," she said. "She just wasn't the type."

"The type for what?" Sonntag asked.

"The type to get into trouble. Nice home. It doesn't fit."

"I'm not following, ma'am. What doesn't fit?"

The slightest pause suggested annoyance. "I keep thinking this is impossible," she said. "Sandy Millbank would not engage in conduct of the sort that would get her into trouble. No, I'll amend that. If she did, she would be...well prepared, if you follow me. She was not capable of fits of passion, you know. She sailed smoothly along, and that's why she became out deputy director. She was simply incapable of reckless behavior. We had every confidence in her."

"But she let you down?"

"Well, obviously, she did. She engaged in conduct that was most embarrassing to the Ranger Girls. The scandal doesn't go away. It percolates just below the surface. Every regional and local administrator is trying to cope with what Sandy's misconduct has done to the Ranger Girls. We have a crisis beyond description."

"Too young, eh?" Silva asked.

"We put much too much trust in her. Perhaps we didn't quite realize how much her scattered and unsettled family had undermined her character."

"And now she's dead, age twenty-one, a whole life ahead of her," Silva said. "It makes me ache, just thinking about it."

"And Camp Ravenswood in ruins. How can we even reopen? That girl!"

"Mrs. Winthrop, I raised a couple of boys and I don't know much about Ranger Girls," Sonntag said.

"Well, then you wouldn't," she said. "It's hard even to describe Ranger Girls to anyone who has no daughters."

"Well, see if you can give me an idea, anyway."

"Ranger Girls are for women entering adolescence and approaching adulthood. That is, we welcome girls at age twelve, and they graduate at eighteen, at the time they finish high school. We like to say we bring in girls and turn them into women."

"The difficult years," Silva said.

"Detective, I don't suppose you know much about that."

"I guess not," Silva said.

His abashed smile didn't help any, Sonntag thought.

"We have a variety of goals and programs, and Camp Ravenswood reflected them all, sir. We teach our girls to become independent and competent. We have strong athletic programs. We have citizenship programs. We introduce girls to the natural world. Nature walks. Birds. Plants. Rocks. We take great pride in our social conscience programs. They learn compassion for the world's oppressed and poor. We provide counsel and instruction to young women going through adolescence and entering the world of dating, boys, romance, husbands—and all that. We instruct them in the difficulties of womanhood, which is something so many mothers fail to do, or don't do well. We have a visiting nurse at Ravenswood, who not only looks after minor medical matters, scraped elbows and runny noses, but also quietly helps young women prepare for adulthood and motherhood. So, you see? Sandy

Millbank let us down terribly. Of course we miss her, but this never should have happened."

"What shouldn't have happened, ma'am?"

She sighed, frowned, and eyed the door. "For someone who teaches how to avoid pitfalls to set such a bad example, sir..."

"Sandy Millbank set a bad example?"

"The record speaks for itself."

"What sort of pitfalls, ma'am?"

"Pregnancy. Ranger Girls all receive counseling privately. Usually from the visiting nurse at our camps, or at special meetings during the rest of the year."

"Do doctors come to the camps?"

"We have a physician on call. A woman, I should say. Ranger Girls takes great pride in running camps independently."

"This nurse, let's see here, she's Mrs. Boetticher?"

"Yes. When the camp is operating during the summers, she's there most mornings."

"Where does she work?" Silva asked.

"St. Luke's. She's in the maternity ward. She also works for someone or other, a gynecologist."

"She knows a lot about all that, then."

"All that, all that, happens to be the most important things in a young woman's life as she marries and prepares for motherhood."

"Sure, and that's very important, ma'am. Now, did Sandy have any close friends in camp?"

"She simply loved the girls flowing in and out of camp. I don't know that she had any close friends. It's a pity she didn't, because someone who knew her better than I did might have talked her out of her recklessness."

"I guess we're back to that. She got reckless with someone, right? Any idea who, when, or how?"

"I will not discuss such things. Especially since it's all speculation."

"Do you mind if we talk to the rest of your personnel?" Silva asked.

"I don't suppose anything I say will prevent it," she replied.

Her unblinking gaze had become a wall.

"I guess we'll be on our way, then," Sonntag said. "If you come up with any ideas, please give me a call. Here's my card."

"The chance of my calling you, sir, is rather slight, I think. But I will keep you card if lightning strikes."

Oddly, she was smiling broadly. Sonntag had the sense that she was smiling because she had utterly defeated two Milwaukee detectives.

It took a long time to drive to the south side, where St. Luke's nestled among the teeming neighborhoods, Poles and Greeks, Bohemians, Slavs, Italians, all jostling one another, where streets ran Latvian in one block and Ukranian the next. Mrs. Boetticher was on duty in the maternity ward and pleased to talk.

"We've got one coming," she said. "But we've some time. The contractions are still a bit apart. When they speed up, I'll have to leave you, okay?"

"Countdown time, eh?" Silva asked.

"Better here than in the back seat of a taxi," she said

The nurse was big, hearty, apple-cheeked, and wore a starched nurse's cap. She looked capable of delivering three babies simultaneously while lifting two-hundred pound bar bells. Sonntag wondered if she was a midwife.

"That poor girl," she said. "I loved her so. She was so giving, you know? All she wanted from life was to give to others. I just plain cried."

"It sure was a loss," Sonntag said. "A loss for Camp Ravenswood, too. A loss for the Ranger Girls."

"Oh, you've been talking to Amanda Winthrop," she said. "She didn't really care for Sandy, and when this business happened...." An loud groan echoed in the hallway. "Oh my, forgive me. Let me check on my little mother."

She dashed into the delivery room and returned moments later. "Ten and a half minutes," she said. "We'll make it."

"We'll make it?"

"We'll be done with our little visit before the delivery. Now then, there was only one loss, and that was Sandy. She died. Nothing else matters. She was blooming, at the beginning of life, and then she died. What else could possibly matter?"

"That's how I feel, too," Silva said.

Frank Silva was oddly at home there, Sonntag thought. These were his neighborhoods, these were his corner taverns, these were his streets. Maybe Silva should take the lead. Joe nodded faintly at Frank. He nodded back.

"It was an accident, you know," she said. "It was one accident after another. I'm sure Sandy didn't plan on conceiving. I'm sure the person she went to didn't want it to end the way it did. But it happened, and you can't roll back time."

"Yeah, well, did she talk about it? With you? That's your field, isn't it?"

"Not a word. I wish she had. I know how to deal with these things. I know how to talk a girl into having her child; how she'll regret it if she doesn't. I know the agencies. People are waiting in line for little babies to enter their lives, ready to adopt, ready to love." She sighed. "That dear girl, she kept it all inside of herself, so no one could change her mind—no one knew."

"You'd be the person she'd come to, right?"

"Of course! I'm there three mornings a week all summer. I meet every girl in those two-week sessions. That's part of what Ranger Girls do. We introduce the girls to their own bodies and natures. It's the nicest and happiest and most rewarding thing I do." She eyed her watch. "Oh, oh," she said, and vanished into the bright-lit room next door.

Another groan came forth, then she returned. "This kid's coming like an express train. You got any more questions? I gotta run now."

"Yeah," Frank said. "Someone did something to Sandy Millbank. Can you steer us?"

She thought a minute. "We had a patient a few weeks ago. Hemorrhaging. A botched abortion. We saved her. Just barely."

"We'd like to talk to her. And to the attending doctor," Frank said.

"That's confidential, you know." She smiled. "But I'll ask."

Sonntag handed her a card. "As soon as possible. We need help."

She nodded, plunged into the delivery room, and left an odd vacuum behind her. Mrs. Boetticher was life itself.

It was strangely quiet in the corridor.

"That's public information," he said. "Physicians are required to report that. We can find it in the records here."

"The office, then. You know what, Joe. I've never been in a maternity ward before. I don't think I should be here. This place ain't for males. I think maybe I'll never walk into a maternity ward again."

"Twice," Joe said. "Terror and joy."

The clerk in the office didn't like cops. He stood nervously behind the bulwark of a counter, while Frank explained.

"Calls to the police? Lots of those. In a log we keep."

"Last three months," Frank said.

"The rest won't be so easy. The emergency room, lots of people in there every day."

"Hemorrhage, from an abortion."

"Let's look at the police calls first," the clerk said.

He pushed the ledger across the counter. It had been kept in many hands, with many inks. Date, time, nature of call. A few shootings, some assault and battery, one child abuse, a starved vagrant, traffic injuries, pedestrian heart attack. Sonntag and Silva fingered their way down the log, week after week, two months, three. No call about a botched abortion. The clerk frowned nervously.

"All right, ER records then," Silva said.

"That's going to take more digging, sir."

"Are things filed by procedure, so many concussions, so many broken arms, so many catheters?"

"Not that way, no. Just a log, daily, describing everything that day. Sometimes there are a hundred, two hundred even, in one day. I could have this reviewed for you in the morning."

"Billing? Would your accounting office have it?"

"No, not in the detail you want."

"All right, we'll check with you in the morning. Mr...?"

"Halvorson, sir. Lothar Halvorson."

They headed for the unmarked cruiser. "That's interesting.

She says they fixed a bleeding woman a few weeks ago. Hospital didn't call us," Silva said.

"I think there may be a lot of that," Sonntag said.

"You know something, Joe? I'm glad they don't."

Chapter Twelve

Sonntag was lucky. A Number 10 Wells Street car was just grinding to a halt when he reached the stop. He boarded; the conductor punched his pass, and he headed down the crowded aisle, preferring a seat at the rear. That was because if the street-car plunged headfirst off the terrible Wells Street Viaduct, which spanned the Menomonee River Valley, he would live a second or two longer than the passengers at the front of the car.

He rode the streetcar over that high trestle twice a day, and never got used to it. It was always a white-knuckle trip, in which he clutched the seat-back in front of him, and waited, terrified, for a gust of wind to blow the car over the edge, and down eighty or a hundred feet. The Number 10 line ran from the East Side westward, and ended up in the suburban village of Wauwatosa.

He often envied Frank Silva, who could catch a Cudahy streetcar and get home on solid ground. He had thought of moving somewhere that wouldn't require that he take the Wells Street line to work. He had thought of driving more. He could go into town via State Street, and avoid the trestle altogether. But until they paid cops more, he was stuck.

All sorts of things could go wrong, and he was certain that some day one of them would happen. Maybe maintenance crews would forget to put the big bolts back in, and the wooden timbers would fall apart and take Joe Sonntag's streetcar with it. Or unruly teenagers would start bouncing around in the car, just when it was negotiating the perilous trip over the viaduct, and tip the car over. Or a drunken motorman would forget the ten-mile-per-hour speed limit on the trestle, and run the car up until it careened off the trestle and landed on the Miller Brewery below. Who could say?

One of the things that troubled him about all this was that he wasn't at all manly. He was a cop, after all, but there he was, cowering every time the streetcar edged out into space. He was secretly ashamed. Why couldn't he be like Captain Ackerman, fearless and tough? Captain Ackerman would cross the viaduct and think nothing of it, and never imagine falling off to his doom. Or landing in the Menomonee River and drowning, trapped underwater in the shattered streetcar.

But there Sonntag was, plunged into terror twice each workday. He had looked to the realm of the head-shrinkers for help, reading Freud and Jung. They were hard to follow, but if he could find a reason for his terror the reading would be worth it. Jung in particular interested him. Sonntag decided he had an Icarus Complex. In Greek mythology, Daedalus built wings with feathers anchored by wax, and gave one set of wings to his son Icarus. Soon Icarus was flying, but flew too close to the sun, which melted the wax holding he feathers, and Icarus plunged to his doom. Just like falling off the viaduct in a streetcar.

Then Sonntag discovered Freud, and soon came to the belief that he had been weaned too soon, and that if he had been kept at the breast a while more, he wouldn't be suffering from the terror he felt every time the orange streetcar edged out onto the lonely track high above the good earth, defying gravity. He thought that if he could drink some mother's milk each day, he'd overcome his unmanly fears. But it didn't happen.

Lizbeth had listened to all these theories with patience, and a faint smile. "I'll drive you to the other side of the viaduct each day, or pick you up there, and you can take the Wells car the rest of the way," she said, practically. But he refused. That would be surrendering to his unmanly weakness. So things remained the same. The viaduct cast a long black shadow over his life.

This afternoon, like so many others, he clenched the wicker seat in front of him, felt sweat pool in his armpits, and waited for doom. It was a gusty day, making the car rock, and making Sonntag clamp his eyes shut. He didn't want to see the car derail and plunge. But then the earth rose up and greeted the streetcar on the west side, and a few blocks later he hopped off and walked toward his little bungalow, down a side street, a place where people had flowers and bushes and trees. It had been a good place to raise boys. He thought briefly of Joe Jr., lost to polio one terrifying August.

He found Lizbeth with her hat on. She wore summer hats full of flowers, and this time it was full of cloth geraniums.

"Get the car out. You're taking me on a little trip," she said.

"What about a drink?"

"The drink can wait until I solve the crime."

"What crime?"

"The Washington Park crime. That's where we're going. You're going to show me exactly where Sandy Millbank was found. I want to know. Why there, why not somewhere else?"

Lizbeth had a knack; Joe hated to admit it.

"What's for dinner?" he asked.

"It won't be Greek," she said.

That was a coded message. He grumpily swung the garage door open, cranked the prewar Hudson to life, nursed the engine until it warmed, and pushed the choke lever back. She was waiting when he backed out.

He drove to the zoo, parked, and escorted her to the place. The PD was done with it, and it was no longer sequestered.

"There," he said.

She squinted at the mangled ferns, the signs of foot traffic that had ruined the fragile ferns. The acrid odor of the zoo cages drifted through the evening air.

"Why here?" she said. "There's lots of ferns around. Sandy Millbank could have been laid to rest like that in a dozen places around here. The zoo has fern beds all over."

She hiked toward the lion cages.

They were in a row, each an indoor and outdoor cage with barred iron imprisoning the big cats. Pedestrians and viewers were separated from the cages by a fence and moat. The closest of the cats was a West African lioness, and next to her was a Transvaal lion, a big fellow with a noble mane.

"Reminds you of MGM, doesn't he?" she said.

The lioness prowled restlessly, working a circle around her patch. Next were the tigers. A sleeping Bengal tiger, a Siberian somewhere inside, and a Malaysian quietly watching the world. The tigers seemed quiet, but next to them were the rest of the big cats; a puma, a lynx, a jaguar, and a cheetah, all in a row, eyeing the public as a dieter would eye his spouse's supper.

"There, you see?" she said.

"See what?"

"It all fits. I knew it. Sandy Millbank's abortionist was in tight with the Ranger Girls."

Sonntag stared. This was alien turf. "Okay," he said, which was his way of demanding an explanation.

Lizbeth decided to let him stew a little. "She was found closest to that lioness," she said. "Doesn't that tell you something?"

"Nope."

"And she's close to the jaguars and cheetahs and pumas. So what does that tell you?"

"I want a bourbon," he said.

"If you knew anything about the Ranger Girls, you'd know. The trouble is, we had boys so you're sort of blank about this. But any woman would know."

"Would you like to take me out for Chinese?" he asked.

"Sandy Millbank was closest to the lioness. Think about that."

"She's never been in West Africa, far as I know."

"But she was a Lioness! That's the highest order. It's like being an Eagle Scout."

"Uh, Lizbeth, let's go eat. Maybe I could get swizzled beforehand."

"A girl starting in Ranger Girls at age twelve is a Bobcat. Then she gets to be a Lynx, and then a Jaguar, and then a Puma, and finally, if she's the best of the best, she gets to be a Lioness. Whoever brought her here was honoring her, placing her closest to the Lioness over there. It was an inside job, Joe. "

"Ah, don't you think maybe it was a coincidence? Someone took her out of a car back there and carried her here and ran."

"Nope. She was brought here as an honor. Next to the lioness over there because she is one, she's a Lioness. Whoever carried her here arranged her in the bed of ferns, in the place of highest honor, a Lioness with the lions."

The thing was, maybe Lizbeth was right. "You deserve a Greek restaurant dinner," he said.

"Tough luck," she replied. "'I've got meatloaf and broccoli in the oven."

He meekly followed her back to the Hudson. He drove home, almost running a stop sign because his mind was on Ranger Girl ranks, and Sandy Millbank being a Lioness. He'd have to check that out.

He parked in the garage and caught her hand before she hopped out.

"Thanks," he said.

She smiled.

In the kitchen he poured two drinks while she cranked up the heat under the dinner, and then she joined him. It was their evening ritual, except that half the time he was late, or doing something urgent down at the station, or so absorbed by something in the *Milwaukee Journal* that she got testy.

"So who would do that?" he asked.

"Well, it wouldn't be a Boy Scout. That's my whole point."

"If she was laid to rest there as an honor, a Lioness come home, who would do that?"

"Beats me," she said. "But I wanted you to see things as we do—women do."

"Yeah, I don't know anything about that."

"Thank God," she said.

There it was again. He was a man messing in the private world of women. This case was shaping up as something almost beyond male comprehension. Which only got his dander up. He was going to invade that world and solve this thing, and knock down barriers if he had to.

"So someone aborts Sandy; everything goes wrong. She dies. Why take her to the zoo? Why not just take her to some field and dump her? Or try to make the body disappear in the bottom of Lake Michigan?"

"That's my point," she said. "Someone in Ranger Girls did it."

"Like the visiting nurse at the camp?"

"Look for the blood," she said.

"We talked to the nurse. She's down at St. Luke's. She may have spilled some beans. About a hemorrhage that didn't get reported to us. We'll know more tomorrow."

"I wish you'd just leave some things alone," she said.

He wanted to tell her he had sworn to uphold the law, but he didn't. She knew it. And she knew that a lot of times, the law wasn't upheld very well, and there were good reasons. Some things were best left alone.

"Where do we look for blood?" he asked.

"Right in the middle of a hospital, where it can be gotten rid of."

"There were two soaking sheets out at Ravenswood. In a laundry basin. But her bed was all made up. She's the only one there most of the time. Or I should say was. Maybe we should have collected the sheets."

"You wouldn't have found anything. Nothing will ever be found at that camp."

"How do you know that, Lizbeth?"

"I just do."

"So the abortion was in Milwaukee?"

"I don't know," she said, turning private again. She got up and started putting dinner on the table. He sipped, unable to collect any of this into a coherent whole. Maybe Walsh could manage it. He understood women.

"That reminds me," he said. "The family will have a memorial service coming up. It's taking time for them to get together. The parents are in Peru. A brother's in California. A sister's about due and can't come. Sandy's buried, but there'll be this memorial, and I'd like to know who shows up. Somebody loved the girl enough to arrange her body in a bed of ferns, next to a lioness, and that somebody's likely to show up. Would you go?"

She knew why. It's because cops always look like cops and can't hide being cops, and stick out. But Lizbeth could go, observe, figure things out, and maybe come up with something.

"I'll be your stool pigeon," she said, smiling again.

"You're the right person. Lizbeth."

"You bet I am. If that abortionist shows up, believe me, I'll know it."

Joe Sonntag believed her every word.

Chapter Thirteen

Wendy Vestal was blue ice. She had greeted Milwaukee PD detectives Sonntag and Silva coldly in her rather expansive office at Pulaski High School. She wore tennis shoes, a white blouse, and Bermuda shorts. She was lean, dark, gray at the temples, without fat or humor or breasts. Her office was all waxed hardwood floor, a wooden desk and benches around the periphery. She was women's athletic director at the high school, and Camp Ravenswood's athletic director during the summer.

Sonntag felt he'd walked into a wall of oak.

"Mrs. Vestal, we'd like to talk about Sandy Millbank," he began.

"It's Miss. I've always been Miss, have no intention of becoming Mrs., and you can draw whatever conclusions you wish."

"Ah, fine. Miss Vestal, we're just trying to find out what happened to Sandy Millbank. Perhaps you could help us. We're looking for someone who might be preying on women who are having some difficulties."

"The difficulty would be the baby, not the abortion."

"Why do you say that?"

"If I could steer every pregnant girl to an abortionist I would do so. The whole thing would be over in minutes and a girl could get on with her life."

"Well, I imagine you have plenty of company. Was that Sandy's view, too?"

"I never talked to her about it."

"You're the athletic director out there. What did that involve?"

"Sports and hikes."

"That's it?"

"What are you looking for? An abortionist on the prowl in the camp?"

"No, ma'am."

"It's Miss."

"I guess we're trying to track how Sandy Millbank found out where to go, and who she went to. We've heard about cards in girls' rooms, like around here. If you need help, call this number. Have you seen any of those?"

"Of course. I leave them right where they're put. Maybe I helped some girl by leaving the cards stuck in a mirror."

"Do you have one?"

"I never touch them."

"Could you lead us to one?"

"Not if I can help it."

"Do you know who stuffed them into mirror frames?"

"I'd do it myself if I could," she said.

Sonntag thought maybe to back off a little. Sometimes you got further along in these interviews just by letting go. "Was Sandy Millbank an athlete, ah, Miss?"

"No, she couldn't. She had an odd malady. She bruised easily. She'd get purple patches under her skin if anything hit her. Very strange. So, no tennis or badminton. Especially no volleyball. She didn't golf. Not even calisthenics. But she loved to hike. She could hike all day, so she did a lot of birding. She was one of he best hikers in camp, and thought nothing of a ten-mile day."

"Did she tell anyone she was...expecting?"

"What do you think single women do—go around and announce it?"

"I guess I don't know," Sonntag said. "I had sons."

"Lucky you."

"I thought maybe the friendship, the bonds, the closeness

formed in camps like that might make women more open with
each other."

"No, they're more likely to elbow each other on the volleyball
court."

Sonntag felt he was swimming against a tide. He nodded
faintly to Frank Silva.

"You have a real nice visiting nurse out there, Mrs. Boetticher,"
he said.

"She's a butcher's daughter."

"I mean, she's just the sort that girls need when they have
questions, you know, adolescence."

"No, she doesn't do abortions, and she doesn't lead stray
girls to abortionists."

"She works in maternity, and also for some gynecologist,
doesn't she?"

"Doctor Barbour, yes."

"So she know all about that stuff."

"What stuff?"

Silva, amazingly, reddened. "The stuff she's trained in."

"She comes out to camp with her Gladstone bag and some
stainless steel tools and scrapes babies out of girls, is that what
you're saying?"

"No, Miss Vestal. But somewhere, somehow, a dead girl
named Sandy Millbank got the name of an abortionist, who probably
botched the job. She was very, very dead when we found her in
the ferns, and we want the person who killed her. We want that
person very badly, so that he doesn't botch any more jobs, or
take the lives of any more sweet girls who're at the beginning of
their lives."

For once Wendy Vestal's frost thawed a little. "It's hard to
be a woman, and you men don't know that," she said.

"Why there? Why there at the ferns, next to the West African
lioness?" Sonntag asked.

"Because someone in Ranger Girls loved and honored her,"
she said.

At last. "Someone in Ranger Girls knew she had reached the
top rank?"

"Everyone in Ranger Girls knew she was a Lioness. There are only a few Lionesses in the United States, sir."

"Someone in Milwaukee, Wisconsin, took her there. Do you know what she looked like when we found her?"

"I'm afraid I don't want to know."

"Someone placed her in a bed of ferns. Do you know what else?"

Miss Vestal simply stared.

"Her eyes were closed, her hair was combed, her legs were straight, her skirt was smooth, her arms were folded over her breast."

She smiled slightly. "That's what you get as assistant director."

"Do you know who prepared her that way?"

"Whoever it was won't pay me the same honor."

"Some one or two or three people carried her there. Someone in Ranger Girls," Silva said.

She didn't budge.

"Miss Vestal," Sonntag said, "the director, Amanda Winthrop, thought that Sandy Millbank let the organization down, and embarrassed it, and created a problem for the camp, by going to an abortionist."

"She's entitled to her opinions."

"Let me ask you an entirely hypothetical question. If a girl in trouble came to you, and you knew where she could be aborted, what would you do?"

"Sorry," she said, with a glacial smile.

"If you know something about an illegal act, and don't tell us, you might be an accessory," Frank said.

"Fine, try me."

"If you think of anything you want to tell us, Miss Vestal, here's my card."

She took the card and carefully tore it to bits.

They headed for the cruiser, which was parked in a no-parking zone in front of the weary old school. Some students stared.

"You cops?" asked a kid.

"How did you guess?" Silva replied.

"Short hair," the kid said.

"Bad suits," said another smartass.

Sonntag thought better of rattling the kid's teeth. He bought his suits at Irv the Working Man's Friend, straight off the pipe racks. No cop should wear expensive suits. People would think they were on the take.

Silva was driving. "It'll take me an hour to thaw out," he said.

"She'll get around to talking a lot more," Sonntag said.

"We should have some female detectives," Silva said. "Women for female cases."

"I'd like a couple, but a case is a case. No male or female."

"Tell that to those ladies," Silva said.

Silva had a point. Even Lizbeth turned silent and walled up when this case came up. He wished he could read the minds, get the real thoughts, of all the women he'd interviewed in the past days. Most of them were mad at him. They were full of things they didn't want to tell him. They were against abortions, but wished he'd just go away. Some of them faulted Sandy Millbank, whose life had been snuffed out, for bringing scandal upon their Ranger Girls organization. Ranger Girls counted a lot more to them than she had. Damned if he could understand any of it.

"Doctor Barbour's office?" Frank asked.

"Good as any. Mrs. Boetticher knows things."

Barbour's office was in a medical building near Marquette. There were two women in the waiting room, suddenly uncomfortable when males walked in.

"Police, ma'am. We'd like to speak to Mrs. Boetticher a few minutes," Sonntag said.

That evoked sudden consternation. The receptionist vanished, only to return with the doctor, who was wearing a white smock.

"I'm glad you came," he said. "You get to talk to both of us. But we've patients waiting so have at it."

The doctor was lantern-jawed and massive. Sonntag and Silva followed him to his office, where the nurse waited.

"It's about the Millbank case," the doctor said. "Mrs. Boetticher was telling me."

"We're looking for an abortionist, sir. We want to know how Sandy Millbank was contacted, or contacted someone, and who it was. Could you help? Either of you? Even the smallest lead?"

"I might," said the doctor. "Women see me all the time about this. Some want an illegal procedure. I tell them I'm not in the business, but I'm in the contraception business, and will be glad to fit them out. That's my answer to abortion, gents. Fit the women out."

"That poor girl," said Mrs. Boetticher. She and Doctor Barbour were two of a kind, massive and strong.

Barbour opened his desk drawer and extracted two calling cards. "I should have given you these long ago," he said. "Maybe they are innocent, maybe not. Some of my patients clutched one and I begged a couple from them." He handed the cards to Sonntag.

Need Help? Women's Counseling.

There was a local phone number.

Sonntag handed one of the cards to Silva.

"Westside number," Silva said.

"Was Sandy Millbank your patient, doctor?" Sonntag asked.

"No, she wasn't. But my dear nurse here talked so much about her, after that tragedy, that I've felt as though she were a daughter."

"Do you know who her physician was, Mrs. Boetticher?"

"I'm afraid I don't, sir. The family's far-flung, and I suppose her doctor was her parents' doctor."

"We can find that out. I'm wondering if she went to someone when she thought she was pregnant."

"If it had been summer, when I was out there, I think she might have come to me. I treated her off and on. She bruised up, regular purple, and I had her put cold-water applications on the bruises. But this is now, not then." She sighed. "This thing just eats at me."

"Is there anything else, gentlemen? I have patients waiting."

"These cards, that's a big help, sir."

"I should have gotten them to the police long ago. But who can say what's behind them, eh?"

"Who can say," Silva said.

They headed into a chill wind.

"Finally, something," Silva said, as he settled into the cruiser.

"How are we gonna do this? Just call them up? Go visit? Try to trap them?" Sonntag asked.

"There'll not be a place. Like some busy office, full of women doing good things."

"Yeah, there may be no place to walk into. I'll call my friend Maxine."

Maxine was the supervisor at the phone company who did magical stuff for Sonntag, usually invisibly, and sometimes without anyone at the company aware of it, and sometimes against company policy.

"You're right, Joe. We need some lady detectives. We need one who's about nineteen and sweet and pretty."

It wasn't far to the station house. They checked in the cruiser, and headed up to the bullpen. It was quiet in there. Milwaukee gave up crime for Lent, Halloween, Thanksgiving, and the first Tuesday of each month. A couple of uniforms were booking a shoplifter, an emaciated old woman with an overcoat full of new brassieres.

"She wears nothing but a smile and a Jantzen," Silva said.

Sonntag found no messages on his desk, and not even Captain Ackerman was around. He lifted the receiver and dialed.

"Maxine Andrews," the voice said.

"Sing Rum and Coca Cola for me," Sonntag said.

"Hi, Joe. I'm outa rum. What nasty thing are we doing today?"

"I'm going to give you a number. I need to know who has it and where it's connected."

He gave her the number. Bluemound exchange, 258.

"That sure doesn't get much use," she said. "Let me see. Right back."

He heard her abandon her post. It seemed to take a long time. Finally he heard her pick up the receiver. "That belongs to Speedy Secretarial Service, 10011 Bluemound Road, way out there somewhere."

"Have they got other numbers?"

"Yes, it's an answering service, and they have a bank of three numbers. The name of that is In Touch."

"That's it?"

"In Touch, yes. The listed owner, two owners, William and Elvira Henderson, CPAs."

"Like in Certified Public Accountants?"

"Who knows, sweetheart. Just CPAs, after their signatures."

"And they have offices there?"

"That's what's on the file card."

"Maxine, you've just kept the Dodgers from winning the World Series."

"That means you want more from me."

"Yep, all calls over the last, say, three months."

"That's a hell of a lot of calls, Joe."

"I'll send you some roses."

"I'm still waiting for the last dozen. Something wrong with this outfit? I'm snooping."

"That's what we're trying to find out."

"Gimme a clue."

"Not this time, Maxine."

"This has to do with that girl they found at the Zoo."

"That's all the clue I can give you."

"Find them," she said. "And then throw away the key."

Chapter Fourteen

The Speedy Secretarial Service was located far west of the city line. Sonntag and Silva pored over county maps, trying to pinpoint the place.

"West of Wauwatosa, near Elm Grove," Silva said.

"We need to go take a look. We also need to work this out," Sonntag said.

"Are we gonna try to lure them out?" Silva asked.

"We've got two businesses here. Maybe one is a front. Maybe the other is legit. Maybe it really is a service for pregnant women, offering shelters, help, stuff. We need to know that."

"Secretarial service. Is that a code word for something?"

"Not that I've heard. They do typing, phone answering, message stuff, and these people are probably accountants. You got any ideas, Frank?"

"Yeah, send someone in who's looking for business services, who's got a little shop going and wants some help."

"Gorilla."

Silva grinned. Gorilla Meyers, the PD's photographer and technician, ran a little photography business on the side; weddings, anniversaries, portraits, sports events, reunions. Gorilla's little business had sometimes come in handy. Nothing like sending a photographer with a big Speed Graphic and a mess of spare flashbulbs to an event the cops were keeping an eye on. Gorilla got his name from his appearance. He was a three-hundred pound slab of cunning.

"So Gorilla goes there with some business needs. An answering service, accounting and billing, and talks. But why does he go way out there?" Sonntag asked.

"He'll think of something."

"Okay, that's part of it. We'll also need some twenty-year-old gal in distress. Do you know of any?"

"How about my Communist girlfriend?"

"Get serious, Frank. Who can start this ball rolling?"

"Lizbeth could do it. She'd know the right things to say."

"Lizbeth? Too old. We need a high school girl, full of all the slang."

"No we don't. We need, like, a thirty-year-old woman, broke, abandoned by her husband, expecting, desperate, with another kid to raise, and no way out."

Sonntag stared. Lizbeth could do that, and do it well. "We'll need to polish the story," he said.

Silva grinned. "Do you think she would do that? Invent a whopper and calmly spin it out to whoever answers that phone?"

"I don't know," Sonntag said. "What we call a story, she might call a lie."

"Maybe we can get someone who really is in trouble, borrow her from one of the shelters. There's one run by nuns out there on the west side."

"That would be tough. Let me talk to Lizbeth."

They had to wait a minute for Gorilla to finish making a print in his pungent darkroom, but eventually he opened the door. "I've been trying to catch the ghost," he said.

"Ghost?"

"The woman up on Farwell who says she has two ghosts and they're stealing from her pantry. I set up a remote camera. Got this."

There was a print in the fixing tray of a blurry hand thrust in front of the lens; cupboards in the background.

"Doesn't look very ghostly," Frank said. "Maybe juvenile cookie thiefs."

They told Gorilla about Speedy Secretarial Service, and asked him if he could come up with a business reason to go there, and a reason to head so far out of town.

"What is it a front for?"

"They may be the ones putting Need Help cards in women's rooms."

"Sandy Millbank," Gorilla said. "Give me a bit to come up with a plausible story."

"We're going out there to look it over. You want to look it over?"

"Let me see if they have any work for me," Gorilla said.

They drove west, out Bluemound Road. Gorilla had his new Leica 35-millimeter camera, with a telephoto lens. The city thinned out and quit. Wisconsin had a quiet, ever-changing beauty about it, woodlands, slopes, meadows, creeks, dairy cattle. But the Speedy Secretarial Service was closer in, and within sight of the tract houses blossoming in the wake of the war. It was housed in a stone farmhouse, guarded by giant black walnut and hickory trees. The farmhouse had been there forever, and was partly yellow limestone quarried nearby. The farmhouse had a second floor, and a barn and outbuildings. It almost seemed to be a working dairy farm, but it wasn't. This place had no livestock.

Frank, who was driving, stopped to let Gorilla click away from the car window.

A discreet sign, black block letters, announced the Speedy Secretarial Service at the driveway. The farm house was a good city block back from the road. The place looked to be the very soul of tranquility. Sonntag found himself wondering how many fetuses had been scraped out of how many women in those upstairs precincts behind those black windows.

Gorilla was clicking away. "Go up the road a little, Frank, so I can shoot back," he said. Frank pushed the cruiser ahead a little, and Gorilla continued to take pictures.

"It sure is a quiet place," Sonntag said. "You're going to need a good reason to come here, Gorilla."

"I might just try calling; maybe discuss price."

"Keep us posted. And I want your impressions. Your hunches."

"Sure, Joe. Do you want to get out and have a tourist shot? You in front of the killing palace?"

Sonntag laughed.

They would need to talk to the county sheriff about this. It was far from Milwaukee city turf. He didn't like that. Was it Waukesha County? He'd have to check on that. He hated jurisdictions. He wished his badge was all he needed.

That upstairs interested Sonntag. It was big enough to operate an abortion mill, pushing the ladies in and out. The barn was big enough to hide a dozen cars. It all fascinated him.

But at this point he had nothing but a number on a card, and his telephone company pal Maxine's trace to this place. Which reminded him to call her when they got back.

It was a long, pleasant drive back to the station house downtown. When he returned to his desk he found a note that said to call Maxine.

"I got the list," she said.

"You've done it again."

"Want me to teletype it? If I do, pleased pull it off the machine right now. I don't want that stuff floating."

"I'll wait for it," he said.

He headed for an alcove. The PD teletype mostly connected the Milwaukee cops with other cities, the FBI, and public agencies. Even as Joe stepped close, the machine chattered and a column of unidentified phone numbers slid into view. All of them were calls made to and from the farmhouse over three months.

There weren't many calls. And none from Camp Ravenswood, or the Millbanks' home. And none from the phones of the women who ran the camp, or ran Ranger Girls. No easy links from that farmhouse to the girl who had died of a botched abortion. But that was how investigations went. The easy ones were rare.

"Frank, find out who owns that property. The real estate," Sonntag said.

Frank wheeled away wordlessly. It would take a while.

Sonntag planned to get more from his contact at the phone

company: whose numbers were the rest of the calls? It was a temptation just to start dialing, and see what he could find out, but Maxine might be faster. He called her.

"Didja find out anything, sweetheart?" she asked.

"Nothing that links that outfit with a certain girl."

"And now you want who the rest of the numbers belong to, right? And the long distance. All to Chicago. Do I get another bouquet of red roses?"

"Yellow roses."

"It figures," she said. "You've run out of red roses. I'll get back to you. Tomorrow morning, maybe."

Sonntag smelled Captain Ackerman behind him. You could always smell the captain before he arrived.

"What else is new?" the captain asked.

"We might have the place, but we don't connect Sandy Millbank to it—not yet, anyway."

"I'm betting on a woman."

"Why?"

"Way the girl was laid out, like in a funeral parlor. Man would just dump her in the river."

"I won't take the bet," Sonntag said.

Ackerman's black marble eyes glowed. "Maybe we got us a real, Chicago-style abortion ring operating here. Out of town, out in the country, real quiet, with a solid front business. Maybe it's a mob deal; there's money to be made. Lotta families, not just the women, lotta families would fork over big money, five hundred, six hundred, maybe more. Lotta girls in Milwaukee, the more religious they are, the easier they get knocked up. That's Ackerman's Law. Milwaukee is all Catholic and Lutheran, so girls get knocked up. We got whole convents full of knocked-up girls."

Sonntag smiled.

The cloud of mustard gas ambled on, and Sonntag checked his watch. Shift was over. There was nothing else pressing. He saw Silva on the phone. Eddy Walsh was still off looking at hospital records, looking for females in emergency rooms, looking for hemorrhages under any other name organized medicine could conjure up.

Sonntag clambered into his trench coat and clamped the old fedora down. He didn't know why he wore either one in warm weather. Rain, he told himself. Because it might rain.

He waited forever for the Number Ten streetcar, boarded, got his pass punched, and found a rear seat, butt-end of the car. The car ground over the viaduct without disturbing Sonntag as much as usual. That's because he was in the rear seat, so if the car went over, it would collapse like an accordion and spare his life.

"So tell me," Lizbeth said, handing him his ritual bourbon.

He did. And what he had in mind for her.

"Drive me there. I want to see it," she said.

"How about after supper?" he asked.

"So you want me to call the number. Maybe I will. I've always wanted to be an actress. If I hadn't married you, I'd be the star of little theater, the queen of summer stock."

That answered one question. "We're going to have to rehearse this. It's going to start out innocently. Why sure, my dear, we can give you a list of shelters. We can help a girl. And you'll need to string them along."

"I know that," she retorted so sharply that Sonntag retreated. This was mysterious female ground, and he was intruding.

"You'll need to be sort of reluctant, and desperate, and not knowing what to do, and keep asking what they think would be best, or maybe what shelters cost."

"Do you think I don't know that?" She was sounding seriously annoyed, maybe even a little icy.

"Okay. We'll go to the station house in the morning, and you can make the call."

"Why there?"

"So we can listen in and take notes."

"I don't want three males listening to me. This is private talk."

"But we need to take notes."

"No, sweetheart. This isn't for men. And I don't need to do it at the police station. I can do it here."

Sonntag knew when to back off. "Your turn," he said.

"I'll call after you go to work in the morning. This isn't for men. I'll call you afterward if I learn something or get somewhere."

"Call me anyway, just to tell me what happened."

She seemed sort of reluctant, but finally nodded. This whole contact was going to go through the Lizbeth Sonntag filtering system.

Then she smiled. "Just you wait and see," she said. "We'll nail that butcher."

That was good enough for him.

"And tomorrow is the memorial service," she added. "I'll be going to that, too."

"Yeah, keep a sharp eye out. Read the guest book. And you'll need some excuse. Why are you there? How did you know Sandy Millbank? That sort of thing."

She glared. He wasn't exactly winning any popularity contests this evening. "I'll take you out for Chinese," he said.

"Make it Greek," she said. "Ever since I got pregnant, Chinese tastes funny."

Chapter Fifteen

Joe Sonntag was itchy. He liked to control every facet of an investigation. What he really wanted was for a trained female investigator to make the call, while two detectives were listening in, taking notes, shoving suggestions her way. But Lizbeth had flatly refused. This would be her call, she'd do it her way, and that was that. He thought of the ways she could blow it, or miss something important, and waited irritably at his desk for the call from her. A call that didn't come.

Meanwhile, Frank Silva was plowing good ground. "That parcel is zoned agricultural, even though the city's encroaching," he said. "It's forty acres, with house and barn, and it belongs to a corporation. It's called Wisconsin Land, and it's chartered by the state. But the owner's out of state. Arizona."

"Arizona?"

"Yeah, about as far from here as you can go."

"You got an owner?"

"Yeah, I do, and here's where it gets interesting. The corporation's wholly owned by one Arnold Cyrus Needham and his wife Marvella. He's a defrocked doctor, used to practice here."

"Defrocked? What do you mean?"

"License pulled for a whole string of things. A surgeon. He was apparently drunk during his surgeries. He was open about it, said he needed a drink to steady his hands. But the result was a disaster. One case, he left a surgical towel in a patient; it festered, the patient died. An autopsy revealed the towel. There were half a dozen of those. He was charged with negligent homicide once, beat it, and got out of town."

"You got a list of all that?"

"I've asked the licensing board to send it."

"Are there any calls from the Henderson number out there, to Arizona? Are they in touch with Needham?"

"Not that we've found."

"Do the Needhams have other property around here?"

"Haven't got that far."

"Try the courthouse. And if you get an address, I'll call Maxine at the phone company."

"This looks good, right? A trained surgeon who can't practice and maybe runs an abortion mill?"

"We're on to something, Frank. You run with it. This is the best prospect we've had since the girl died."

"Yeah, but it's a long way to come just to do a quick abortion or two."

Sonntag nodded. Needham could make an easier living down there, doing the same thing.

Silva nodded, and headed out. Impulsively, Sonntag pulled a ragged phone book from his desk drawer. He'd solved cases with phone books. There was a B. J. Needham on the west side, and a Q. E. D. Needham on the north. Now what the hell was that? Didn't it mean here's the proof, or something like that? He headed for the Webster's on a stand in a corner of the bullpen. Captain Ackerman hated the dictionary, and said it shouldn't be in a police station. Any cop who needed a dictionary shouldn't be a cop, he said, Q.E.D. Sonntag knew he shouldn't be a cop anyway, so he looked it up. *Quod erat demonstrandum.* What a name to pin on to that Needham. How are you, Quod old boy? Or old girl? He decided maybe Q. E. D. Needham needed some looking into, if nothing else showed up.

At last his phone rang, and he yanked up the receiver.

"Joe?" Lizbeth said, "Joe, I don't know about this."

He knew she didn't even want to talk, so he just waited until she was ready.

"I called them. It's not the deal you were looking for. Or sort of, I don't know."

"It all helps," he said.

"Yes, but this is sort of different. It's an adoption society, but with a twist. They think they have a good thing going."

She was on the brink of hanging up, so he just waited her out.

"I told the woman a little about, you know, what we decided. The story. Me being some thirty-year-old mama to be, broke and alone and all."

"Good," he said. "Did they ask how you got the number?"

"The card, I said. I found it."

"Good."

"This woman, she was chatty, sort of, just oozing with cheer. She said her society was looking for babies to adopt. But here's the thing. People who want a baby want to know what they're getting. I'd say they don't want a pig in a poke, but that sounds awful. They want to meet moms, and even pops if they can, and they want to decide about adopting after they have a few visits with the mom."

"Yeah, to see if the mom's a drunk or a dimwit."

"How can you be so cruel?"

Sonntag retreated and dug himself a little pit of silence and waited.

"So if the couple likes the mom, the deal is that the couple supports her through childbirth, and pays for the prenatal and stuff. And then gets the baby. The woman signs a contract giving up all rights. And then she gets an allowance, whatever it takes to get her through. It's really sort of nice, don't you think?"

"Yeah, if you're what they're looking for. Did you talk about anything else?"

"I said what if I don't want that? What if I don't want anyone to know anything? She said she had a list of shelters. There's a couple here, others around the state. The one run by the nuns is the biggest, and not just for Catholics."

"You give her your name and phone number?"

"No, I just told them I'm Lizbeth, and I'd think about it, and maybe call back."

"Any hint, anything at all, pointing in some other direction?"

"Just that she said they always wanted to meet the pregnant woman in person, even if it's without names, in a coffee shop."

"Did you ask where the office is?"

"I did. She said it's temporarily an answering service place, but soon there'd be a regular place for the foundation, the Matchmakers, over in the downtown. Near you, I guess."

"Okay, Lizbeth. What do you think?"

"I don't know."

"Try a shot."

"I didn't believe a word she said," Lizbeth said.

"You gonna call her back?"

"When I'm ready," she said. "I don't like this. Babies are sacred."

"Sweetheart, they are to me, to a lot of us, and you've done us a great favor."

"I don't like being an actress. It's not just little theater. It's small, small and mean theater."

"I'll take you to dinner tonight."

"Did I do okay, Joe?"

"You were a star."

"I wanted it to be okay. I want to help you."

"You did."

"Don't forget, I'm going to the memorial service for Sandy Millbank at two."

"I wish I could put you on the force."

"It would beat pushing the Electrolux around the living room. I put an extra Oreo in your lunch bucket. Don't get fat."

An adoption service. He should have expected that, but he hadn't. Look over the girl, look over the adopting parents, if they really existed. A safe front all around. But only a front.

He decided to head for the morgue at the *Journal* to see what might be found out about Dr. Needham. The afternoon daily had a fine morgue, and the ladies in there loved to help a cop.

The stuff from the state medical licensing board was coming, but sometimes reporters got it better and deeper. This was a developing case. It wasn't dead-ended. Each day opened up new prospects. He liked that. He was going to nail that butcher.

The paper was a quick walk, but there were towering cumulus with flat black bellies, and he wondered if he'd regret leaving his trench coat. He entered the stately doorway of the state's preeminent newspaper, and trotted upstairs to the newsroom, hoping he could dodge Matt Dugan, the paper's superb crime reporter. Dugan had the best intuition of any newsman Sonntag had known, and could prove to be embarrassing at times, especially when the department was trying to keep a line of inquiry quiet.

He made it past the news staff, and ducked in. The morgue was vast, with golden oak files, floor to eye level, stuffed with packets and folders filled with clippings. Each clipping had been dated. The folders were labeled by topic. It wasn't always effective, and clippings got stuck into wrong folders, but mostly it worked.

One old gal knew Sonntag; the rest were new.

"Lieutenant?" she asked. "Back again, eh?"

He set his gray fedora on a table, as if to claim possession. "You're Flora, right?"

"Flora, Fauna, whatever you wish. What sort of heinous crime are we going to solve today, sir?"

"A doctor. His license was pulled by the state board. His name is Arnold Cyrus Needham. You got anything?"

"You just hang on there, and I'll dig up Arnie for you. He's an old pal."

"Old pal?"

"Figuratively speaking, Lieutenant. He's been clipped a few times. Who'd want a doctor named Arnie?"

"What's wrong with Arnie?"

"If you had your choice of being slit open, head to toe, by an Arnie, or slit open by, say, a Thomas, which would you choose?"

"I'd choose Harry, who told me I didn't need the surgery."

She cackled. Her ancient blue fingers clawed open a drawer, and flipped past folders, and finally found one. She studied it, beaming.

"There you are, Lieutenant."

There were, indeed, a dozen clips in the folder. He examined them briefly, and organized them by date, starting with the most recent, hoping to save some time. None had a photo, which disappointed him.

The most recent, and perhaps the most interesting to Sonntag, was datelined Phoenix. Needham was appealing the licensing board's decision, and wanted to be restored to practice. It was the dateline that caught his eye. Needham had hired a Madison attorney to pursue the matter before the medical board. It referred to Needham as a medical consultant, presently living in Phoenix. Sonntag wondered who consulted Needham, and about what.

The next oldest was the story about the board's decision. Milwaukee Doctor Disqualified, the head said. The story was fairly long, but didn't detail the evidence against Needham, who was a general surgeon specializing in abdominal surgery. In fact, it dodged specifics, and alluded to accusations of malpractice.

An earlier clip outlined a malpractice suit filed in district court. That turned out to be the one involving the surgical towel. Another clip put Needham at the head of a hospital staff committee recommending changes in operating rooms. Another clip, this one of some interest to Sonntag, was about Needham doing medical charity work in a children's wing. The doctor was an avid golfer, and won competitions at Brown Deer and elsewhere.

Not much else.

"Flora, you have anything on any other Needham?" he asked.

She looked and shook her head. "Not filed under that name, at least," she said.

"What would you think of someone named Q. E. D. Needham?"

"I'd think the new mother had a Quick Exclamation of Dismay."

"Flora, you should be an editorial page editor."

"I'm too liberal for the *Journal*."

She stuffed the clippings back into the folder while he gathered his hat, and headed out.

Matt Dugan was lurking there, ready to pounce.

"You see? Newspapers are the biggest stool pigeons of all," Dugan said. "You're hot in pursuit of an abortionist."

"We're making some progress, too."

"So have I," he said. "There's an abortion mill operating around here. I'm getting some noise, just by asking."

"If you get something we need, I hope you'll—"

"Cough up. So that I'm not an accessory." He was grinning. "I've got a whole collection of cards that say Need Help?"

"Yeah, we have a couple."

"These cards," Dugan said, "have you looked closely? They're home made."

"They're what?"

"Someone with a silk screen and a paper cutter made them. They weren't gotten from a print shop. Whoever made them didn't want any print shop to do them, and maybe give the ball away. Here," he said. "I'm carrying."

He handed a card to Sonntag.

"I'd hardly know a hand-made one from a printed one."

"That's what I like about you detectives," Dugan said. "Whoever made those cards must have had a few office things, like a hand press, stencil set, a paper cutter, some card stock, some inks. Like an office supply place, or a stenographer with a shelf full of that office stuff."

"Yeah, Dugan, you're right."

Sonntag smiled, slid away, and planned to set Gorilla Meyers loose as fast as he could.

Chapter Sixteen

Gorilla was superb. Sonntag sat in the side room, phone glued to ear, as Gorilla explored the Speedy Secretarial Service.

"Hey, is this Speedy?" he asked.

"Sure is," a woman responded. "What can we do for you?"

"Well, I'm a company photographer, and I've got a little business on the side, just stuff I pick up, weddings, portraits, reunions. I just need to get it organized better. There's not much in it, so this is no big deal, but I could use some help."

"Well, name it, sir, and maybe we can help."

"Well, do you have an answering service? Real low key, maybe one or two calls a week. Get the message and get in touch with me?"

"We can do that, at bargain prices, sir. Who'm I talking to?"

"Ray Meyer. I do insurance photography."

"Never heard of that."

"My company wants a picture of everything it insures. Real estate, cars, you name it. I get to take the pictures. Eight hours a day. Anyway, I've got this little side business, see? And I'm no businessman. I need someone to keep the books, someone to set up appointments., send out invoices, collect checks. Do you do printing? I need some business cards."

"We custom print, Mr. Meyer. Unique, handcrafted cards that make an impression."

"Yeah, that's good. Maybe if I drive out there, you can show me some samples. Now that brings up something. You're off and gone on the west side, and that means a lot of driving."

"Oh, you'll hardly need to come here, Mr. Meyer," she said. "First, check our prices. You won't beat them. Second, remember that we can do almost all of it by mail or phone."

"How come you're out there?"

"Cheap rent. We know the owners, and they want someone in the place to keep it up. So we get to run a business without overhead."

"Yeah, that's good. Mind if I drive out there and talk? I like to know the people I work with. Talk prices, and show me some of those sample cards, okay? Maybe we can set up something on a trial basis. I don't earn much with this, so I'm not sure about any of it. I've got the afternoon free; you want to yak a little?"

"We're here. I'm Elvira, okay?"

"I'm downtown. It'll take a while, Elvira."

"We're open till five. That's the store. I take calls any time."

Gorilla hung up, and Joe clicked off, hoping the lady wasn't listening.

Sonntag grinned, and gave Gorilla a V for victory sign.

"That was damned good, Gorilla."

"I should be in little theater."

"That's what Lizbeth says. Maybe we've got our toe in the door out there."

"What should I look for?"

"Sample cards. We can have our lab people see if it's the same ink and card stock and stuff as the Need Help cards. See if you can learn what's upstairs. Where the stairway is. Who lives up there? Don't push any of that. See what the phone system is. The Get Help cards have a different number from the Speedy outfit. Is this Elvira answering both phones? Wearing two hats? We may get some technical people in and try a wire recorder. When Lizbeth calls, is it the same woman as your Elvira? And talk about being an insurance company photographer. Maybe they'll talk about the farmhouse."

"Jaysas, you don't want much. I'm just a shutterbug."

"There's a big fish out there, and he killed Sandy Millbank, and we're going to get him."

"Maybe he killed a lot more than a woman, Joe. Maybe he killed the future brothers and sisters and sons and daughters of lots of us."

There was something very solemn in Gorilla's face, so solemn that it made Sonntag wonder a little. Gorilla was out of there, driving his own Studebaker, within ten minutes.

"That was good," Captain Ackerman said, somehow arriving ahead of his own stink. "Real good."

Sonntag knew better than to ask how Ackerman knew. Ackerman spent most of his day spying on his cops. Let a pair of cops spend too long on a coffee break, and Ackerman mysteriously knew it, and threatened demerits or docking some pay. How he knew all that stuff was beyond Sonntag. Ackerman should head the PD investigations bureau, Joe thought.

He found a special delivery package on his desk. The state medical licensing board had acted swiftly. He noted its receipt in his log, and slit it open. It was the formal decision to pull Needham's medical license, and there was an ancillary document listing the charges. Best of all, there was a glossy black and white of Needham. The man looked a little like an owl, with horn rimmed glasses, curved beak, jowls, and a pouty lip. His hair was receding, giving him a high brow. He was wearing a white shirt, dark bow tie, and tweed jacket. He wasn't old, upper forties, maybe.

The charges were much the same as those in the papers, but largely using medical terminology. The stuff didn't seem very sinister to Sonntag. Needham was a sloppy man, a careless man, a forgetful man, and on some occasions a drinking man, and the evidence considered by the medical board seemed to boil down to muddle-headedness. Not very criminal, Sonntag thought, but not the sort of man who a woman could trust to scrape a fetus out of her without killing her.

He'd look it over at his leisure. What pleased him most was that formal portrait. He'd have Gorilla make a few copies, and give one to each of the detectives, including Eddy Walsh and Frank

Silva. In a sense, this investigation was a manhunt, and the photo might be very valuable. He only wished that Gorilla had seen it before he took off.

He waited for Gorilla until his shift ended. Frank Silva, who worked a later shift, could get the story when Meyers returned. And call Joe if there was anything hot. That's how it was in a big investigation. You came to the end of each shift, and sometimes you left things hanging. It was a big police department, and here were other men, some of them good men, who would keep on during the next shift, and there'd maybe be some progress overnight. But he sure wished he had been able to talk to Gorilla before clapping his fedora on his head.

He headed into the world. It was always an odd moment, when the day was done in the station house, when he stepped outside, away from burglaries and rapes and vagrants and now an abortionist, and into the soft breezes. Milwaukee didn't have many days like that, where one could get to the street car without freezing, sweating, getting fingers numbed, or losing one's hat to a gust of wind. But this was a good day, and a car was waiting, and he got his monthly pass punched and it clanged off, the smell of ozone on the air.

For once he got home ahead of Lizbeth. That memorial service was up on the north side, at Niebauer Funeral Home, and that involved three streetcars and two transfers. A round trip meant riding six orange streetcars. But she sailed in, looking hawkish, set her straw hat aside, smiled, and then settled in to spin her story.

"I think I got something," she said. "About half of Camp Ravenswood was there. I mean, everyone administering the place, and the ladies from Ranger Girls. But it wasn't full, I mean, it wasn't a big crowd. The Millbanks haven't been in Milwaukee all that long."

"Was anyone from that camp not there?"

"How should I know that?"

"Yeah, you're right. Can you remember who?"

"Well, sure. The director, Amanda Winthrop—she's a snob. Mrs. Boetticher, the visiting nurse. The cook, Sylvia Purdy. Wendy Vestal, the athletic woman, those were the camp people."

"Plus girls? The Ranger Girls?"

"No, in school," she said. "Or maybe discouraged from attending."

"Was anyone curious about you?"

"Me? No, I had a line all figured out. I said I was from the church. If they said who are you, I said I was Lizbeth from the church."

"That was a stroke of genius."

"Yeah, I think so. Tell them you're from the church, and they all accept it, or at least don't get curious. I didn't even have to name a church. What is it about ladies from churches?"

"And Sandy's family?"

"Brother Darren and parents, John and Linda, no other relatives. That's interesting. No aunts and uncles, no sister—she's expecting—no grandparents. It's like a real small family. And Sandy's brother is a half-brother, and sister is a half-sister. Linda's the second wife, and Sandy was the only child of that marriage. That's what the nurse, Mrs. Boetticher told me."

"Tell me about the parents."

"They sure were quiet. They'd come up from South America on a Pan American Clipper, and then took a train, so they were plenty tired. Neither wore anything black. Darren, the half-brother, he wore summer tan. It's like this family either doesn't want to acknowledge death, or thinks it's nothing—just passage to somewhere else. Linda wore a blue suit. John wore tweeds. There're families like that. The last thing they want or do is hang crepe or wreathes. Oh, that's another thing. No flowers in there. Not one red rose. I don't get people like that. All the things people do to grieve, they set aside. There were some bouquets out in the foyer, but not in the chapel."

"Was it a service?"

"Mostly a few of Sandy's friends from elsewhere, remembering her. Like two-minute snapshots. One of her teachers from somewhere, not here."

"He's an engineer, the father?"

"I guess so, building something down there."

"And no one cried?"

"Ranger Girls don't cry. They don't get mushy. They don't get sentimental. Ranger Girls are strong. Ranger Girls are always on top of everything."

"Okay, Lizbeth. This woman died of a botched abortion, and these people were attending her memorial. Tell me about that."

She shrugged. "I kept waiting for something. Nothing, Joe. At least maybe an elaborate effort to avoid it, but there wasn't. It was if it didn't exist."

"Was there a reception afterward?"

"Coffee and sweets. Yes, I attended. It was, oh, fast and empty. Like they all had to go through it and get out. Like the parents and brother shook a few hands, nodded, and it was all done. Like no one much cared, and in fifteen minutes they'd had a cookie and sipped a cup and headed out."

"Were the guests there because they had to be?"

"Of course. Sandy Millbank had embarrassed the Ranger Girls, and they'd never forgive her for it, and if they could dodge this, they would have."

"Hey, beautiful, ya done good."

"It was the saddest thing I ever saw," she said. "A girl being politely remembered and silently condemned. She'd slept with someone, gotten into trouble, chose the wrong way out, embarrassed an organization, and everyone there wanted to put it behind them. The whole memorial service had happened because they couldn't escape it."

"Are the parents heading back to peru?"

"I don't know."

Something was bothering Sonntag, and he couldn't quite fathom it. He sipped his bourbon, trying to pluck the right straw. And then he knew.

"Someone loved and honored Sandy Millbank. Someone carried her body to the zoo, to the lioness cage, and stretched her out in the ferns. Someone straightened her legs and skirt, folded her arms across her chest, set her face upward, maybe closed her eyes, and arranged the ferns around her. Someone knew she was the highest ranking Ranger Girl, the lioness, and honored her."

"I think there may be someone at Ranger Camp you haven't interviewed," she said.

"The cook. What was her name?"

"Sylvia Purdy. Not a regular-looking cook. She was so thin I thought she must fast."

"I guess I'll go talk to her. Somebody loved her. Maybe that somebody was the abortionist."

"Joe, do you grieve the unborn child? Or do you grieve the mother? I mean, if you think abortion's wrong, tell me why—and who."

He tried to dodge all that. He didn't know. There were people who thought it was murder. There were laws saying so. But if it was, it didn't come close to the loss of a young woman from medical negligence. A living, sentient, beloved woman, someone's lover or wife, someone's mother. That was a real loss. The other, scraping away a few cells, didn't compare to that. He thought of Sandy's only lover, Wenzel, who had been visited by an angel, a crippled man whose life had been transformed for a little while by Sandy, the Miracle.

"You know something, Lizbeth. It's sad to see a tiny bit of protoplasm never reach life; it's a lot worse to see someone's beloved woman, a person in the fullness of her life and years, perhaps a mother, perhaps a wife, be swept away. What's worse? I vote for the woman, like Sandy."

Her response was utterly unexpected. "I'm glad you love me," she said.

Chapter Seventeen

The investigation was going nowhere. Sonntag was wondering what to try next. Gorilla had picked up some sample business cards out at the farmhouse, and it looked like they were made on the same card stock as the Need Help cards, but a lab would settle that. Gorilla had a good visit with the Hendersons, who seemed like an innocuous couple with a small business. He did learn one thing: the Hendersons lived there; the secretarial outfit was in the front parlor, and the rest was their home. They had rooms upstairs.

But there was no connection between this place and Sandy Millbank. No evidence of an abortionist operating in the area.

"We could stake out some women's rooms. Someone's distributing those cards," Silva said. But the idea didn't appeal to Sonntag. Some female would have to hide in a stall, bored to death. Or park herself outside, note everyone entering the restroom, and rush in to check for cards whenever someone left. Not a good deal.

Q. E. D. Needham turned out to be another dead end. Phone disconnected winters, almost never used. An abortionist couldn't maintain a business seasonally. Still, the name intrigued Sonntag, and he filed it away. Nothing connected Sandy Millbank to anyone doing illegal procedures. In fact, he had no real evidence there was anything like an abortion mill operating in the area. But that didn't mean that things added up. The Matchmakers. A bright, legit opening for girls in trouble. Why operate out on the edge of town? Why not put out word with the social services organizations? A new option? Bring the adoptive parents in early? But that wasn't the way that thing was set up. Sonntag wrote Matchmakers on his yellow legal pad, and underlined it. And underlined it again.

There'd be a break soon. He felt it in his bones. He laughed at his own intuitions, but this one kept crowding his mind. Meanwhile, maybe he could plow some old ground. He clapped his hat on, let Eddy Walsh know where he was headed, got a cruiser, and drove over to Vliet Street. He made his way to the door of Arnold Wenzel, knocked, and waited for the heavy and hesitant thump announcing Wenzel's presence.

"You, is it, sir? What have I done now?"

"Mind if we talk?"

Wenzel waved Sonntag in, and followed, painfully behind.

"We're still trying to find out how Sandy Millbank died—how and why. I thought maybe you could dig up a few memories for us."

"I guess you can't depress me more than I am now," Wenzel said.

"I'm sorry. I know how this eats at you, sir. But this thing needs resolving, and maybe you can help us. I guess what I'm after is this: why did she abandon you? What did she say? What was her reason?"

Wenzel reddened. "So it's going to be about all that again. Why can't it just be that she led a handicapped man—polite word for cripple—out on the dance floor and soothed him past his terror and shame, and then filled his heart with valentines?"

"You make me like Sandy a whole lot, sir."

"She was all apologetic. That was it, a whole string of apologies, so I knew what was coming. She was breaking up."

"Did she give a reason?"

"Trouble. She was having some trouble."

"What kind of trouble? Mental, physical?"

"She didn't say."

"Did she imply she was pregnant?"

"Too soon, much too soon, sir. This was only a few weeks after—she welcomed me."

"Emotional trouble, sir?"

"She was afraid of something, something bad. I'm just an old bachelor in a dump, and I couldn't figure it out, sir. But she was all apologies. When I look back, that's what I remember, her saying she didn't mean me any harm, she wasn't breaking off because of anything I'd done, but just that she had troubles and she had to not come here any more."

"She was in good spirits?"

"No, sir, she was scared of something."

"Do you have any idea? Any hunch?"

Wenzel looked pale. "She was upset. It was like something was making her sick."

"That's just a guess, right?"

"She was just about in tears, and I got so blue I couldn't work for a couple of days."

"This was too soon for—you know, a procedure."

"I console myself with that."

That was the sum total of what he could get from Arnold Wenzel, who looked more forlorn than ever.

"I'm sorry, Mr. Wenzel."

"Everybody's sorry," he said. "They look at me and suddenly they're saying they're sorry. Those are the most familiar words in my life."

"You've helped me, sir. Say, one last thought, and if it's not something you want to answer, just say so, okay? Was ah, intimacy painful to her?"

Wenzel sighed. "We were both amateurs, sir. I don't wish to say more. Just fumbling, bumbling amateurs."

Sonntag left, more puzzled than ever. Sandy had left him long before should could be sure of her condition. And she was deeply upset about it.

Next stop was *The Milwaukee Sentinel*, and another visit to the grand dame, Dorothea Blue. Maybe she'd be ready to talk a little more, now that she had weighed the danger of being an accessory. He was glad that Frank Silva had brought it up.

She was looking pale and imperious—and there was a little anxiety in her face this time.

"Madam, we're making some real progress," he said. "We're getting close. We thought maybe we could enlist your cooperation."

"You're getting close?"

"We're going to find whoever destroyed the life of a sweet young woman, and when we do, it won't be pretty."

She stared.

"You hear rumors, I imagine. Gossip, I imagine. Some rich girl, ah, I should say a young lady from a prominent family, she gets into a little difficulty, right? And that sure makes the rounds, right? And some girls get hustled off to Mexico or Phoenix and return, good as ever. Right?"

"I don't have facts, sir. Sometimes a little gossip."

"All right, then. Just answer me this one question. Is there a local abortionist around here?"

She hesitated. "I think so."

"And does anyone talk about the cards that show up in women's rooms?"

She finally smiled. "Those are a joke. Girls collect those cards and make fun of them."

"But do they call the number?"

"They call and tease the woman who answers, and make up wild stories, and try to rattle the woman."

"They tease the person who takes the call?"

"Sure, they say they're five months pregnant and want the brat eliminated, and right now, and they'll pay any price. That's sport. That's part of having fun. A little daring, but fun."

"And these girls aren't in trouble at all?"

She eyed Sonntag. "The rich are different from you and me."

Sonntag smiled. He hadn't smiled for a hell of a long time. "I think detectives and reporters are in the same business," he said.

"Don't you wish," she said.

"Okay, so we've got an abortionist around here. How do

you know?"

"Wedding reception. Very entertaining."

"Okay, what?"

"Well, you see the bride was wearing an Empire style gown.
Maybe because she had to."

"You know, I'm a flatfoot, and I don't get it."

"An Empire gown hangs loosely from the bodice. It's very
good at concealing an expanding middle."

"Okay, so there's a little gossip at the reception?"

"Just a few sly comments, some ladies who were tight as
ticks."

"About the bride?"

"That led to some talk. They knew someone who'd gone to
an abortionist, and were having a good time bringing it up. They
knew I was there, eating cake, and that made them all the more
reckless. They knew a young lady who'd done it. They said it cost
a thousand dollars, and that ain't hay, honey. A thousand in mixed
bills, nothing over a fifty, and it was all over in no time, fast and
easy, and she was home in a few hours."

"You know the name of that gal?"

"It wasn't revealed to me."

"Can you guess?"

"I could make a list of fifty, and be pretty sure."

"Do you know the women who were talking about it?"

Now she hesitated. "Do I have to?"

"No, you don't have to. At least not unless it gets formal, or
reaches court. But I want to talk to them. I need to get to that
young lady. She's the key to it all. I can keep it all so quiet that no
one knows, but I do want a little talk with her. She's been there,
seen him, paid him, gotten herself fixed up."

She sighed, stared out of the grimy window of the Hearst
paper, and weighed matter.

"You might try Signe Swanberg. Fox Point."

"She's the most likely one in that list of fifty?"

Madame Blue nodded, uncomfortably.

He smiled. "You've been a help," he said. "If you think of
anything else, call me. Here's my card."

She fingered the card, not wanting to hold it. But she managed a smile, and oddly, Sonntag thought it was sincere. He liked her. The rich might be different from the rest of us, he thought, but she wasn't.

Sonntag plowed through warm weather to the station, his thoughts on the difficulties of getting a young woman who'd had an abortion to open up. He'd need to think about that. She wasn't off the hook herself; probably complicit in an illegal act. But his whole instinct was to dodge that. All he wanted was a name, a place, and an account of what happened. Which was asking a lot, actually. And truth to tell, he couldn't guarantee her any privacy. She could find herself on the witness stand.

He wished he'd had a daughter. This whole thing was clawing at him and making him feel like he didn't belong on the case. Maybe he should turn it over to Eddy Walsh, make him the lead investigator. Eddy was a ladies man. Eddy knew all about everything female.

Almost as if to verify all that, Sonntag found Eddy waiting for him in the bullpen.

"Okay, I've made the hospital rounds," Eddy said. "I don't think there's any abortionist cutting on young women and calling it something else. Not at all."

Sonntag settled his fedora on the peg. It was hot and damp in there, and fans weren't helping any. The room was sticky, and his own feelings were sticky.

"Female surgeries, mostly hysterectomies and getting tubes tied."

"What's that? I'm the flatfoot and you're the expert."

"It's rich women's birth control. Tubal ligation. It's expensive. They call it getting fixed. Up in Whitefish Bay, they reach a certain age and get themselves fixed."

"I'm helpless," Sonntag said.

"It's the fallopian tubes. They get tied off or cut or whatever, and that ends it. They can't reverse it. No more babies. It's abdominal surgery, and that means there's some danger, but not a lot. And that puts it out of shot for most people. But the rich like it. Most hospitals won't do them. Catholics say it's birth control. Lots of doctors are uneasy about sterilizing young women, and won't do them. So it's done in a few places by a few doctors."

"Twice in the last couple of days people have told me that the rich are different from you and me."

"They sure as hell are," said Eddy. "They have all the fun, and don't care who knows it."

"I got a name this morning, Dorothea Blue semi-volunteered it. A girl she thinks might have gotten an abortion. I don't know how to talk to her."

"I'll talk to her. They love to tell me that stuff."

Eddy was grinning.

"I'm hoping to do this discreetly."

"Discreet hell. Let me at her. I'll tell her I know she got herself fixed up and I want her story and I want it fast."

"Let's think about this, Eddy."

"Nothing to think about. I'll have it this afternoon if you want it. We aren't in the nicely nicely business."

"Signe Swanberg, Fox Point."

"You're lucky I'm on it. If Frank Silva was on it, he'd make it a class issue. I'll get back to you, Joe. You just sit on your ass and wait for old Eddy."

Chapter Eighteen

L eave it to Eddy Walsh. He was one of the best dicks Sonntag
had. He was old school, a tough interrogator who got what he
wanted by scaring the crap out of people, or sometimes jollying
them along. Sonntag had watched Walsh kid a suspect into spilling
the beans. He always thought Walsh was more effective than himself,
in most types of investigation. Walsh wasn't polite and didn't try
to win cooperation from a hostile suspect. Sonntag did that intuitively; be nice and the criminal might talk. It sometimes worked,
sometimes not. He saw that as a weakness in himself; he wasn't
tough enough. But Walsh was, and Silva could be hard, in a different way, his mind finding angles, and his tongue lashing a suspect
mercilessly.

But Sonntag knew he had his virtues, too. He put people at
ease, opened them up with some innate empathy. Maybe it came
down to this: the world was filled with different sorts, including
the criminals, and it took different sorts of cops to pry truth out of
them. So Eddy volunteered to rattle the teeth of a rich girl up on
Fox Point, and would probably return with the big prize: a name,
an address, a description of a back-alley abortion right there in
Milwaukee.

Sonntag waited impatiently. Whatever it took to resolve a crime investigation, he was all for. Meanwhile there was no point in waiting around. He consulted his list. There still were some names, people associated with the Ranger Girls, or Camp Ravenswood. Maybe he could squeeze something out of them. But these were all long shots. Maybe it was time to talk to Mrs. Barbie, the regional director of the Ranger Girls. There were some undercurrents that might prove useful to the investigation.

He called her, and she agreed to see him, so he collected a cruiser and drove up to her suburban home, where she welcomed him brightly and nervously, and they settled into cream wing chairs in her blue-colored parlor.

"We're making progress," he said, half-way believing it. "We may have this cracked pretty quickly now."

"It's not going to look good for the Ranger Girls, no matter what," she said.

"No, it probably won't be. No one can escape that. She was the off-season camp director, and there seems to be a lot of Ranger symbolism in the way she was left at the zoo."

Mrs. Barbie nodded somberly.

"I'm going to raise some delicate questions," Sonntag warned. "Your group differs from the Girl Scouts in certain important ways. It's a group for girls entering puberty and adulthood, moving into, say, womanhood. It's a group that focuses on that very thing. These Ranger girls coming into camp, they're being prepared for, what?"

"It's difficult to discuss, sir, with a...policeman."

"Well, that's all right. Were any of these things part of the camp's curriculum?"

"That's hard to say, Mr. Sonntag. We did encourage our visiting nurse to discuss anything the girls wanted to know with them, privately. And...well, there were and are people who want change."

"Could you tell me about that?"

She smiled, nervously. "Well, let's say there are factions in the Ranger Girls, and I'll give them names. The traditionalists, and the moderns. The traditionalists are, well, just that. Private matters are private. Let new wives discover what needs to be learned. Let them follow the dictates of church and conscience. The moderns are, well, more liberal, and well, things aren't so rigid, and women should have more freedom, especially, well, the freedoms that might require birth control."

"I think I get it," he said. "Feminists? Some were feminists?"

"We're all feminists in Ranger Girls, detective."

"Okay, some wanted to steer girls one way, some wanted to steer them another way?"

"It was a very fierce debate, sir. I'm somewhere in the middle, myself, but then again, I've always been daring, and that's how I ended up as a national director for this region."

"How did this affect what went on in the camp?"

"We worked out compromises. There were classes on feminine hygiene, but they differed with age. Young girls, our newest members, were instructed in a rather, oh, rigid manner. Older girls, there was an effort to inform them about their bodies and their, how shall I say it, options."

"And neither side was satisfied?"

"It is the thing that eats up our board meetings, detective."

"Was abortion ever discussed?"

"The older Rangers were warned against it."

"Discussed in terms of what it was, or its legality?"

"I think by that age our girls had figured it out. No, it was simply warned against."

"Are there women who think that's much too cautious?"

"Absolutely. We have our very liberal wing, sir. Amanda Winthrop, the camp director, was adamant about opening up the lives of our girls; so was the athletic director, Wendy Vestal. For them, there should be no difference between what girls do and what boys do—or pretend they do."

"Could any of these more liberal women have attempted to help a pregnant girl who came to camp?"

Mrs. Barbie stared, lips forming words and then compressing. "I could not answer such a question, sir, and I hope that doesn't reflect on the organization."

"Wendy Vestal told us that she knew about those Need Help cards floating around, had some, and said she'd gladly give a card to a girl. How does that strike you?"

Mrs. Barbie stared at her blue parlor. "It's her own view, sir, not the view of my organization."

Sonntag sighed. 'I know this is painful. Is there any chance that anyone, or any group, was using Camp Ravenswood as a, well, recruiting place for girls in trouble?"

Mrs. Barbie pulled a handkerchief from a pocket, and began dabbing her eyes. "If they did, I didn't know about it," she said.

"I'm wondering whether an abortionist had agents there, women committed to that option."

"Mr. Sonntag, I don't know a single woman who wants or approves of abortions. And that includes the entire staff at camp."

"But might there be any who would simply wish to give a girl in trouble a quick way out?"

She sighed. "I think you know that's possible."

"The athletic director?'

She nodded. "And our cook, Sylvia Purdy. She was the most outspoken."

"What about your visiting nurse?"

"Dear heaven, not Mrs. Boetticher. She has the biggest heart. I know personally that she helps two or three women every summer find their way into shelters, where they will be cared for and their child put up for adoption."

"She does deal with all that?"

"Constantly, sir."

"Where might I find Mrs. Purdy?"

"She's a hospital cook. Milwaukee Hospital. She takes summers off to cook for us."

"When you say she's outspoken, what does she say?"

"Well, she's not on our board, sir, so what she says is not of any account in the executive board."

"But she has views that, well, run to extremes?"

"She's a very good cook, Mr. Sonntag."

"Is she controversial?"

Mrs. Barbie sighed, and nodded.

"Mrs. Barbie, do you have any idea, even just a hunch, how Sandy Millbank found an abortionist, managed to link up, and have one? Or where she got the money?"

"No, not the faintest, sir."

He left it at that. Somehow, the interview was leading somewhere, but he didn't know quite where. He drove the rattling patrol car back to the station, so immersed in his thoughts he almost ran a stoplight. Women's bodies were battlegrounds. The churches had their own ideas. The law had its rules. Feminists were staking out ground. Traditional people had long lists of what was permissible and what wasn't. He had missed it. He had boys, and somehow missed it. Nothing had prepared him for the discovery that a fierce war was raging among those ladies about what could or could not be taught or discussed or shown in a camp for girls reaching womanhood. About ideals, beliefs, acts, and taboos. The only people who didn't have much say about their own bodies were the women themselves. No wonder Lizbeth was acting funny about all that stuff.

He would check with Eddy. Maybe Eddy had a name, a number, a way. If Eddy got that, the Milwaukee PD would soon have whoever killed Sandy Millbank.

"Hey," said Eddy, "you're lucky. You get to travel."

"What are you talking about?"

"Ask the captain for a nice trip to Italy. Catch the Queen Mary."

"Dammit, Eddy."

"Struck out," he said. "Miss Swanberg's spending her summer in Florence looking at art. She's in the Smith College Year Abroad program."

"Anyone else in the household who can talk?"

"Her mother's with her. Her daddy's in London."

"How do you know?"

"I knocked on the door and got chatty with the maid."

"There went the best lead."

"Yeah, but you can bet she's not the only doll around town who got fixed up."

"Then find me some more," Sonntag said. He was feeling peeved.

"Leave it to Eddy," Walsh said.

Sonntag drove to Milwaukee Hospital on the near west side, a grim place that shed gloom and turned a sunny landscape dreary.

He advised a receptionist that he was a police detective, and wanted to talk to a cook, Sylvia Purdy.

The cook proved to be compact, with black hair braided and pinned to her head, and hostile.

She followed him sullenly into an empty cafeteria area with empty food counters.

"It's the Sandy Millbank thing. I heard you were poking around."

"Yes. We're looking for the abortionist."

"Well if I knew, you'd have to fight me to get it. But I don't know."

"Why would we have to do that?"

"Because I wish there was one on every street corner, and I wish any girl could get help, and I hate the very thought of shutting the man—if he's a man—down."

She sat there, a food-stained white apron armoring her, a wall between the cop and the cook.

"You knew Sandy Millbank?"

"Look, I'll save you the bother. I knew her, I didn't know she was pregnant, and if she wanted to get rid of it, I'd approve, and no, I didn't help her and I didn't know of anyone who could help her. Does that take care of it?"

"She died from a man's carelessness, Mrs. Purdy."

"Why do you think I'm married?"

"The ring."

"That's to keep men away. Men have no idea how many women wear cheap rings. Okay, it's like this. When I was a girl I was molested by my stepfather, and he got me pregnant, and I ran away desperate to Chicago, and by asking a lot, and going somewhere else, Gary, Indiana, next door to a steel mill, I found a woman who'd do it, and she did it, and I got rid of it, and I never looked back, and I'd do it again, and men can go to hell. I spent the next two years making small payments until I got her paid. She did it without wanting money in advance. She trusted me to pay. I don't know what happened to her. I hope she wasn't caught."

"You know something, Sylvia—may I call you that? I think in cases like incest and rape, a lady ought to have that right. I'm sorry the law's written the way it is. I'm stuck with enforcing a law that needs reforming."

"A lady ought to have that right anytime. I'm against reform. I'm for repeal. Now are you done with me?"

"Well, pretty near. There were some politics in Camp Ravenswood. I'll call one side the traditionalists, and the other side the feminists, just to put labels on them. Were you in on that?"

"I was the cook."

"I guess I'd like to ask that again since you didn't respond."

"Yes I was in on it. I wanted every girl who left that camp to leave with a good knowledge of how to survive as a female in a male world. And I didn't mind telling the girls. We had dishwashing and table crews and we talked. Did I ever. Any girl who had a question about it, they came to me and I told them."

"What's a Lioness, Sylvia?"

"You'll have to ask the people who run Ranger Girls."

"Sandy Millbank was left in repose, next to the lioness at the zoo. What do you think of that?"

"I wish it was me," she said.

Chapter Nineteen

Milwaukee was building west, swallowing green meadows where Holsteins and Guernseys grazed, throwing up cracker box tracts in a hilly, bucolic hinterland that had supported diaries from time immemorial. Out there it wasn't suburb but it wasn't country either.

Joe Sonntag drove the rattling black Ford, with Frank Silva beside him. They crossed the Milwaukee city limits and kept on out Bluemound until they reached the old limestone farmhouse. The lab work made it specific. The Need Help? cards had been made from the same card stock, and employed the same inks, as the samples that Gorilla had collected from the Hendersons. It was time for some hard questions.

"Do you want to take it?" Sonntag asked.

"Sure, I'll take it."

"You have a way about you."

Sonntag turned into the farmhouse drive, passed the little sign announcing Speedy Secretarial Service, and braked on the gravel drive at the front door. A bright blue Plymouth was parked under an elm. The place looked for all the world like a rural home, but for the small plaque on the door announcing the business. "Please Ring," it said. This was not a walk-in shop.

So Sonntag rang.

Elvira Henderson opened, and William was standing back a bit.

"You're the Hendersons, right?"

They nodded.

"We're with the Milwaukee police, and we're hoping to ask a few questions about your business cards, if you have a moment," Sonntag said.

"Business cards? Oh, those. We do a little custom work."

"Yeah, well could we talk a bit? Like in your store here?" Silva said.

"You're pretty far from Milwaukee," Henderson said from behind his wife.

"Yep, that's true, sir. I'm glad we caught you here because it's a long drive. We're sure hoping you can help us. It's real important to us. Maybe you can help solve some trouble over in town."

Henderson and his wife exchanged glances, and she slowly widened the door and nodded.

"Thanks a lot, ma'am. I'm Frank Silva. And this is Joe Sonntag."

They entered a front parlor that had been converted into a small shop. There were a few items for sale, such as steno notebooks, ledgers, and file folders.

"Just starting up an office services company," Henderson said. "More than supplies. Secretarial. No competition out here."

"Not many customers, either," Silva said.

There weren't chairs for the four. That was fine. People didn't like being interrogated standing up, and tended to rush ahead sometimes just to get it over with. On the desk on one side was one of the new multi-line consoles.

The Hendersons looked unconcerned but not entirely at ease. But people weren't exactly relaxed around cops.

"Nice place here," Silva said. "You get to work in a quiet place. Me, I'm not one for country life. Too many snakes. But nice here. I wonder why you set up here?"

"Free rent. My wife's relatives own the place and wanted someone in it. So we've got a home and store for not much rent."

"Well," Silva said, "we're looking into these cards. Like this one here." He handed a Need Help? card to Henderson. "They're printed here, right?"

"Well, some."

"Yeah, on a little hand-print deal, silk screen or something. Now these cards, they've got us asking some questions. Who's putting them in women's rooms around town, and why? What kind of help? So we'd like to know who's getting these cards from you, and who's putting them all over the place, and why. You got the name and number of who's ordering these?"

"No one's ordering them, sir; that's our new business," Elvira said. "Matchmakers. We're a new kind of adoption agency, just getting going."

Silva eyed the card, and her. "Well, isn't that something," he said. "So is this your number? Is that the phone there, with this number?"

"We have several numbers, sir. Speedy Secretarial, and Matchmakers..."

"Okay, this is good. We're getting somewhere. Tell me about this Matchmakers."

"We're matching girls who are going to put a baby up for adoption with the parents beforehand. The adopting parents get to meet the girl, pay for her shelter and delivery, and then get the baby. We get a commission for it. We think it's the most wonderful innovation in the whole adoption field."

"Where do you find the parents-to-be?"

"We have a small personals ad in both papers, sir. It says, Adoptions Arranged. Know your child. And our phone number."

"Let me get this straight. You put these cards out to draw calls from girls, ah, young ladies, who are in trouble. And you put ads in the papers looking for couples wanting to adopt, and you tell them about the girl, and she needs support, and after that they get the baby, right?"

"That's the whole idea, sir, yes."

"Well, okay, ma'am, you've got this fine service, but you spot these cards around in women's rooms, stuffed in mirrors, instead of using the personals columns in the papers to connect with girls in need. That's sure a puzzle to us, Elvira."

"Oh, well, that's simply how we chose to do it."

"Who puts these cards out?"

"Spend one day a week in town doing it. Schools, places like that."

"You just walk into, say, Shorewood High School and stuff a few of these in the mirror frames? Do you tell anyone?"

"Oh, no, sir, I just do it."

"Wouldn't it just be easier to put an ad in the personals? A girl's gonna see it there. That's the first place she'll look if she wants help. How come you float all over Milwaukee doing this?"

"It's so personal, sir. This is the only effective way to contact girls who've gotten into difficulty."

"Yeah, well, it's got us looking into it. I guess you know why."

"Oh, sir, Matchmakers is not, not, not that sort of thing. Not at all! We're going to appoint a board of directors, prominent women, and we're planning to publish some brochures about the new service. And of course, let the other adoption agencies and shelters know. We really believe in this."

"So a woman calls you, and you take the call right there, at that desk, and she says she's in trouble. Then what?"

"We find out everything we can about her circumstances. If she's a minor, has she told anyone? Her parents? Is she living at home and afraid of her parents? Does she have any way to support herself if she leaves her parents? If not, would she consider meeting adoptive parents who might pay for her sheltering and then get the baby? We try to get all that down, and then get back to her with some potential parents, see? This whole thing is just the opposite of anonymous. Right now, in most places, everything is kept secret and apart. The adoptive parents don't know the girl; the new mother is kept from the adoptive parents. We're going in exactly the opposite direction."

Elvira Henderson sounded so enthused that Sonntag wanted to believe her. Only he didn't. Silva was doing a great job, bringing her out and getting her talking.

"I guess you've talked to all those people, like the sisters who have that shelter, and the state agency, whatever its name is," Sonntag said. "Let them know, right?"

"Well, not yet. We want to make it work first. There's no law preventing us from setting up our own agency," William Henderson said.

"Yeah, well let's get back to these cards. How many calls you get?"

"Oh, hardly any, sir."

"Well, how about letting us talk to some of these girls? Like the ones who've had their baby, given it up, and there's happy parents now."

"That's all confidential, sir."

"Yeah, well how about letting us see your records? You know, call received, gal wants help, needs money, all that stuff."

"All deeply private, sirs," Henderson said.

"Yeah, well adoptions have to be recorded by the state."

"That's between the girl and the new parents, sirs. We don't do that and don't even know whether it's been done in all cases."

"Let me get this straight. You're running this new adoption service, and you don't keep records and don't make sure the adoption's lawful?"

"We're just getting started, sir," she said.

"Okay, a girl's pregnant, but she doesn't want to do it this way. She doesn't want to give her baby up. She doesn't want the new parents to support her. What other stuff have you got up your sleeve?"

"I resent the way you put that," Elvira said. "We refer them to regular agencies. We give them the phone number of that convent where they'll be taken in."

"What if they're looking for, you know, a little procedure?"

"We tell them there's nothing we can do for them," she said.

"Do they ask for that much?"

"No, not in my experience. Most just are afraid of their parents, want to escape to a safe place, have the child and start life over."

"Tell me," said Sonntag. "You've got two unrelated businesses here under one roof. Does your secretarial service take messages for clients?"

"Yes, we have two or three clients who want our message service. We take the message and call them."

"Who's that? Why's that?"

"Some people don't want to be interrupted, sir. Others want the messages screened. We call them and tell them the message, and they decide whether to respond."

"You have some like that? Can we talk to them?"

"No, sirs, that's their business, not ours."

"You live here?" Silva asked.

Henderson nodded.

"You mind giving us a tour? Nice old farmhouse like this? I bet you've got comfortable quarters."

"Well, what you see is just about all, sir. Just two bedrooms and an old bath upstairs."

"I'd sure like to see it. Might give me ideas about remodeling."

She smiled. "Oh, come sometime when I've had the chance to straighten up."

"I like old barns. I'm a real barn man. Give me a barn and I'm crawling all over it, just because I like barns," Silva said.

That sure was news to Sonntag.

"You know what a city guy like me, what I'd like? A barn tour. I want to see the whole dairy."

"Not much to see in there, sir," Henderson said.

"Yeah, well teach a city boy a little, okay?"

The Hendersons eyed each other, and then William nodded. "Sure," he said. "Mostly some diary stanchions."

"Never saw one before. They stick the cows in and milk 'em?"

"Yep. Now if you gents will follow me, I'll show you. I guess it's be strange stuff for a couple of city fellows."

Henderson herded the cops out just as the phone started ringing. Elvira ignored it, and smiled. Sonntag itched to head back there, but let himself be herded down the front steps and onto the gravel drive. The phone stopped ringing.

"This was a dairy until the middle of the war," Henderson said. "There wasn't anyone to run it. Hired help all drafted. So they shut it down, I guess nineteen forty-three or so. Cows got sold off."

Sonntag wished he could be listening in on the phone call back there.

The decaying barn was spacious. A dozen stanchions marched down either side of the wide aisle, pipe racks and concrete. Clamp a cow in, milk her, go on to the next. A shed at the rear turned out to be the milk room, a place to wash containers, collect raw milk, send it off to the dairy. Not much to see. All the paraphernalia was gone. An enclosed stairwell with a padlocked door rose at the far end.

"Where does that go?"

"Hayloft."

"How does that work?"

"You can fork hay down to the cows from there."

"It's locked. Any chance I could see how that works?" Silva asked.

"I don't have the key, sir. Owners have it."

"Yeah, who are they?"

"Wisconsin Properties."

"Yeah, but who's the person? Her relative that lets you live here to keep up the place?"

"You know, I'd have to ask her, sir."

"Maybe she has the key."

"Neither of us have a key to that padlock, sir."

Silva grinned. "I got it," he said. "Out in my car there, I've got a deal that lets me pop any padlock. A genius invented it. You sort of try a few, wiggle them in, and it sort of pushes around in there and bingo! It pops open. You want me to give it a try? You as curious as I am?"

"No, sir. It's not my business, and I don't think it's anyone's business but the owner's."

"Just thought I'd ask," Silva said.

They were done there. Sonntag fired up the old cruiser, and they rolled out.

"What's that padlock buster device?" Sonntag asked. "I never heard of it."

"Neither have I," Silva said.

Chapter Twenty

It was odd how neither of them talked. At least not until the city line. Then when they were in Milwaukee, everything changed.

"That was a lot of Shinola," Frank Silva said.

"You can't put a shine on it," Sonntag said.

"We're on something here, but what?"

"There's something rattling in my head about adoptions. Births, that's public record. Adoptions are public record too, but sealed. That's it. It's sealed. The law says that the birth mother and adoptive parents are confidential That's to keep the mother from trying to get the child back, and tearing up a family."

"So Matchmakers is illegal from the get-go?"

"I dunno. We'd have to look it up."

"I was gonna hit the public records. Birth certificates, adoptions, see what Matchmakers is doing."

Sonntag eyed him. "There won't be a public record. There can't be. And no adoption agency will deal with them. It's either a front for an abortion mill, or it's an illegal and shadowy child-trafficking deal."

"How do we get at it?"

"Find a woman who's had an abortion and is willing to talk."

"Lots of luck, Joe."

"Or if it really is a child-trafficking deal, with no recorded births and no adoptions, but babies moving into homes without benefit of any documentation, then we're chasing something different. A whole world of trafficking that no cop or judge or state attorney knows about."

"Or maybe both. A front and a baby mill."

"Why would a couple want a child by that route?" Joe asked.

"Damned if I know," Silva said. "Maybe to check on the girl's looks. You know, race, ethnicity. Some little mothers don't make the cut."

The radio squawked. The things didn't work half the time, especially outside of town.

"Sonntag, you there?" the voice said. "You and Silva? Where are you?"

Silva picked up the mike hanging from the dash. "Fifties on Bluemound."

"At last. You've been blank. Why didn't you call? We've got a suicide on south Forty-fourth. It doesn't add up, and you go take a look."

Silva wrote the address, and Sonntag turned off on Forty-fourth.

"No suicide adds up," Sonntag said.

"I think they all add up," Silva said.

"No one should quit," Sonntag said.

"Tell that to the one who just cut his wrists," Silva said.

Sonntag didn't like suicides. They were quitting instead of fighting. He knew that Silva was the exact opposite. He thought suicides were brave people, choosing the best path out. Sonntag liked the law making suicide a form of murder. Silva thought the law was absurd. They'd argued it a dozen times, and no doubt this would start it up again.

Sonntag found the place, a small Milwaukee-style bungalow. There were two uniformed cops there, and an ambulance crew, and a couple of neighbors.

Inside, a distraught woman sat in a tiny parlor, wringing her pale hands. In the sole bedroom lay the deceased male in uniform, a man who had lost part of a leg, all of an arm, an eye and an ear,

NIGHT MEDICINE 151

and the remaining hand was crippled. Another veteran, Sonntag thought. The world was full of ruined men, destroyed men, tucked silently away and out of sight, the debris of a long war. The nearby Wood soldiers home was full of them now, these hidden men, the men that warmongering politicians didn't want the world to see.

"I'm Lieutenant Joe Sonntag; this is Detective Frank Silva."

"I'm Manfred, sir, and outside, that's Hesserl."

"This here is Eden Stumpf," the cop said. "Sergeant, hit at Anzio. He was at Wood, couldn't stand it, somehow got this place. She told me."

"Who's she?"

"Next door, also his caretaker. He paid her a little to look after him."

Stumpf had gotten dressed up for his exit. His wool uniform didn't fit well now, but it was on, the leg pinned up, the sleeve pinned up. The unpinned sleeve had three yellow chevrons. Stumpf was freshly shaved. It must have been a hell of a task just to shave himself. He lay on his back in repose.

"Here's the letter he left. It was on his chest," the cop said.

The letter was short, painfully printed out by a man with little use of his hand.

"I can't go on. I served my country. I died at Anzio, not now. Don't blame anyone but me. Sergeant Eden P. Stumpf."

Joe felt a sudden sadness. Anzio was 1944, he thought. A few years of living death in a veterans warehouse and this bungalow and now it ended. No future, no wife, no children, no career or job. Apparently deaf too, so maybe no music. Maybe not much reading, either. Just whatever war washed ashore.

"How?" Silva asked.

The cop pointed to an empty blue bottle with a label pasted on it. Seconal, it said. It had been typed. Just the one word. A powerful barbiturate.

"He'd need a bunch of those for this. Where'd they come from? This isn't a drug store bottle or label."

"We'll find out," Sonntag said. "Anyone touched that bottle?"

"I'm afraid so, sir. It was on his chest. The ambulance people did, we all did. That's when we called central for help."

They got the story from the woman, Agnes Louk. She always came early afternoon, collected his mail, came in, checked on him, handled his dishes and food, sometimes did some washing in an old wringer Maytag, and did errands, such as drug store runs.

"He tried to be independent; he didn't like it when I had to help, and it maddened him sometimes," she said.

"You know where this blue bottle came from?"

"It was there on his chest, empty. The water glass was empty, beside his bed. I was so frightened. I touched him and he was cold, but I already knew. He was in his uniform, and that told me everything. He doesn't have a phone, so I went next door and called."

"Had he talked of this?'

"Never, sir. He was stern."

"Did he have visitors?"

"Once in a while. Veterans people, they came by."

"Did you see this blue bottle before today?"

"No, sir, I never did."

"Did anyone other than veterans people come by, or leave a note?"

"I don't watch that closely, sir. But we had a signal. If the light was on in his window, he was all right. If he turned the light off, he needed me."

"Was the light on today?"

"Yes, and it still is," she said, gesturing.

"How did he reach people if he had no phone?"

She pointed to a stack of opened letters. "He would sit in this chair, here, and study letters, and write some himself. It was hard for him, but he did, and I stamped and mailed them for him."

"You got his prescriptions, ma'am?"

"Yes, at the veterans home. They're in his medicine cabinet."

"Any Seconal?"

"I'll look," Frank said.

He brought two bottles back. "Low dose, ten milligram, and there's a few in here."

The Wood Veterans Home pharmacy bottles had black and white labels, with hand-written doses. The other was digitalis.

"He hurt a lot," she said.

"Did he drink, ma'am?"

"That's a funny thing. He didn't, but he asked me to get him a pint of rye the other day, so I did."

Silva headed for the kitchen and returned with the pint. It was mostly gone. He eyed Sonntag. Alcohol was a good way to speed up the Seconal. It was a favorite way for celebrities to check out. Drink a few, and then swallow capsules, and it goes fast. Like Carole Landis. Like the celebrity evangelist Aimee Semple McPherson in 1944.

Sonntag eyed the body. Next to Stumpf was a folder. He flipped it open. Honorable discharge. Purple heart. Battlefield citations, some for valor. High school diploma. Honorable mention in civics essay contest. Birth certificate. A life, extinguished at age forty-one. There was nothing about relatives or family, other than what was on the birth certificate.

The ambulance guys were waiting, looking bored.

"You found him like this?" Sonntag asked.

"Gone. Cold. Ambient room temperature. We have protocols for that, mainly call the cops."

"We're done with him. He goes to the morgue. Autopsy."

"We can go?"

"With Sergeant Stumpf. And treat him as you would a saint or a king. He's been dead a long time, since Anzio Beach."

"Yes, sir," said one. They didn't know what Sonntag was talking about. It didn't matter.

He asked Agnes Louk whether Eden Stumpf had ever said anything about a family, or what he wanted after he died.

"That was off-limits, sir. But the Veterans Administration would know."

"And give him a funeral," Sonntag said. "Let me ask one more time, if you have any idea or guess where that blue bottle came from."

She shook her head, a little frightened. "Someone brought it," she said.

"Okay, thank you, ma'am. You've been very helpful. Here's my card. If you connect that blue bottle to anything, like a delivery truck or a mail order, anything that comes to mind, I'd be grateful if you'd call me right away."

She took the card. "You're the first police officer I've ever talked to," she said.

"You did everything a person could do, ma'am. You helped us. You're a very good neighbor and citizen."

"I try," she said.

"The officers are going to check a few things here, and then lock up, and leave the key with you. We don't know how this'll wind up. If anyone comes around here, please call us at once. We'd really like to talk to anyone who comes to this door."

"Oh, I'll keep an eye out, and you can count on it," she said, her eyes brightening.

He smiled, and she beamed.

He watched the ambulance men carry the body out. They were gentle, as if carrying something indescribably beautiful.

Some neighbors had gathered. "Okay, you go home now," he said. But they didn't.

He collected the blue bottle, the pile of mail, the folder with his citations, the rye bottle, and some envelopes he found in a waste paper basket. He added the two bottles from the Wood Veterans Home pharmacy.

Silva studied drawers, closets, shelves, clothing, and the whole kitchen. And then they headed out to the decrepit car. Sonntag hoped it would start.

It did. The cops and neighbors watched them drive away.

"Somewhere in here, there's a felony," he said, knowing it would set Frank off.

He rose to the bait. "Some felony. A guy needs a little help ending his miserable life, and some compassionate person helps him do it. And because of that, we send him up the river for twenty years."

"It has to be that way. The state has to respect life, all life, in all circumstances, and there can't be exceptions. The moment there's exceptions, there's holes in the wall, and then the state's letting people get killed."

Silva scowled, and said nothing. But Sonntag knew it wouldn't end there, and it didn't. By the time they got to 35th Street Silva jumped in. "We don't own people's bodies. The state doesn't, the cops don't, the politicians don't, and attorney general doesn't. People own their own bodies. Eden Stumpf had every right to quit if he wanted, and whoever helped him had every right, law or no law."

"Okay, there's a commandment," Sonntag said. "No exceptions."

"Don't pull that on me," Silva said. "The man who just killed himself was busy at Anzio killing Germans and Italians and wasn't paying any attention to commandments."

This was old ground, and Sonntag felt tired. "Frank, does that blue bottle bother you?"

"What about it?"

"Someone delivers a bunch of Seconal capsules to a suicide, so why a bottle with a label? Why not just an envelope full of the capsules?"

"That's a good point," Silva said. "The enabler was someone who's been around medicine and has some habits. Like a pharmacist. They can't stand loose pills that aren't labeled. They can't imagine a bottle with pills and label. It goes against their instincts. That's also true of nurses and doctors."

"So someone took an ordinary gummed label from the dime store, typed the label, and pasted it onto a bottle and added a lethal dose of a deadly drug. Why?"

"Beats me," Silva said, "but let's find out. Maybe we get to arrest the only compassionate medical man in town."

Chapter Twenty-One

Neil, the motorman, was heading his way. "You getting off, Lieutenant?"

Shocked, Sonntag peered about. He was at his 56th Street stop. Neil had been operating this car for years, and knew his passengers.

"Oh, sure, yeah," Sonntag said, bolting up and out of the wicker seat.

"We get to thinking about other things," Neil said, heading to the front of the car and his motorman's seat. Sonntag stepped down, and the door clanked shut. The Wells Street car whined away, passengers staring at him from grimy windows.

Sonntag marveled. He'd been so preoccupied he missed his stop, and missed his terrifying ride across the viaduct. Here he was. He crossed Wells and hiked toward 57th, and his bungalow on a dead-end stub where Lizbeth patiently waited with a drink and dinner, as she did through the thousands of days of life.

Crimes of compassion, he called them, but still crimes. Someone had assisted Eden Stumpf to take his life. Someone who could get enough Seconal to do it, and get it to Stumpf by some hidden means. Someone who was maybe trying to help a man out of his misery.

Sonntag hated crimes like that, where some criminal was motivated by mercy. It could just as well be lots of bucks. Maybe a thousand dollars for a few pills. Make something illegal and you put a high price on it.

One nice thing about a dead-end street; kids could play without a lot of traffic. Some young parents knew that, and Joe and Lizbeth found themselves with young neighbors, and roiling bands of children.

He walked inside, pitched his fedora toward the hat rack, and headed for the kitchen.

Lizbeth greeted him with a perfunctory peck. "What's eating you?" she said.

"Does it show?"

"You can't hide it, buster."

"Oh, just another dead-end day," he said.

"That's where I live," she said.

He wasn't going to talk. She'd take some other viewpoint. She and Frank. He didn't feel like fighting her. The law was the law, no exceptions, no reasons to disobey it, but now she was finding reasons. Like saving the life of a mother. It was odd how this case was changing her beliefs, separating her from him.

She sensed it, and disappeared into the kitchen. They'd eat earlier, since no one was going to say anything that night. Sonntag didn't care. You can't have exceptions. First thing you know, some Willy will be in court arguing that he shot his uncle George to end his suffering from constipation, and the life insurance didn't matter because his motives were compassionate.

He pretended to study the front page of the *Journal*, and pretended to read the comic strips in the Green Sheet. He pretended to ignore her, but she was staying invisible so there was no one to ignore.

She served meatloaf and mashed potatoes, with some Brussels sprouts, which he didn't like but ate manfully. Then she put away the food, washed the dishes, and started playing solitaire, while he stepped outside and stared at the factory smoke layering the valley. That's how the evening played out. She went upstairs early. He sat in the canvas lawn chair smelling the hops from the breweries while the night cooled and the factory smoke lifted. Soon he could see a few stars. Lizbeth had the radio on and the sounds wafted through the open window. They were playing "Nature Boy," by the Nat King Cole Trio, on WEMP.

His thoughts weren't lightened by the tune. The whole country was full of the walking dead, he thought, ruined men from the war, hidden from sight; men without sight or parts or limbs or taste or hearing; men useless to themselves and the world; men no politician talked about except an occasional solemn reference to those who gave their all. But these ruined men didn't quite give their all. They lived on and on, bored, in pain, despairing, lonely, bitter, and hopeless. They were mostly young, but waiting to die. Eden Stumpf was one of them, forty-one and looking for a way out—which he found. That's what made Sonntag mad. There shouldn't be any exceptions, but he thought Stumpf did what he needed to do. Sonntag thought he'd do the same.

From the radio, Kay Kyser's orchestra played "On a Slow Boat to China," and then Margaret Whiting began the melancholy love song, "A Tree in the Meadow." The radio clicked off in the middle of it. Sometime much later Lizbeth appeared in a white robe, stared at him, and vanished inside again. He finally quit. The clock in the kitchen said two-thirty. He went to bed and didn't sleep, and then it was six and he needed to get up and head out and report for duty and do it all over again. Stumpf had figured out what to do about inhabiting a ruined body. Sonntag hadn't figured out how to inhabit a ruined world.

He made coffee. Lizbeth deliberately stayed apart. He loaded up his black lunch bucket with a sandwich, cheese and white bread, and some Oreos, and headed out the door in the awakening of the day. He'd find the bastard who helped Stumpf do it, find him and throw the book at him. The man probably had broken five or six laws.

>> | <<

The bullpen looked alien to him. There were a couple of uniformed cops writing out reports. He didn't want to sit at his desk. He didn't want to run through Eden Stumpf's correspondence, all the envelopes and debris that he and Frank had scooped up. It was too quiet in there, and the naked lights hurt his eyes. He poured some ancient coffee, mostly to procrastinate. He didn't feel like pawing through a veteran's stuff, but he did. He sorted it into piles. Bills and invoices and receipts, correspondence, and postal money orders. The man had no bank account, and his finances went through the postal window at the Wood Veterans Home.

There was no personal correspondence, no friendly letters received from anyone. He was a forgotten man as well as a ruined one. His helper woman must have done a lot for him, including the groceries and bill-paying. Sonntag looked over some pharmacy statements from the Veterans Home. Veterans got their medicines free, apparently. There were postal money order stubs for rent, sixty a month, Wisconsin Gas and Electric, Mrs. Louk, seventy-five a month, and a monthly grocery bill.

The card caught his eye. Pain Relief, it said, and a number. He fingered it. The card looked oddly familiar, and he thought it was the same card stock and same blue ink color as the Need Help cards he had collected. It had a different number, but still in the Bluemound exchange, 258. He pulled from his wallet one of his Need Help cards and compared the two, and then sat there, astonished. Same deal.

He wondered if they'd recognize his voice. Probably not. Frank Silva had done all the talking. It was worth the gamble.

He dialed, heard the ring, and heard a man's voice. "The Pain Relief Clinic," the voice said. It sounded like William Henderson.

"Yeah, I found your card and I'm a veteran, and I never stop aching where my arm got shot off, and I was just wondering—I mean, what do you do there?"

"Relieving pain is our object, sir."

"You have a clinic? I could come out there and get diagnosed and get some help?"

"There's no need for that, sir. We achieve complete diagnoses by asking you a series of questions, including body weight, and things of that sort. Then our experts will determine what you need."

"I'm really desperate. I hurt so much I can't stand another hour of it."

"Well, now, we need to confirm who you are, sir, before we can begin to evaluate your condition. How did you find out about us?"

"Veterans Home," Sonntag said, making a stab at it.

"Well, let us prepare a form for you. We'll need your number."

"You know what? I want to think about this. I'll call you later if I'm still interested," Sonntag said.

"We can help even the most desperate," the voice said.

"Not as bad as I am," Sonntag said. "You got nothing for that."

Sonntag hung up, stared at the black phone, and thought that the Hendersons might have yet another business, that of assisting suicides. Or maybe it wasn't the Hendersons. Maybe they were fronting for something bigger. Somehow, Eden Stumpf got his Seconal, and probably right there. But to think it was to know that was absurd. How many suicides a year in the county? How many assisted? This was Sonntag's first case of this sort. He had yet to look it up. Accessory to murder, maybe. Maybe first and last case. You can't make money assisting suicides when there aren't any customers.

Silva showed up, and Sonntag handed him the card.

"I called. It probably was Henderson. They're peddling pain relief, without doctors appointments, phone questionnaire. I backed out."

"How many Eden Stumpfs are there, looking for a way out?"

"That's what I thought, too."

"Why do you look so tired?"

"I want my criminals to be criminal."

For once, Silva grinned. "We could go after hubcap thieves."

"Someone sent Sandy Millbank to her grave, trying to help her out. Someone sent Eden Stumpf to his, also trying to end the suffering. Maybe the same person. That's why I hate this."

Sonntag called the coroner.

"Yeah, we're done. I was just writing it up. Deceased died of toxic overdose of Seconal. There were four undigested hundred milligram capsules in his stomach. The toxicity range was thirty to fifty."

"That's a lot."

"That's a massive dose. No surprises. You know what? Merciful dose. Oh, yes, blood alcohol too. Speed things along. It took some knowledge. I'll send the report as soon as it's ready."

Sonntag hung up. "Merciful dose, he says."

Silva smiled. "There we go again."

"I want to go to his funeral," Sonntag said. "I want them to fire twenty-one times, or whatever's the top salute. I want them to give someone the folded up flag, someone who cared about him. The man died for his country."

"The dose from the Veterans Home pharmacy was ten milligrams," Silva said. "Not a merciful dose."

"Frank, we've got to look at all suicides for the last couple of years, let's say forty-seven onward. I'll put you on that. Eddy Walsh is looking for girls with stories to tell. I want to get back to Sandy Millbank."

"What's left to do?"

"I want to know exactly how a Lioness gets to be one. Like the initiation."

"Who'll tell you that?"

"Amanda Winthrop, camp director."

"Why do we need to know?"

"Because Sandy Millbank wasn't dumped in a ditch somewhere."

"You should take the day off. You look like hell," Silva said. "We should take the case off. I wish these were just shut down and forgotten."

Sonntag wanted to come at the Millbank case from the other direction. Who put her in the ferns, all straightened up, and why?

He headed for Captain Ackerman's lair, knowing he'd absorb enough cigar stink to offend Amanda Winthrop and make Shorewood High School reek.

"Fill you in," Sonntag said.

"I don't need filling in. I'm ahead of you. Henderson and his wife are operating the biggest racket in the area. You're awfully slow, Sonntag. If I were running this, I'd have it nailed down by now."

"I'm heading out to Shorewood to find out about Lionesses."

"Sonntag, you're cracked in the head."

"I don't know what Lizbeth found in me," Sonntag said, and plowed out, just before Ackerman put a torch to the next dogturd cigar.

One thing about Amanda Winthrop. He knew where to find her.

And indeed, when the noon hour bell rang and the kids swarmed out, he was there at her classroom door.

She stood up and pursed her lips.

"Five minutes?"

"I'm stuck," she said.

"Tell me how a Lioness is selected."

Oddly, she liked that. "Sit down there in front of me, front row, and I will lecture you."

He did. The student desk was quite comfortable.

"A Lioness is the highest rank in the Ranger Girls. It is a great honor. Only a few girls, each outstanding, are selected. I am one."

Sonntag enjoyed that. So did she.

"Lionesses are regarded as fulfilled women," she said. "Women of independent stature. Women who represent the highest ideal of womanhood."

He nodded. So far, this was a little vague, but maybe that would clear up,

"It's not like the Boy Scouts. So many merit badges, so much community service, so much leadership, so many skills. Pass all the benchmarks and you're the perfect boy. Nothing like that. Instead, the governing women look for certain qualities in a Ranger Girl. And if a candidate measures up, and we consider her the ideal independent woman, we make her a Lioness. And it takes a unanimous vote. One blackball sinks the girl."

"Was Sandy Millbank ever blackballed?"

"Once. But girls come up again after a six-month period. The next time, she passed and became a Lioness."

"She was found closest to a lioness in the zoo. Was that deliberate?"

"Obviously."

"Someone put her there deliberately, as an honor?"

"I'm afraid officers don't understand women."

"No, ma'am, I guess I don't, but I'm wondering if someone in Ranger Girls had something to do with her death."

"That's the way men think," she said.

Chapter Twenty-Two

Amanda Winthrop was enjoying herself. Her eyes lit up. She was clearly amused.

"I'm not looking for a sparring partner, ma'am. I've looking for answers. I think you know some of them, and aren't talking. Who put Sandy Millbank's body where she was found?"

"If I knew, I wouldn't tell you. But I don't know."

"Why wouldn't you tell me?"

"I'm afraid you'll just have to keep on guessing, officer."

Still sparring. He curbed his deepening irritation. "Let's go through this a step at a time, okay?"

"I wish to eat lunch and prepare for afternoon classes. So, no, let's not go through this a step at a time."

"There was not a speck of blood on her body—and very little within it. Where did it go?"

She smiled. "Men are afraid of blood," she said.

"Someone washed and dressed her in fresh clothing. Who was that?"

"Aren't you the prurient one."

"Someone washed her face and combed her hair. Who was that?"

"Oh, my, she's been turned into a goddess."

"Someone, or maybe several, put her in a place of honor, at least among her colleagues, and failed to report the death to the police, and concealed evidence about the way she died. Who was that?"

"Why, you might call national headquarters and get a list of suspects. What's the line in that movie? Round up the usual suspects."

Sonntag eyed the lady. "Ma'am, let's go to the principal's office. You won't be conducting classes this afternoon, and he should know. We're going to the station house."

"I'm in Shorewood, not Milwaukee. Your powers stop at the line."

"I think you'd better come along, ma'am."

"What are you charging me with?"

"Maybe you'd care to name it," he said.

"You're charging me with being a woman," she said.

The funny thing was, Sonntag sort of liked her. "Nothing but women locked up in Waupun," he said. "Pretty soon we'll get the rest."

She caved in. "Let me get my purse. You can tell the principal you're going to give me the third degree."

A while later, he drove her southward, into central Milwaukee, and pulled up at the station house. She was pretending to enjoy it all.

"Throw me into my cell," she said, getting out.

"Do you belong there?" he asked.

"I'll be a martyr if I must."

He led her to one of the interrogation booths along one side of the bullpen. These were pretty gamy, and sometimes stank, but someone had wiped the wooden table and chairs that morning, getting rid of the vomit and debris that seemed to build up on them. Eddy Walsh was at his desk, so Sonntag nodded to him.

Amanda Winthrop settled on one side of the table, Walsh on the other.

"Coffee?" Sonntag asked.

"Yours wouldn't be worthy of the name," she said.

Sonntag nodded to the steno sitting outside of Ackerman's cubicle. She picked up her machine and joined Walsh.

"Okay," Sonntag said. "This is Amanda Winthrop, director of the Ravenswood camp. Amanda, you're here because we consider you an uncooperative source. The stenographer here will record your answers. Eddy Walsh here, one of our staff investigators, will be asking questions. It's a crime to mislead an investigating officer, one that might land you in jail."

"Hey, you're one smart lady," said Eddy. "You got us all on the run. All right, the real big question for us is why you're not cooperating. You got any thoughts about that?"

"I'm enjoying it."

"Enjoying trying to keep us from solving a crime?"

"By the end of this interview, I will have the pleasure of stopping all your legions cold."

"It's you against us? The cops?"

"Against men," she said.

"Yeah, I feel the same way sometimes," Eddy said. "Men drive me nuts. Is that why they made you director of Camp Ravenswood?"

"No, the goal of Ranger Girls is to make every woman independent. You may take it or leave it."

"So what's independent? What's that about?"

"If we could live in a world entirely without males, we would gladly do it."

"How come you don't like men?"

"Mr. Walsh, put away your toys. You want to know what you imagine I know. You want to find out who tried to abort Sandy Millbank's child. You want to know how she found the person. You want to know what Ranger Girls found her dead and moved her. Isn't that right?"

"Nah, we're pretty well along on that. We want to know why you don't want to cooperate with us."

"And you already have that answer; unless you're even more dimwitted than I thought, I see no need to repeat myself."

"Me, I'm just a flatfoot that got promoted, okay? So you'll have to explain everything twice or I won't get it."

"I'll ask you a question. How do you know Sandy Millbank went to an abortionist?"

"She died of a hemorrhage according to the coroner's report."
She sighed. "You see? You don't know what you're talking
about."

"Yeah, guess I don't," Eddy said. "Beats me, ma'am."

"So, there's no point in telling you," she said. "Now, why do
you presume that my organization placed Sandy Millbank where
she was found?"

"Beats me," Walsh said. "You're a lot more sophisticated
about this stuff than I am."

"You think it was symbolic," she said. "A Lioness placed near
a lioness, and that this is how Ranger Girls think, and what they do."

"Yeah, it crossed our minds."

"Why do you think that? Who told you that?"

"Well, if we got it wrong, maybe you'll get us straight on
that," Eddy said.

"What's your IQ, Mr. Walsh?"

"Well, I think it's higher than I can count on my fingers."

"Is it higher than idiot, or imbecile, Mr. Walsh?"

"Maybe at night, after I've had a couple of whiskeys."

"Taken to a place of honor next to a female lion, by devoted
Ranger Girls. For symbolic reasons of course. Even though she's
stone cold dead from a crime committed with her secret
cooperation. Is this idiocy, or is it imbecility, Mr. Walsh?"

Joe Sonntag had never seen anything like this. Eddy Walsh
had turned her into the interrogator, and she was questioning the
cops. Eddy, he was just busy being dumb.

"Sounds pretty unlikely, now that you put it that way, ma'am."

"And how do you know there was an abortionist, Mr. Walsh?"

"Well, we don't know for sure, but we've got a coroner's
report, ma'am."

"Does it name the abortionist?"

"Name him, nope. It's just full of stuff about what killed her.
The sudden departure of a lot of blood did the job."

"So you're just leaping to conclusions, as usual, sir."

"Well, we're a bunch of males around here, Mrs. Winthrop,
and we sort of get this stuff second hand, and not very much. I
guess you have other ideas."

"The most common abortions are self-attempted, Mr. Walsh. A coat hanger suffices."

"Well, I learn something every day, ma'am."

"Meanwhile, is it your purpose to indict the entire administration of Ranger Girls, and Camp Ravenswood?"

"Well, it might not be a bad idea," Walsh said.

Sonntag was aghast. How could Eddy say that?

"I imagine you'd like that. The Ranger Girls running an abortion ring outside of Milwaukee. Lieutenant Sonntag, there, would be promoted to Captain. "

"You got it, ma'am. More pay," Walsh said. "That's how it goes with cops."

Sonntag raked his memory, wondering whether this notion of an abortion camp ever came up. He couldn't remember thinking anything of the sort, nor could he remember any talk or any questioning leading in that direction. She had moved the whole investigation to new turf.

"I imagine you keep an eye out for stuff, running the place," Walsh said.

"It wouldn't be a bad idea, a camp for knocked up girls," she said. "Maybe the Ranger Girls could even the score."

"Maybe it already is, ma'am," Walsh said.

She laughed. "Don't you wish."

Then she was fencing again, and things were going nowhere, and Eddy couldn't get her back on track. He wanted her questioning the cops again. That's when she was revealing the most, when she was driving the interview wherever she wanted to take it. But it was over.

"You going to lock me up for the night?" she asked.

"No, we'll have an officer drive you back," Sonntag said.

"I must not have done well," she said. "I get a Lieutenant taking me here, and a private taking me back."

Sonntag smiled. Why did he like her? He shouldn't like her at all.

She collected her purse, left some rumpled cops and a stenographer behind, and followed Sonntag to the street.

"I don't suppose you want my card, if you think of anything," he said.

"Here's my card," she said, "call me if you're desperate."
She smiled triumphantly.

He watched her climb in, instruct the uniformed guy, and pull away.

"Well?" asked Captain Ackerman.

"I was ready to try the cigar treatment, but I'll save it for next time," Sonntag said.

Ackerman grinned evilly, sucked on the yellow cigar, and exhaled a volcanic plume.

Sonntag found Eddy and Frank sitting in the interrogation room, looking worn.

"I've got a way with women," Eddy said.

"Grovel and smile," Sonntag said.

"What do you make of all that?" Silva asked. "I missed most of it."

"I think I no longer have any theories," Sonntag said. "I don't know what happened to Sandy Millbank. I don't know why her body ended up where it did, and why."

"Do you believe that coat hanger stuff?" Eddy asked.

"No."

"That's for working class girls," Silva said.

"You're the expert."

Silva looked pained. "All I'm saying is, girls with money don't try that."

"Do you believe she's right? That no one in Ranger Girls would put the body next to a lion cage as some sort of honor?" Sonntag asked.

"You know, she's right. That's all crap," Eddy said. "We don't know why Sandy Millbank's body ended up there, and there's probably no meaning at all in it. That's where she got dumped."

"Stretched out, hands folded over her chest, skirts straightened?"

"Oh, hell, I don't know."

"Do you think Amanda's trying to cover up anything?"

"Like what?" Eddy asked.

"Like Camp Ravenswood staff teaching the girls where to go, what to do, how to cope with sex?"

"I hope they are," Silva said. "I just hope the whole outfit's doing it, and that's why it exists."

"You're the Progressive," Eddy said.

"Yeah, you could call it that. I hope every girl who goes to camp gets educated. I hope every girl who walks out of there after a two-week summer visit knows how to deal with it."

"You'd be popular there, Frank," Eddy said.

"I think not. I think it's done, but so secretly that no parent or clergyman has a clue. I think Amanda Winthrop and gals like Mrs. Barbie don't want anything said about it. It's like an unspoken service of Ranger Girls, one that would start an uproar, maybe even an official investigation by every blue-nosed prosecutor around here."

Sonntag thought he might be right. But it was all hypothesis. And it wasn't leading to any new insights about the mysterious death of Sandy Millbank, and the mysterious treatment of her body.

"Okay, where should we go with this?" he asked.

"What have we got?" Frank asked. "Millbank at the Zoo. Some country club gossip about a Fox Point girl now in Italy. The Hendersons, fronting for someone, and full of Shinola. And some speculation about the Ranger Girls."

"Not much," Sonntag said. "Also, Wenzel's statements, the unlicensing of Dr. Needham, Dorothea Blue's gossip, the Millbank family, the visiting nurse at the summer camp, Mrs. Boetticher, the cook Sylvia Purdy, the camp athletic director Wendy Vestal who is frankly for abortion, and the autopsy by Dr. Stoppl."

"Needham," said Frank. "He's the owner of that farm, or his corporation Wisconsin Properties is. He could do abortions. I don't know what he's doing in Phoenix. That's a long ways away. Maybe he figures he's farther away than the long arm of the law."

"Yeah, but right now we don't have a big abortion mill going. We have one death and one bit of gossip about a rich girl. So where does a big abortion ring come in?"

"Well, there's the assisted suicide," Joe said. "Someone slid that wounded soldier a lethal dose of Seconal, and that someone had a card printed by the Speedy Secretarial Service."

"That's a separate deal," Eddy said.

"Maybe not," Frank Silva said. "You put a doctor out of business, and what can he do? He can slide narcotics to suicide candidates, for a price. And fix up desperate girls, for a price. And call himself compassionate, even if the law doesn't."

"Needham," Sonntag said. "Let's find him."

Chapter Twenty-Three

Q E. D. Needham's house turned out to be compact and cream-colored brick, with neatly trimmed hedges and manicured gardens. That color of brick was a Milwaukee hallmark. It was eight or ten blocks inland from the lake, in an old, tree-lined neighborhood.

"Car's there," Frank Silva said.

Sonntag clambered out of the black Ford, and Silva followed. Sonntag rang, and Arnold C. Needham opened. Sonntag recognized him at once: owl beaked, receding hair, jowly, with horn rims. The photo was a good once.

"Dr. Needham?"

"Ah, so you've found me out! Latin is still the universal language."

"Well, sir, I'm Lieutenant Sonntag, and this is Detective officer Silva, the PD, and we'd sure like to talk to you."

"Well, that's good because I'd enjoy talking to you. Do come in, gents. That's my wife Marvella, there."

That was unexpected.

Sonntag and Silva were escorted into a small parlor that looked totally unused, one of those places to receive guests that didn't come. Homes like that usually had lived-in dens off somewhere else.

"So, my veneer didn't last long," the doctor said. "I employ it to screen callers. How do you know Latin? School?"

"I had a year in junior high school, sir. I got a C minus."

"Well, you know, doctors need a working knowledge of Latin. You can't get through medical college without it. That's what makes doctors so magical and mysterious. We can talk in a learned tongue and mystify listeners. I thought Q. E. D., well, quite entertaining. Especially for an unlicensed doctor. Take away our robes of Latin, and we're just as plain as anyone else."

It was odd. Here was a doctor who'd lost his license oozing good cheer. He fairly bounced with it, like a loose basketball. And there was Marvella, oozing cheer and curiosity, with none of the reserve of people being questioned by law officers.

Still, there came a questioning pause, and Sonntag got down to business. "We're here about a real estate company called Wisconsin Land."

"What about it? Are the books wrong?"

"Well, could you tell us about it, sir?"

"Certainly. After I lost my license, I was faced with the dilemma of making a living. The first thing we did was sell our home in Whitefish Bay, big pretentious thing we didn't need, and employed the profit first, to buy this little place, and second, to purchase various properties that might yield us some income. We have three or four here, and more in Arizona. I have all the books, and you're welcome to examine them. I don't quite know what you're after, but I'd be pleased to help."

"Tell us about Arizona," Silva said.

"Oh, I'd love to tell you about that place! We love it so. There's a little hamlet outside of Phoenix called Scottsdale, in the Sonora desert, filled with saguaro cactus and a dozen other things, and we found an old adobe ranch house, a true desert house, and some land, and that's where we winter. I've got some work with the Indian Bureau—there are reservations in every direction, and they need physicians, and I can do month long rotations there for the bureau. They know all about my licensing difficulties here, but they're federal, and they pay reasonably. At any rate—I'm going on and on, aren't I?—any rate, that desert costs almost nothing, a few dollars an acre, and we've been buying what we can of it, and putting it into our little holding company. Some day, we think, it'll help us retire, and meanwhile we own some of the most delightful desert."

"I guess it has rattlers," Silva said.

"Beautiful, rare, pink desert rattlers," Needham said. "I'd love to show them to you. I have some slides. I can set up a screen."

"Ah, no, thanks, sir."

"Do you have any children, sir?"

For once, Needham lost his cheer. "We did. A son. Cyrus. He died at Guadalcanal."

"I'm sorry."

Marvella's face seemed to cave in. "Our only one," she said.

"That's when I started on the Scotch," Needham said. "Wasn't very bright of me, was it?"

"I'm hoping you can tell us about your properties here, sir."

"You haven't told me what you're after, but I can guess it has to do with the farmhouse out on Bluemound Road."

Sonntag and Silva stared sharply at one another.

"Perhaps you'd like to tell us about that one, doctor," Sonntag said.

"I have some renters in there, good income from it, but they worry me some. I imagine that's what you're here about."

"Who are they?"

"A couple, forties maybe, Henderson's the name. They pay me three hundred a month for that property, and I get more from leasing the cropland. The farmer put it into field corn for his dairy. So that's five thousand a year, a tidy amount."

"Are they relatives of yours, sir?"

"No, never saw them until we advertised for a tenant. They're from some place, Illinois I guess."

"They rent all the buildings?" Sonntag asked.

"Yes, sir. If it was just the old farmhouse, it'd be a hundred fifty. But he wanted the barn, too, so I gave it to the man."

"What does he do with it, sir?"

"He stores something, I imagine. He cleaned out the hayloft and stores something. Lots of space in a big old dairy barn."

"You were going to tell us about the Hendersons, sir. Why they worry you," Silva said.

"That's why you're here," Needham said. "They've got these businesses. They live in the house and run a couple of businesses. Secretarial service, but the other one's the one you're here about. I don't know what to make of it. They counsel people looking to adopt, and they look for ladies with babies coming along. I got a call from a friend a while ago, telling me that maybe this isn't up and up. I ignored him, and now I wish I hadn't. Is that what you're looking into?"

"It could be, sir," Silva said.

Needham smiled. "Look into it for me, will you? If I can help, call on me."

"Do you think there's something not right about the adoption service?"

"Not right! Of course it's not right. I've asked if they're licensed, who am I to ask that, eh? But I have, and the state says they've never heard of the Hendersons."

"If we went up in the hayloft, sir, what would we find there?"

"I don't know. But if you need permission from me to go look, you've got it."

"I would like that, sir."

"I'll write it out. Marvella..."

She headed at once into a rear room, and returned with paper. Needham pulled out a fountain pen and wrote: Permission is herewith granted to the Milwaukee Police Department to examine my entire property on Bluemound Road. Then he dated and signed it.

"That should get us into the barn, at least. Have you a key for the padlock?" Silva asked.

"No. I examine my property twice a year, and saw it there, but Henderson said it wasn't his padlock, and I didn't pursue it."

"How do the Hendersons pay you, doctor?"

"First of the month, there's a check in the mail."

"You know the bank?"

"First Marine."

"Is it a business check?"

"Speedy Secretarial Service."

"Next time you get one, could you call me?" Sonntag asked.

"Detective, I'll drive down there and show it to you," Needham said.

Needham talked about the other properties. A rental duplex, a dental office building, and a heavy equipment storage yard. "They and the Bluemound property keep us afloat, and the Indian Bureau rotations, that's how we live now," he said.

"What kind of surgery did you do, sir?" Sonntag asked.

"Ancient history, I'm afraid. Appendectomies, colon cancer and diseases, stomach ulcers, prostate and bladder cancer, hernias, the whole gamut. All gone now. I don't even have my surgical kit. I don't do surgeries for the federal bureau."

"I think that covers it, doctor. Here's my card if you think of anything else about the Hendersons. Say, do you have a card, doctor?"

"No, not any more. Not here, anyway. The Indian Bureau gives me one in Arizona."

Sonntag and Silva drove back to the station house, mostly silent.

"You got any ideas?" Silva asked.

"Only that I'm a born skeptic."

"You want to get a hacksaw and go look at that hayloft?"

"Yeah, pretty quick."

"His story and the Hendersons don't add up. Like, she's a relative of the owner and they're living there rent-free to care for the place."

"It sure would be a good place for an abortion mill," Sonntag said. "Only we don't have one yet. No connection to Sandy Millbank. No connection anywhere else. A girl in Italy, maybe, maybe not."

"No connection to that suicide, Stumpf, with the blue bottle, except for the card," Silva said. "Funny, there's no abortion mill yet, and no suicide mill yet, so why do I keep thinking our answer is out on Bluemound Road?"

"We may be closer than we think. Blue medical bottles come from somewhere, and Seconal comes from somewhere, and we have a dead soldier who got them somewhere. Maybe that's the trail that will lead us to an abortion mill, which will lead us to Sandy Millbank."

Silva started laughing. "Whenever I hear Walter Winchell on the radio, I think of you. The Communists are coming. The suicide squad is coming."

That ticked Sonntag off.

"There's that pharmacy wholesale place on Water Street, south of the avenue. Let's stop for a visit," he said.

>> | <<

Sonntag parked in a no-parking zone at N. Water and E. Chicago. An anonymous building of cream-colored brick stood there, a small legend in black letters in its window: Wisconsin Pharmaceutical Supply.

They entered a chill anteroom, as silent as a cemetery, and waited. No one showed, so they rang a countertop push-bell, and then some old gray guy in a bib apron showed up.

"Milwaukee police, sir. We've a few questions, if you don't mind."

"Police, eh? I'll need some proof of it," the old guy said.

Both Sonntag and Silva flipped open their badges.

"Fine, fine. Where there's dangerous drugs, there's an element that wants them."

"How does this work?" Silva asked.

"We're a wholesaler. We supply drugs and pharmaceutical items to drugstores everywhere in Wisconsin, usually broken into much smaller amounts."

"People need prescriptions for that?"

"No, sir, licensed pharmacies, hospitals, doctors order these things in whatever amounts they need, and we fulfill. Some things, over-the counter items, don't require that."

"Okay, if we wanted some blue bottles, the kind drug stores use," Silva asked, "could we buy them here?"

"Certainly. In several sizes, with ounces and milligrams displayed."

"That's just walk-in?"

"Well, we have minimums, you know. You couldn't just buy one. A case of twenty-four is standard."

"So who could buy Seconal?" Sonntag asked.

"A licensed person."

"A doctor? Pharmacist?"

"Yes, sir. An accredited person from a hospital or nursing home."

"Has anyone unqualified tried to get some?"

"It's very rare, sir. What we do, when there's doubt, is tell them the order has to be shipped, and we'll send it out in a bit, and what's the address? And they usually just tell us they're out and need some now. And nothing is transacted."

"How do they pay?"

"We invoice them, and they pay with checks. Most do, anyway."

"We understand hundred milligram Seconal is a big dose. Do you have much call for that?"

"That's a rare dose, sir. A dangerous dose. No, only one or two places order those."

"You mind telling me which?"

"Let me look, sir."

He vanished into the silent netherworld back there. After what seemed forever, in which Sonntag's toes were starting to frostbite, even in mid-summer, the man returned with a slip of paper. "One's the Wood Veterans Home. I can well understand that. The other's the Burleigh Rest Home and Convalescent Center, on the Northwest side. They take two thousand a month of the hundred milligram ones. Lots of places take the smaller dose."

"That's helpful, sir. Are there any other places that order the hundred milligram?"

"Yes, but only occasionally. Most hospital pharmacies have some."

"But that's not a regular market, right?" Silva asked.

"Correct, sir."

"You've been a real help, sir."

"I try to do my civic duty," the man said. "There's evil lurking out there."

"Oh, one last thing. You have any invoices or receipts for anyone who's walked in here and gotten blue bottles?" Sonntag asked.

"Well, that's questionable. A man can order a case of bottles, pay me cash, and walk away with my invoice, but I haven't a clue who he is. There's no requirement, you see."

"Could you check and see?"

"It'll take a bit, sir."

They waited for him a long while. And then he returned. "The last case of bottles went to that Burleigh Rest Home, along with the Seconal order."

"Hey, you fixed us up," Silva said.

"That's a strange way to put it," the old man said.

Chapter Twenty-Four

The morning was amazingly hot for October. When Sonntag got to work well-dressed couple was waiting for him. She was collected, with the seams of her nylons marching straight up to the hem of her New Look skirt, while he was already showing signs of wilting in the steamy heat.

"Lieutenant, I'm John Millbank. This is my wife, Linda."

"Oh, Sandy's parents. Let me tell you how saddened I am by your loss. Would you like to go to that interrogation—that conference table, and talk?"

They eyed the tacky area, and Millbank declined. "We're on our way, and just needed to talk a moment. We'll be on the Hiawatha in an hour, and then off to peru again."

"Long trip, sir."

"Yes. New Orleans, and then a Pan Am flight. I have to get back on the job."

"You're an engineer?"

"I'm overseeing the installation of turbines in a hydroelectric project in the Andes, Lieutenant. They were built here. Linda keeps a pension in Lima, the most beautiful city in South America."

"But it'll be a sad trip back."

"Sadder than you may know. How far are you? I mean, with the investigation?"

"We're close, sir. But it still seems to dodge us, just when we think we've got something."

"We'd hoped to see that criminal behind bars before we left. I guess that won't happen. Is there anything you can share with us?"

"Only that we're pretty sure there's a ring doing these procedures, and we know who's fronting it, who's making contacts. But just when we seem to have something in hand, we end up clutching air. But we're close. This ring's run by smart operators, who put layer after layer between themselves and the world."

"We're deeply interested in your success," he said.

"I can keep you informed, sir, if you'll leave an address with us. In fact, I'd like to know how to reach you if anything should arise."

"Yes, surely," he said. He withdrew an engraved card from a small card-packet he carried.

"Here's my company address. They can connect you at once, or forward mail. I am also available through the American embassy there."

The card was engraved.

"You have a son and daughter also, I believe?"

"Darren and Marge, my children from a previous union, sir. Sandy was, in a way, an only child. Linda has a condition that makes bearing children risky, and we were fortunate to receive Sandy into our family without complications. How much we rejoiced about that. And now she's gone, and we are saddened more than words can express."

"We've been talking of a lawsuit," Linda said. "If you catch this man, we would like to know about it. Do you think a suit might be successful?"

"Not my department, ma'am."

"It was like losing the Mona Lisa," she said. "Just like that."

"I understand."

Millbank looked at his Patek Philippe. "Time to go, Linda.

I'm glad we had this chance, sir. You keep on with this, please. You keep on and never quit until that killer's behind bars."

"I'm fairly confident about this case, sir."

"Good! We're off, then."

Sonntag watched the couple head outside, where a checker cab was waiting, its engine idling. They got in; the Millbanks were gone.

Sonntag wondered how he'd feel if he had a beautiful young daughter who perished at the hands of a careless abortionist. There was pain in that, pain coming from all directions. And the mother's only child, too. Medicine was a mystery, and he wondered what had made her maternity so perilous. Maybe Lizbeth would help him—if Lizbeth chose to talk at all about that. She sure was edgy about this case.

He found Captain Ackerman licking the slimy end of his day's first dogturd stogie.

"We're going out to the Burleigh Rest Home and Convalescent Center."

"To check in, I suppose," the captain said.

"They use a lot of hundred milligram Seconal."

Ackerman lit up, and grinned.

He collected Frank Silva, and they were given Cruiser 974,which had a bad carburetor and died whenever you pushed on the gas pedal too fast. Luck of the draw. But at least it started up fine on that boiling morning. He headed out State Street. On 35th he would turn north.

"The Millbanks are catching a train. Going back to peru," Joe said.

"I supposed they wanted the abortionist signed, sealed and delivered."

"They're hurting, Frank."

"People with money don't hurt very much."

"Sandy was her only child, Frank. The others, Darren and Marge, are from a previous marriage. She said she has some kind of condition, it was dangerous, but Sandy was the result, and now the girl's gone and there can't be another."

"What kind of condition?"

"I don't know."

Frank shook his head. "I'd sell them a couple of new children for a hundred thousand apiece."

>> | <<

The rest home was out on the Northwest side, where cracker-box houses were springing up by the square mile to feed the pent-up demand for housing. There was nothing alluring about the area.

The rolled down windows helped not at all, and merely blew steam bath air into the car. The place wasn't even on Burleigh Street; it was on 60th, across from a big hot cemetery.

"Nice view for a convalescent home," Frank said.

"Inspiring," Sonntag said.

The Burleigh place was one story, concrete block, and new. The concrete was painted cream on the outside, and proved to be hospital green within. You didn't need to explain what that was to anyone. Everyone knew exactly what shade hospital green was; it had conquered every medical building in the upper Midwest, and half the schools too.

"What are we looking for?" Silva asked.

"We want a tour."

"This place is a warehouse," Silva said. "A box. Look around here. No baseboards, no cornices. No carpets. Small windows. Nothing hanging on the walls. I can guess what the rooms will look like."

There was no receptionist in sight. Just long corridors, with branches, floored with a fake tile linoleum. There were, at least some discreet signs with arrows: Administration, Convalescent Wing, Rest Home Wing, Food Services, Wellness Center. They peered down hallways. They saw old men in wheelchairs. They saw an orderly in stained white clothing carrying something.

"Let's get the grand tour," Sonntag said.

The Administration suite had a glass window fronting it, with a receptionist behind it. She peered up impassively.

There was a small circular hole in the glass, for speaking purposes.

"Milwaukee police here," Sonntag said. "We're hoping someone can give us a tour of the place. Show us how it all works."

"Police? Is this an inspection?"

"No, we're simply investigating."

"Oh," she said.

She vanished into the offices behind her, and emerged with a man in his shirtsleeves, florid faced and beefy. He pushed through a doorway and into the corridor and extended a massive hand. "Art Pendergast, fellas. Call me Artie. I'm where the buck stops."

That was in vogue. Harry Truman had a sign on his desk that read "The Buck Stops Here."

"Lieutenant Sonntag, and Detective Silva, sir. We're hoping someone can show us your place."

"Is this an inspection? Like sanitary?"

"Nope, we're just looking at how old people's homes work."

"Oh, then, just wander around and see for yourself. I don't get this. You lads looking for something?"

"Yeah," said Silva, "how the terminally ill are cared for."

"Ah, now we're down to brass tacks," Pendergast said. "We're the most efficient and economic rest home in the state. We've got costs down so low that we're the envy of the Upper Midwest."

"Yeah," said Silva. "We heard you have a good program."

"Good! You can't beat it. People with morbid conditions can't wait to check in here, because we give 'em what they need, and they like that. You want to see some? I'll have Mabel there give you a quickie. We got a whole wing full of grateful terminals, and more wanting to check in. The program's so big we're talking about a new wing."

"You can't take us yourself?"

"Hey, I got payroll, inventory, an unhappy wife, and an unfed parakeet."

"They come here to die?" Silva asked.

"Wholesale. We're the best place to die in Milwaukee County, and word's out. I gotta go, fellas, nice to see ya, I'll put Mabel on your case."

He pumped hands and vanished within. Moments later, the receptionist emerged, with a shawl over her head.

"We always cover our heads, you know. When we're with those who are passing, we show our respect. Come this way, sirs, and we'll look at the Terminal Wing. That's our word for it. On our signs it's the Peace and Dignity Wing, you see. That's the way everyone should pass."

They walked into a somnolent area with shiny, new-waxed floors. Most of the doors to the tiny rooms were open, and within lay ancient and pale men and women, staring upward, or dozing. In a few rooms, relatives or friends sat at bedside in metal chairs. Here there were a few cheap prints on the walls, sunrise or sunset scenes, garden scenes.

Sonntag spotted one room with a blue bottle at a bedside stand. "Those blue bottles the sedative?" he asked.

"Our terminals always have an option," Mabel said. "We are deeply compassionate, and give them their choices. They can choose the dosage—their choice, their schedule. It's a blessing beyond words, you know. Cancer especially is so brutal."

"Yeah, but what if they deliberately take too much?" Silva asked.

"It's because they wish to, you know," she said.

"You let that happen?"

"We neither encourage nor prevent it, sir."

"Do you help them out, any?" Sonntag asked.

"That wouldn't be legal, sir. No, never. If they wish to float away in peace, they must achieve it on their own."

"How many people do that?"

"Oh, I couldn't say. No records are kept of that sort. We lose two or three of the terminals a week, though."

"Buried across the street, over there?"

She nodded. "They can gaze from their windows here upon their last resting place. It's a great comfort to them."

"Those prescription drugs, does some doctor prescribe? Keep track?"

"We have prescriptions on file for all our patients, sir. And the doctor gives our nurses whatever options they need."

"Do you lose capsules?"

"Certainly, Lieutenant. What often happens is that the terminals forgo immediate relief, and hoard a few capsules for the time when their needs are more urgent."

"Do they give capsules to relatives?"

"We do our best to discourage that, sir."

"Could we see your Wellness Center?" Sonntag asked.

"Is there a reason?" she asked.

"Everything is so modern," he said. "Most modern place I've ever been in. Yes, we'd like to see it."

"It's restricted, but I think I can see my way to letting you peek. If no patient's there, of course."

She went ahead and peered around. "Free and clear," she said.

The Wellness Center had three consulting rooms, two hospital-type treatment areas screened by drapes, and the rest was devoted to medical supplies in large boxes. And a row of blue bottles. The place was so clean it hurt. The treatment areas looked so unused they seemed to just come out of the factory crates.

"How do you get your customers—ah, patients?" Sonntag asked.

"We run classified ads offering sedation for the ill. We have doctor referrals. We have brochures about our specialty."

"Do you work with veterans?"

"Oh, yes, sir, outreach. Many are wounded and in pain, and our outreach people try to help them if possible. That's the least we can do for those who sacrificed so much for our country."

"Even though many are poor?"

"There are usually death benefits that repay us, sir. Often GI life insurance, which our contracts make over to us. There are social security benefits too, which we arrange to repay us. So yes, it is a good business for us, and that is why we have a serious outreach program, especially among veterans."

"The Burleigh gets it all, then?"

"As much as is needed to repay us from the estate, sir. Our program for the disabled and terminal can be very costly."

"And profitable, I suppose," Sonntag said.

"Mr. Pendergast has a saying, sir. Sleep is our business."

Chapter Twenty-Five

They drove in silence back to the station house. Even shifting gears seemed noisy. They were both lost in thought, and Sonntag was grateful that Frank Silva wasn't probing it out loud, or starting a debate.

There was a bright line in the law. Suicide was self-murder. Abetting or assisting suicide was a felony, with the abettor complicit in murder. There was a part of him that wanted to arrest the whole staff and send them up the river. But the bright line had blurred, and he couldn't say whether leaving pills around for people in desperate pain, or lost in hopelessness, or simply people who had given up and yearned to pass away, was anything for the law to be concerned about.

If the staff had left a sharp knife on the bedside table, would it make a difference? Maybe. Knives were painful, while hundred milligram Seconals produced swift painless oblivion. The knife would be less an invitation to suicide than the pills.

But who was to say that a desperate and suffering mortal shouldn't want to fly away? The moralists said so; life was too sacred. Death was so final. Yet the same moralists who thundered against this had no compunction about sending men off to war to kill and be killed. The same moralists who might have opposed the death of Eden Stumpf, who lay there in his uniform, his leg and sleeve pinned up, serene in the death he sought, had no difficulty drafting him and sending him to the killing fields.

It always annoyed Joe Sonntag when realities crept in and upset his certitudes. Today he had visited a rest home that had turned his moral universe topsy-turvy, and that left him restless and not good company. He knew he should put all that aside. His sworn duty was to ferret out illegal activity and bring the criminals to justice. He needed legal information. He needed to know where that bright line stood before he organized some sort of dragnet to haul away the top echelon of that Burleigh warehouse for the maimed and ruined and decayed.

It wasn't until they were about to climb out of the car that Frank opened up.

"Do what you have to do," he said. "I hope you can leave me out of it."

"I don't have to do anything, Frank."

"Of course you do. Self-interest. A racket. Pendergast and his gang are cleaning up. They're pocketing GI life insurance, veterans death benefits, and social security death benefits. They're turning a profit on leaving some Seconal handy. Lot of disabled veterans haven't a dime until they die—and then there's plenty. Pendergast's a vulture. Which is what I can't stand, because suicide is the release from torture some of those old vets and cancer-stricken people want so badly they think of nothing else. So I can't stand it."

"Frank...Frank."

But Silva was vanishing at the door.

Frank had pulled deep inside of himself. But Sonntag knew he was there, too, and not just about the assisted suicides that were against the law. The abortion case was doing that to him, too. And that was making him feel as rotten as Frank was feeling. Two cases, each dealing with the compassionate use of medicine, in ways that state and city law forbade. How the hell could a good cop deal with it? He had done hard things in his day, and it looked like he would do hard things again.

He didn't feel like walking into the station house. The asphalt parking area was damned near melting his shoes. He felt like hiking

over to Lake Michigan and jumping in. He didn't want to walk in
and update Ackerman on it, which would probably result in a whole
task force of cops landing on the Burleigh Rest Home and hauling
away enough personnel to fill the county jail. He thought maybe
for the time being, he'd say nothing. Ackerman always knew when
Sonntag was doing that, and always wormed the story out of him.
But Sonntag thought he would do it anyway. He wanted a little
elbow room until he could sort things out.

He forced himself to head for his carrel. He wanted to check
with Eddy Walsh, find out if the ladies' man on the force had
uncovered any additional little procedures. But Eddy was out and
Silva had vanished. Not even Ackerman was around. The heat
was making the bullpen fetid. It was a day to escape any enclosed
place if one could. The PD was operating in slow motion this fierce
day.

It might be a good time to get out himself. He phoned the
pathologist, Dr. Stoppl, who had done the post mortem on Sandy
Millbank. There were some questions to ask. Sonntag wanted to
know what made an expert abortionist and what made a back-
alley one, and how a good examiner could tell. Stoppl answered at
once, and Sonntag recollected that pathologists rarely needed
secretaries or receptionists because they didn't normally see
patients.

"Lieutenant Sonntag here, sir. I'm wondering if you have a
few minutes?"

"I always have a few, Lieutenant."

"I'm looking for a little education. I'm trying to sort out what
makes a skilled abortionist and what is the telltale mark of some
back alley one."

"Oh, that'll be a pleasure. Shall I be seeing you shortly?"

"Few minutes."

"Good. I'll make a little display of the tools of the trade for
you."

Stoppl's office was within walking distance, but Sonntag
sensed that if he tried it, he would soon be soaked, and there
would be black patches under each armpit. He'd drive, even if the
car was a furnace. He found the cruiser he had abandoned a while

earlier, and turned it over. It started right up. That was hot-weather driving for you. The carburetor didn't flood and the battery didn't give out. But heat sometimes caused vapor lock, so nothing was ever perfect.

It took only a few minutes, even though he had to circle the block three times to find a parking slot. Stoppl's offices filled the lower flat of a duplex near Marquette. He welcomed Sonntag, who found himself feeling the pleasant cool rush of air pumped downward by a ceiling fan. Stoppl was big and intense, and not used to dealing with the public. He was an expert, back in his warren, resolving medical mysteries presented to him by other physicians.

Stoppl led him into a lab, with gleaming stainless steel counter tops, microscopes, glass slides, and rows of bottles. At its far side was a rolltop desk, and that's where the pathologist settled. "A good question," he said. "Did the abortionist have some sort of medical background? Maybe a doctor or nurse or midwife, eh? Or not."

"That's what I'm trying to nail down, sir. It helps me narrow down the person I'm looking for."

"Very good. Now the task at hand is to remove the embryonic tissue from the placenta that is growing on the thin wall of the uterus. These instruments here, which I've laid out for you, are curettes. They vary in shape and purpose, but they're all curettes. Most now are stainless steel, but earlier ones were steel or other metals, often with bone handles. They are medical tools, and are well designed to perform an abortion. This one here, with the loop on its end, is commonly used to work the fetal tissue free. Here's a curved version of the same device. Here's one with a spoon on the end, and here's one with a curved blade edge. They can be employed with a light source and a speculum to hold things open. Are you following?"

Sonntag was itchy, but he nodded.

"So a trained physician works the material free gently, aware that the walls are thin and riddled with new, wide blood vessels that will provide blood to the placenta and remove wastes through a filtering process. Now, a trained physician can do this relatively safely, but not entirely. There's always risk, and the unexpected looms. But the untrained abortionist, sir, and I must include the woman herself, usually lacks appropriate equipment or circumstance. The coat hanger, bent into a thin U-shape, is famous. These things are sometimes attempted without a speculum or light, and are reckless by their very nature. These people would scarcely know how to deal with a hemorrhage if it happens. So yes, there is a vast difference between a trained person and, say, a rogue midwife or hospital orderly doing it for cash on the barrelhead. That procedure is so dangerous that maybe thirty percent turn out badly, sometimes killing the woman."

"That's what killed Sandy Millbank, sir?"

"Well, now, that's a puzzle that still plagues me. She died of a massive hemorrhage, but there was no particular evidence of an abortion. I could find nothing. What's more, there's the question of whether she had conceived. Certain things happen rather swiftly, cellular changes, blood vessel changes intended to bring fresh blood to the embryo. But a biopsy was ambiguous. I did a second and third, with the same result. A cluster of small blood vessels. So the question became, was this an early miscarriage followed by bleeding? And I could not properly answer it. But I think it probably was. A hemorrhage, absolutely. From there, yes. I was able to discover the source. But what started it and when, I cannot say in any positive way."

Sonntag sat there, stunned. "She might not have died of an abortion?"

"Oh, quite likely she did, Lieutenant. There are natural abortions we call miscarriages, which occur by the hundreds of thousands, mostly so early that a woman is not aware of them. If you want to stop abortions, sir, you'd best put Mother Nature in the dock and indict her, because she's the main culprit."

"But Sandy Millbank might not have even been to an abortionist?"

"Correct, sir."

"And what does the death certificate say?"

"That she died of uterine hemorrhage, Lieutenant. That is exactly the case."

"Could you be mistaken? Was the abortion done so skillfully that you found no lacerations, no tiny wounds, nothing to reveal that it still happened?"

"It's more important, Lieutenant, that I found little placental development."

"You're saying Sandy Millbank didn't conceive?"

"I'd rather say she had an early miscarriage. Very early. One that somehow started the hemorrhage."

"A young man she was keeping company with said she broke off suddenly, after a few weeks, and wouldn't give him a reason."

Stoppl shook his head. "I have no mind-reading powers, sir."

"What would you speculate happened?"

"I'm not trained to speculate, sir."

"All right, have we covered all the possibilities?"

"I would say so."

"Would this hemorrhage have come in a rush, or gradually?"

"Given what I examined, I would say gradually, sir. But there is a mystery about all this that eludes me. Maybe some day we'll know more."

He stood suddenly, his way of dismissing his company. Sonntag thanked him and left, smacked by the wall of wet heat outside. He drove back to the station, sweating profusely. He felt like his brain was sweating too, dripping stupid theories, darkening the armpits of his mind. By the time he got back to the station, he thought he was sitting in a pool of his own sweat.

He clanked the car door shut, and pulled at his sticky pants to free them from his butt, and then headed inside. About half way up the stairs he remembered that there was no phone contact between Sandy Millbank and the Hendersons out on Bluemound Road, fronting for God knows what around there. Did Sandy Millbank have an abortion?

He headed for his desk, wondering what next would knock him flat, when Frank Silva beckoned. So he headed over there instead, still trying to unstick his pants. Frank was talking with a big gal, maybe late twenties, with a mess of freckles and a lot of coppery hair and a faintly Asiatic look to her eyes.

"Hey, Lieutenant, this is Wanda Wisniewski, from my neck

of the woods. She and I go back to high school, where we both belonged to the socialist club. So I've known her a long time."

"Wanda, is it? Any friend of Frank's is a friend of mine. I'm Joe Sonntag."

"Wanda's on the night shift at Allis Chalmers," Frank said. "She makes orange tractors."

"I make a dollar and seventy-two cents an hour," she said. "How can you beat that?"

"That's because she's union, top to bottom," Frank said. "But she's not here to organize the cops. She's here to tell me about a little something that might interest you. Let's call it an abortion."

Chapter Twenty-Six

Suddenly everything was different. Wanda Wisniewski gazed upward at him with a certain defiance, or at least reserve, in her freckled face.

"Well, this is something," Sonntag said. For some reason he didn't want to say this was big, or this was important, or this was the break-through, or this was hot stuff. Abortions were different. They were something down there in the silence, something unspoken. This big girl had been courageous even to walk into the station.

"I've heard the story," Frank said. "So maybe you can just let her tell it herself."

She eyed Sonntag somberly. "It doesn't need telling very much," she said, and then grinned. "Any friend of Frank's is a friend of mine."

Somehow, Sonntag knew it would be all right.

"I got knocked up," she said. "That's the church for you. This guy and me, we were seeing each other, and I sort of got a little careless—in more ways than one."

Sonntag sensed that he should sit down; he shouldn't be standing there, while she spoke up to him, so he corralled a chair from the next desk, and joined her.

She smiled, acknowledging what his gesture meant. "So what to do, right? I take care of my mother. I'm it. She's not on social security yet and she doesn't have two nickels to rub together, right? So I'm the one who keeps us going. But it's not a very exciting life, and I get lonely sometimes, and I meet this guy, Sten, and me and Sten, we have some good times, mostly Saturday nights, Frank Sinatra on the juke box. We both like him."

Sonntag nodded patiently.

"Hey, I should cut this story short. I got knocked up and I didn't want to tell Sten, and I didn't want to marry and maybe give up my job. I screw gear shift levers to the transmissions, right? So I'm thinking, I don't want this baby. I don't need it. I got less mother instinct in me than a black widow spider. It always comes down to money. I get more money on the assembly line than most women ever see. So what to do? I'd seen these cards once. Need Help? It doesn't take brains to figure that one out. But I didn't have a card. So I spent the next few days looking for cards, every women's room I could bust into, and finally I got smart and headed for the schools, and I found a card in the girl's room of Pulaksi High School, and that was good. I had a phone number."

"You want some coffee?"

"No, but a double shot of brandy would be nice." She laughed.

"Okay, I call this number and this gal gives me a long song and dance about her Matchmakers service, and getting the baby into the right home, and they take care of the gal, and all that. So I told this lady, that's all bullshit, and I want to get rid of it. I don't want any kid. I want a good, fast, safe job. So she says she'll call me back, and pretty quick she does, and I tell her to call later after my ma's in bed, so we can talk, and she does, about nine after we listen to Edgar Bergen and Charlie McCarthy and Fibber McGee and Molly, and have some ginger ale—she's a fiend for ginger ale. And she says, well, she doesn't think it's a good choice for me, but she's heard of someone, and if I insist she'll call. Me, I'm the practical one, and I say how much? So it's a grand. That's big money. I don't have anything like that. I'm not going to hit up Sten. I don't want him to know."

"But Sten's the father—"

"Yeah, well, Sten wants to marry me, and if I told him, he'd insist, and I'm damned if I'd get sucked into that. He's a Lutheran, and I'm a Catholic atheist. So, I've got maybe a hundred stuck in my dresser drawer, and also a couple of gold rings, one with a garnet, maybe I can sell them, but that's not going to raise a grand."

"Could you negotiate the price down?" Sonntag asked.

"No, this lady said that was it, period, take it or not, so I said I needed a little time, and she laughed and said I didn't have much time."

"The union helped her," Frank said.

"Yeah, the brotherhood, they don't ask questions. The brothers put a dollar in the pot, just because I said I needed it fast, and because I was a loyal sister, so the brotherhood raised five hundred seventy one, Allis Chalmers, that's a big place and that's a big night shift. So with that and selling my gold rings, I had about nine-seventy, and I got ahold of my mother's silver teapot, and got the last thirty, and then I called the woman on the Need Help card, and told her I had it, just barely, and she said keep it small bills, not big stuff, and gave me a place to get picked up, which was on the corner of National Avenue and Twenty-Seventh. So I told my ma I'd be gone a while, and go to bed herself."

"What did they tell you about the procedure?"

"They said they'd drive me to a place, after I showed them the money, and I'd get a careful, safe abortion, and they'd keep me there an hour or two, to make sure it was okay, and then drive me back here, but not to my house, and I could walk the rest."

"Did this contact try to reassure you about how it would go?"

"Nah, she was too busy saying she had nothing to do with it. She said it wasn't her deal, that she was pushing the Matchmakers service, but she just made this contact as a favor. I didn't believer a word of it, if you want to know the truth. She was just another BS person. There's a mess of those around."

"Okay, the time comes, and what happened?"

"I wait on the corner. It's night, dark, and I'm wearing a babushka, like they ask. And a car pulls up and the guy says hop in back, so I get in. I can't see his face that way. He says, let's see the cash, so I put the money in the front seat, in a manila envelope, wondering if he'll just boot me out and I'll never see it or him again. But he counts, and says okay. He drives away, and pretty quick I don't know where we're going, but it's a lot of driving through dark streets and finally out beyond the city, and he pulls in somewhere, gravel drive, and into a big barn or something with big doors, and it's real dark except for a stair going up, where there's some light, so he tells me to go on, and when I'm done he'll drive me out. I sure don't know what I'm getting into but if I don't like it up there, I'm going to get out and run."

"A barn then. A diary barn?"

"I can't tell a cow from a hamster, sir."

"A big aisle down the middle?"

"Yeah, he drove in there. So I climb up, and there this person is, and I think it's she, and then I know it is. She's got a surgical mask on, and those hospital scrubs, and a surgical cap, the kind with elastic that you can stuff a lot of hair into, and she's kind of big like me, and wearing rubber gloves."

"Okay, honey, we'll do this quick and careful. There's not anything to worry about if it's done right, she says. I'm glad it's her, not a him, because I got to let her do all this stuff, and I'm just glad it's her."

"She sounds like someone with a medical background," Sonntag said.

"Well, she had that hospital stuff. It was cold, that place up there was sort of a study, with some stuffed chairs, and a few shelves, and some electric heat that wasn't turned on."

"Not a medical setting?"

"You mean like a doctor's office, with Formica tables and stainless steel. No, this was sort of a den, like a place to curl up with a book."

"Did she talk?" Frank asked.

"Not much. I got over my embarrassment. It was all just business. She didn't take long, but it was cold, and I feel something going on, but then it's over. She told me to go rest there on the old sofa up there, and she'd check me in a while, and if I'm okay to go, I'll be taken back. I liked that. She was checking up. This wasn't in and out. She had things in a black bag, like a medical bag, things she might need if there was trouble. But there wasn't. She left me there for a while, and I read *Popular Mechanics*, there was only one little bulb lit, so I had trouble reading, but after a while she came back up, still in the surgical mask and cap, and examined me, and said I was okay, and good luck."

"So you got driven home?"

"Not home. A block away. I was home by midnight. He drove away and I walked the block. I let myself in and went to bed, and it was a strange night."

"What kind of car?"

"Four-door sedan, brown or something close."

"No brand?"

"Hey, it was dark. Not a Ford. I know Fords."

"Did he talk?"

"Not a word except instructions."

"Did the woman who did the abortions say anything?"

"A few things. She tried to assure me. Said she'd done many of them, and it was routine, and I'd be fine, and in a day or two I'd forget it."

"Nothing about herself?"

"No, not a word. But she'd sure been around doctors. She didn't have to say it; you just knew it. I wondered if she was a real doctor."

"She was stocky?"

"Well, it was cold. You put a woman in a wool shirt maybe, and put a surgical gown over that, and maybe she wasn't so stocky."

"Did she say anything afterward?"

"Just okay, it's done, it's fine, you'll be okay."

"No medical terms? Medical words?"

"Nope."

"What direction did the driver take you after he picked you up?"

"West, I think, but don't make anything of it."

"Why are you here, telling us?" Sonntag asked.

"Frank said she killed a woman. Maybe she shouldn't be doing it."

"How do you feel about it and the law?"

"My Catholic self says it shouldn't be allowed. But I'm a big girl now."

"Do you regret coming here?"

She glanced briefly at Frank. "Yes."

"Your testimony might be needed in court," Sonntag said.

"It's too late to think about that," she said.

"How did you know about the Need Help cards?"

"I heard about it after Mass a few months ago. A girl I knew disappeared, and some of us were gossiping."

"How did you know to look in school rest rooms?"

She looked annoyed. "Even a dope could figure that out," she said.

"What happened afterward?"

She blushed. "Me and Sten broke up anyway. Something came between us."

"This abortionist. Take some guesses, give me some impressions?"

"She likes helping girls who get knocked up."

"Not just money?"

"More than money."

"What do you think she does with her money? That's a lot of money."

"You sure are asking stuff I don't know. But I think she doesn't keep it."

"I'm not following you there, Wanda."

"That's the first time you've said my name. So maybe you don't disapprove any more."

Sonntag retreated into himself. Why was all this so hard for him?

"Hey, I don't like abortions," she said. "Who does? The church has one view; life begins at conception. I don't. That's just a blob of cells. You're not aborting a person. I think that little bunch of cells becomes more and more person as time goes by. By the time she's born, she's just beginning to be a person. By the time she's my age, she's a person. By the time she's your age, she's a full person. If there's ever a hard choice between a real person, like a mother, and a bunch of cells, I'm for the real person. Period."

She shut up suddenly.

"I guess I'm done here, okay?" she asked.

"You helped us a lot, Miss Wisniewski."

"Back to Miss now, am I?"

She laughed, and Sonntag wondered why he was so embarrassed.

Chapter Twenty-Seven

So close, so close, Sonntag thought. He caught Frank Silva returning from the men's room.

"We'd better sort this out," Sonntag said.

"She's a sweetheart."

"We've got some things to go on."

"So, you think the abortionist is that nurse, Mrs. Boetticher?"

"She sure qualifies. Been around hospitals, access to all that stuff, like surgical masks and gloves and hair catches. And she's been right there in the maternity wards and the obstetrics offices."

"There must be a few dozen other nurses like that around town. We can't just put her in a lineup and have Wanda finger her. The woman was wearing a mask, had her hair wrapped, wore gloves, and all that showed was two eyes. Not enough, not even close."

"We've got a woman abortionist. But that's not necessarily the whole story," Sonntag said. "This is a big ring, and maybe there's more than one, maybe still a male."

"How do we know it's a big ring?"

"Lots of Need Help cards floating around."

Silva disagreed. "Maybe that's because there's not much business."

"There's something else here, something she talked about just a little. Wanda was guessing, just guessing, that this wasn't a money deal; this was inspired by something else, like women's needs. Did you get anything from that, Frank?"

Silva stared. "I'm an issues man. I do things because I believe in them. Money's not the deal. You're right, Joe. Maybe this ring isn't just a get-rich deal, or a mob deal, or a unlicensed doctor's way of putting cash into his pockets. Maybe it's something else."

"Like a women's deal?"

"Follow the money."

"Only it'd have to be the reverse. Look for loose money and try to trace it back."

"You thinking what I'm thinking?"

"Maybe Mrs. Barbie can show us the books, if she's got them," Sonntag said. "This ain't gonna be pretty. We got anything else going?"

"Search that barn hayloft. Not me. Someone else. I don't like snakes."

"Snakes?"

"Well, you never know what's in a barn."

"If we search that hayloft, we tip them off. Are we ready for that?"

"No, not by a long shot. We've got one sure abortion, and maybe a death from one, and a few rumors, and an abortionist who's shown nothing but her eyes. We've got to collect a lot more before busting over there."

"What do you think we'd find up there in the loft?" Sonntag asked.

"Probably nothing. Some old furniture. Anything that could be evidence gets carried out, every time. Unless they're awfully dumb, and I don't think they are."

"The Hendersons were dumb enough to keep that door padlocked and not let us have a look," Sonntag said. "Smart people have their dumb sides."

"Back to Ranger Girls. You got a working theory?"

"It's all what-ifs. What if there's a real edgy minority, ones who don't like the way the world treats women. What if Camp

Ravenswood is an ideal place not only to recruit more of these, but to help women. Maybe not just pregnant girls, but women suffering abuse. What if there's a whole sort of underground thing out there, right under the eyes of the directors and the executives who run the outfit? Suppose this abortion ring is part of it, and is feeding cash into the whole deal?"

Silva was grinning. He loved anything that had to do with factions, including women's issues.

Sonntag grinned back. "It's your baby. You can see if they'll open the ledgers. I think the whole deal is paranoid, but I'm not a politician."

"Yeah, how about the other cards? The Pain cards, printed out there by the Hendersons, and used to promote mercy suicides.?"

"Beats me," said Sonntag. "Suddenly there's people trying to dodge the law, and for reasons they consider merciful. That just eats at me. If that's what's happening, we're not dealing with mobsters; we're dealing with nice people."

"Nice people who might be bumping off their grannies," Silva said.

That somehow ended it. "Okay, you work on the money, Eddy is working on getting more debutantes to fess up, and I'm working on the Hendersons and the Burleigh rest home," Sonntag said. "A suicide mill and an abortion mill. That's going to make some great headlines."

It had been a good day. He collected his lunch bucket and headed into the rare October heat. It would be a tough ride home, because his pants always stuck to the wicker streetcar seats when it got this hot. He boarded a crowded Number Ten car, and the close air almost flattened him. But he got a hand on a strap hanger, and rode west, grateful for each stop, when the folding door opened and a little air swirled in. When the car reached the viaduct over the Menomonee River Valley, he was certain the whole trestle would collapse. The car had fifty more people in it than the viaduct could possibly support. But the car slowly ground across, and Sonntag was all the sweatier when the car rolled onto solid earth. Somehow, the streetcar was safe, but he couldn't imagine how or why. He got off at 56th and hiked home, hoping Lizbeth wouldn't object if he took off his shirt and had his evening drink in his undershirt. This was Indian Summer with a vengeance.

She met him at the door, wearing her version of a sun suit, a halter and shorts.

"You look bushed," she said.

"It was a good day."

"I've got stuff on ice; you got home on time for once."

"Barely made it across," he said. " I think there's some bolts missing but the city doesn't do anything."

He headed for the bedroom, got out of his sticky shirt and undershirt, washed and toweled himself, pulled on a tee shirt, and joined her on the back patio. Anything was better than inside.

She waited. This was a ritual. She loved to hear about his cases, and he told her about them after he had downed half a drink. He needed half a drink to prime his pump. She'd been acting strange ever since Sandy Millbank had been discovered. Instead of rejoicing at his progress, she was dark and often sharp with him. It made him feel like this case was all female, and he shouldn't be handling it.

"We got a witness today. Frank got her in. She'd had an abortion, and it probably was out there on Bluemound."

"She should be put in jail," Lizbeth said. "If it weren't for women like her, there'd be no abortion ring."

This was going to be one of the bad evenings, he figured. He sipped, and went on, knowing nothing he said would admit him into her winner's circle.

"This gal, she's at Allis Chalmers, got taken out there, and it was a female, maybe a nurse, that did it, but only her eyes were showing; she had a surgical mask, and a hair thing, and gloves. So that's a start."

"What did she pay?"

"A grand in small bills. Her union brothers chipped in."

"They would, being guilty."

"We think we know who did it, and we're going to find out where the money goes. It may not go into pockets at all. It might go for social purposes."

"Social purposes! Is that what it's called?"

"It's just a theory we're working on, Lizbeth."

"It's so any girl can sleep with anyone, and there's no price to pay," she said. "Maybe that's what the Ranger Girls are about. What Camp Ravenswood is about."

"Why do you say that?"

"I just know it. I'd never send any daughter of mine there."

"It's not in their program. It's not in the camp courses. The ladies who run Ranger Girls don't even think that way."

"They don't know what goes on," she said. "This is like a big thing that's all sort of hidden from view."

She looked testy, and was getting irritated fast. It wasn't the first time that Lizbeth had hunches that somehow proved important.

"You're the sweetest gal I've ever met," he said.

She didn't tumble for it. She arose suddenly, and vanished into the kitchen, and he heard pots and pans clanging. She emerged a little later. "You can get your own dinner tonight," she said, and walked away.

He didn't know what he'd done, or what he'd failed to do, or what ticked her off.

He found her in the bathroom. "Lizbeth, let's go for a drive. Fresh air."

"No."

"I was thinking of driving to Camp Ravenswood. It'll still be light, I think."

She opened the bathroom door suddenly. "Who's there?" she asked.

"We'd just be wandering around the grounds."

She was grinning. He didn't understand it, but neither would he zip up a smile like that.

Moments later, while he cranked up the coupe, she joined him, wearing slacks and a blouse, and they were off. The open windows caught the cooling air of an Indian Summer eve, and turned the trip into a road show heaven. Light was short when he pulled into the gravel drive of the girls' camp, but there would be time to show Lizbeth the place where undercurrents were flowing.

"That's Sandy Millbank's cottage there," he said.

The place looked forlorn. But there was light shining in the camp office, and a Studebaker parked in front. Someone was present.

"We'll go get permission," he said.

He spotted the camp's athletic director, Wendy Vestal, peering out at them. The encounter was not going to be pleasant.

She opened the door and stood in it, to bar the way. She was as wiry and mannish as he remembered her, in shorts, tennis shoes, and a white tank top.

"Good evening, Miss Vestal."

"What are you doing here?"

"Taking an Indian Summer drive. I thought I'd show Camp Ravenswood to my wife, if that's all right."

"No, it's not. This is private property, and unless you have official business, you may leave."

"We'll go then," he said. "What brings you here on a weeknight?"

"Someone has to maintain the camp, pay bills, do books. So I elected myself to do it."

"I'm glad someone is looking after this beautiful place," he said. "This is my wife, Lizbeth. She's curious about it. I've been talking about it. Lizbeth, this is Wendy Vestal. She's the athletic director."

Miss Vestal nodded curtly.

Sonntag pointed. "That's Sandy Millbank's cottage there," he said. "She was the off-season administrator. She often spent days alone here. They close up for the winter after Thanksgiving, and run weekend programs until then. Am I right, Miss Vestal?"

She glanced at her oversized watch, which seemed to be a men's model. "Look, I'm in a hurry," she said.

She sure was struggling to be civil.

"Could I give Lizbeth just one peek at the cottage?" he asked.

Miss Vestal shook her head. "I'm busy."

"That's where Sandy was found, right?"

"Yes, but it's late and I'm not going to unlock, and it's time for you to go."

Sonntag smiled. "We'll go, then," he said.

He led Lizbeth back to the old coupe, and seated her. Miss Vestal was still silhouetted in the doorway. He cranked up the car, backed, and headed out. In his rear view mirror he finally spotted her going back in. She had made sure he was leaving.

"Why are you smiling?" Lizbeth asked.

"Because another piece of the puzzle fell in place."

"What piece?"

"She said, 'Yes, that's where Sandy was found.'"

"Oh, Joe..."

They traversed the gravel road for a way, reached the narrow highway, and passed through some woods.

"Joe," she said. "Pull over in some shady place where we can watch the moon. See, it's just coming up. An Indian Summer moon, bigger than ever."

That seemed like a good idea, so he pulled into a gravel byway, and found a place that opened to the heavens.

"Not a bad idea," he said, as she snuggled into him.

"Kiss me, Joe. We're going to neck."

"Neck, hell," he said. "I'll meet you and raise the ante, Babe."

"I've got four aces," she said.

"You win," he said.

Chapter Twenty-Eight

Sonntag got hold of Hannibal-the-Cannibal over in the district attorney's office. Bill Hannibal had acquired the nickname after he prosecuted a bookseller who ate her parents. But now the subject was suicide.

"Suicide's illegal. The law says it's homicide. But we rarely prosecute someone who tried and failed," Hannibal said.

"What about assisting a suicide?"

"Generally, illegal."

"What about encouraging a suicidal person to go ahead?'

"Illegal."

"What about making it easy for the suicidal person to attempt it? Like leaving a razor on a bedside table?"

"Illegal."

"What about leaving pain pills, like Seconal?"

"You'll need to tell me more."

"Okay, a nurse leaves a pain pill for the patient to take whenever he needs it, but the patient squirrels away the pills until he has enough to kill himself."

"Could be illegal. If the dosage is small and clearly for pain, it might pass."

"Hundred milligram Seconal?"

"Which makes it easy? Probably illegal."

"What if a society, they're called Hemlock Societies, advocates suicide?"

"Probably legal."

"What if they describe ways and means?"

"I don't know."

"What if a suicidal person subscribes and gets what he needs in the mail, a how-to manual, and puts it to use?"

"I don't know that, either."

"What if a person is peddling pain pills, or sleep pills, and is approached by someone who says he hurts, and suicide is never mentioned, but the person in pain uses the pills to kill himself anyway?"

"Are the pills licit? Prescribed by a doctor for that patient?"

"No, underground distribution for a profit."

"Arrest the bastards."

"What's the underlying legal idea, Cannibal?"

"Homicide is the taking of human life. No excuses. No putting someone out of his misery. No relieving someone of unbearable pain. The law is uniform, and one reason is to keep someone from bumping off Uncle Willy, who's suffering dementia and piles, for the life insurance."

"And aiding or abetting suicide, that's bad?"

"That'll put Aunt Matilda in the slammer."

"If a rest home is letting wounded and destroyed and hopeless veterans hasten their departure, what do I do?"

"Nail them."

"And if they make money on it, from GI life insurance, what?"

"Nail them."

"If someone helps an old veteran to die, but has no private interest in it, is he guilty?"

"Absolutely."

"Okay, if a guy's dying of cancer, few days to live, and hurting so much he's in agony and delirious and incoherent, and if a doc injects a little more morphine in him than pain requires, and the guy dies a few days early, what?"

"The doc's bought a one-way ticket to Waupun, Sonntag."

"Would you change the law in any way if you could?"

"It's a good law, Lieutenant. It's universal, makes no exceptions, and is grounded in a respect for life."

"Okay, Cannibal, I've got my marching orders."

"I guess you do, Sonntag."

The line clicked dead. Lieutenant Sonntag sat and wrestled with still more law that would rarely hit thugs, crooks, and sadistic bastards. It would apply mostly to people trying to be merciful What kind of law was that?

"So?" asked Frank Silva.

"So, the law's about the same. A mobster hires a hitman to kill someone, and gets sent up the river for life. A beaten old veteran, tormented by what's left for him, hires someone to bring him Seconal, and swallows a few hundred milligrams and dies, and the guy who brings him the pills gets sent up the river for life."

"That's called evenhanded justice," Frank said.

"So do we shut down the Burleigh Rest Home and throw them all in the can?"

"Joe, there are times I wish I'd quit the force and go out pushing pamphlets on street corners."

"What if we just go over there and tell the CEO, what's his name, Art Pendergast, that we know what's going on, and cut it out or there'll be big trouble."

"Sure, and he'll smile and say okey-dokey."

"We'd need stuff we don't have. They're tied to the Hendersons, and so are the abortion dealers. The Hendersons are fronting for several things: suicide providers, abortion providers, and maybe off-the-books adoptions, or trafficking in babies. They're running Seconal out of that Burleigh outfit to those who want it. They're tied up somehow with some faction in Ranger Girls who want to grow balls. But we don't have it nailed down. We can't name the abortionist, maybe plural if this is a big business. And we haven't caught Pendergast's people doing anything illegal—yet."

"Maybe that's good," Frank said. "We don't know the who, when, or what, so we can't bring charges. But we can let them know we know a lot, and maybe shut them down."

It was a temptation, but one Joe Sonntag rejected. He had to know. He had to know every detail and every name, and then he'd see about some sort of clemency. The spider web seemed to spin outward from the Hendersons, so maybe another visit was in order.

"Come on, Frank, we're going out Bluemound Road. If Gorilla's free, I'll want him with us."

An hour later the unmarked gray cop car pulled into the gravel drive, and ground to a halt at the somnolent farmhouse.

"It's a nice farmhouse, all that limestone dressed nicely by a fine stonemason," Gorilla said. "I guess I'll take a picture of it."

He had his Speed Graflex with him, a big camera that used plate film he loaded in his darkroom. He had brought it deliberately; it was somehow more terrifying to people under police observation than his new 35-millimeter Leica. That was what this was about. Put some heat on the Hendersons. Indian Summer was over. Silva and Sonntag stood in the yard, wrapped in trench coats, while Gorilla worked clear around the farmhouse, and then began photographing the barn. About the time he disappeared behind the barn, William Henderson erupted from the farmhouse.

"What's this? What's doing?"

"We're collecting evidence, Henderson," Sonntag said. "We always do a thorough job. We'll want photos of all the interior spaces too. You can show off your new furniture."

"We don't have any," Henderson said. "Now, if this is some more Milwaukee police trying to harass me, you can just pack up and get out. You're not even in your city."

"Why would we harass you?"

"I don't know, but you're doing it."

"Seriously, Mr. Henderson. Tell us why we're here."

"I wish I knew. We're just a little services company. Now why don't you just leave me alone?"

"Oh, we'll go soon, Henderson, but it would be a good idea if you speeded it up. All you gotta do is answer questions."

"Do you have a search warrant?" Henderson asked.

Sonntag turned to Silva. "Are we searching for something?"

"Not that I know of," Silva said. "Mr. Henderson, what should we be looking for?"

"Why are you here, then?" Henderson asked.

"Because someone we're interested in buys cards from you, and maybe you can help us," Sonntag said.

"We have lots of customers; hand-designed, artistic cards we're proud of. That's how I spend most of my time, designing the card that speaks right up and promotes a business."

"Yeah, well, it's cold out here, and why don't we go in and learn about your card business?"

"Mr. Henderson," said Silva, "have you got chickens here? I always thought I'd like to have chickens and eggs if I lived in a farmhouse."

"No, we don't do any farming."

"I guess you just like country living," Silva said.

Henderson let them in, and they collected in his little parlor that was now a sales room with office stuff on shelves and tables.

"Where's the missus?" Silva asked.

"She's away," Henderson said.

Gorilla Meyers showed up, and immediately began photographing everything in sight. The flashbulbs flashed and sizzled.

"Hey, this is a private residence," Henderson said.

"Looks like a store to me," Gorilla said.

"What are you going to do with all those shots?"

"I like to submit them to photography magazines, and win contests." Gorilla took a picture of the phone console.

Silva extracted one of the Pain Relief cards. "You printed this one, right?"

"I'd have to check, sir. I'm not sure."

"Come on, Henderson, you printed it."

"I don't know for sure."

"Well, today we're narcs. We think maybe this is a cover for a ring distributing hard stuff. Real bad stuff. You know what the Federal Narcotics man says, you start someone on marijuana, and pretty soon he's on heroin. So we're really going after this. Now, this here number, it's your answering service number, and we don't know who we're dealing with"

"I'm sure our answering service has nothing to do with anything like that, officer."

"Yeah, well, if we can stop innocent teenagers from trying their first reefer, man, we've done some good around here."

"I think we're just dealing with a group trying to relieve suffering, sir. You know, people hurt a lot, and patients are in great need of help."

"Yeah, if that's what it is, we'll just walk away. We're not worried about pain. We're worried about the drug fiends, and the criminals that prey on them. You want to help us?"

"Well, we keep our clients confidential, sir, but if you were to return with a search warrant in a few days, we'd comply. I'm sure my client would be pleased to help out. But I'd need his permission to reveal anything to you."

Gorilla shot a photo of Henderson, gesticulating. Gorilla popped out the sizzling flashbulb and let it rattle on the floor.

"Hey! I wish you wouldn't startle me like that."

"I'll send you a matted print for your wall, if you want," Gorilla said. "Just give me one of your business cards."

"Oh, I'm not vain," Henderson said. "Just a forgettable face. I'd rather you didn't shoot all these photos."

"So who orders the Need Help cards?" Sonntag asked.

"That's Matchmakers. They're a fine outfit."

"Well, Bill, we need to get in touch with them. I'm told there's some state laws they may be violating. Confidentiality statutes. So we've been asked to look into it. What we'd like is to get them to change their ways, and report to the state, the way more traditional adoption agencies do. You think you could help us there? We just want to make sure things are done right. I'm sure you're in favor of that, aren't you?"

"Oh, you bet. We're just an answering service for them, you know. We answer calls, and make references. I've never looked closely at who runs it."

"Well, you must send them invoices for cards and the phone service. Where to those invoices go?" Silva asked.

"Well, that's a mystery to us, too. I wish I could help you. I don't know why you're confusing secretarial services with the actual people."

"I don't either, Henderson. It sure has us baffled," Silva said.

Gorilla shot another photo of the three others, all grouped close. "That's a good one," he said. "I'll call it Henderson and the detectives. I wish the missus were in it, too. Where's she?"

"In town," Henderson said. "Look, fellas, I don't know anything else."

"Hey, there's something else. We want to see the old hayloft you got fixed up. I heard it's a study, with nice old stuffed chairs and tables in there so you can read. You mind showing it to us?"

"It's not even a study," Henderson said. "Just some used furniture stored up there."

"Well, then let us have a look, okay?"

"I haven't cleaned up in there."

"That's okay, Henderson. I'm not such a hot housekeeper myself, being a bachelor," Silva said. "My place would embarrass me if the cops showed up. The Schlitz bottles, man, there's enough to give the chief a heart attack."

"Come on, Bill, be a sport," Sonntag said.

Henderson looked trapped. "Nothing there," he said. "I guess you can look."

He pulled his keychain, found the padlock key, and headed for the barn.

He flipped the padlock open and swung open the door, revealing a dim stairway rising into darkness. "I'll stay down here," he said.

"Nah, come on up and give us the cook's tour," Silva said.

Henderson led them up the creaking stairs and into a big dark area. He pulled a light cord, and the loft snapped into shape. He was right. An old sofa, a few beat-up stuffed chairs, a big oak dining table, some straight-back chairs around it. A wastebasket.

"Hey, whatcha got in the wastebasket?" Silva asked.

He lifted it up and turned it over. A pair of rubber gloves fell to the plank floor.

"That's just Elvira's cleaning gloves. She scrubs up around here," Henderson said.

"They sure are interesting," Silva said, and stuffed them in his pocket.

"Hey!" Henderson said.

"It's okay, Bill, we're not gonna keep them long," Silva said.

Sonntag began lifting pillows. "I always look for loose change in old furniture," he said. "Hey, here's a dime. It's yours, Henderson. I'll see what else I can find."

"Get out of here," Henderson cried. "Just get out."

Gorilla's flashbulbs were popping regularly, and he went through several more plates as he shot the sofa, the table, the chairs, and the stairwell, and then it was over.

"We're on our way, Henderson. Thanks for the tour," Sonntag said."

"You see? There's nothing here," Henderson said, locking the padlock behind them.

"Here are your gloves, pal," Silva said, handing them to the man. "You can clean up after us."

Chapter Twenty-Nine

Frank Silva came up with some good stuff. "Here, lookit this," he said, dropping a photocopy into Joe Sonntag's hands.

It was a marriage license, issued at the county courthouse, dated September 9, 1944, for Elvira Smith and William Henderson.

"So I went to the *Journal*'s morgue for that date and the days following. Here's what we need."

It was a brief wedding story: Corporal William Henderson, of West Allice, on leave from the 42st Field Hospital in Italy, wed Elvira Smith, a recent graduate of Milwaukee Deaconess School of Nursing, on September 12. Miss Smith, who received her nursing cap that June, is the daughter of Alphonse and Marian Smith, of Waukesha. Henderson, a medical corpsman, had completed two years at the university in Madison before being drafted.

"No wonder they're fooling around with medicine," Sonntag said. "Nice going, Frank."

"Do you think she's the phantom abortionist?"

"She's moved to the top of the list. It'd help if we knew what kind of nursing she did. He went back out, and she nursed somewhere until VE day or later."

"I'll find out," Frank said.

That was easy. She had been a maternity ward nurse at Milwaukee Lutheran.

In spite of the GI Bill, Henderson hadn't gone back to college. Apparently she had supported him. Nothing showed up about him until they started the Bluemound Road operation.

"Might be another war-shock case; there's a lot of those," Frank said. "Men wandering around in a daze years later."

"If he's helping wounded vets to check out, maybe it's become a kind of a vocation, I mean a commitment," Sonntag said.

"Between then, they know enough medicine," Frank said.

"And know enough about dodging medical law."

"Want me to call her?"

"Not a bad idea," Sonntag said. "She'll have heard all about our visit."

A bit later, Silva rang her up.

"Elvira, Frank Silva here, investigator. I've got Lieutenant Sonntag on the line, too. All right if we ask a few questions?"

"No, it's not all right. You people are harassing a legitimate business."

"Well, this isn't about business. We hoped you'd be there yesterday, but you were in town. Distributing more Need Help cards, I imagine."

"I was grocery shopping."

"We got a lot of groceries, ma'am. What I'm wondering is, you're a nurse, right?"

"Where did you get that?"

"Milwaukee Deaconess Nursing School. Got your cap in forty-four, and married Bill when he got home on leave, right?"

She didn't reply.

"Worked in the maternity ward, right? I guess that gave you a good window on all the problems, women and girls, having babies, right?"

"I wasn't there long."

"But you saw the problems. Sometimes everything was happy, new baby in the family. Sometimes sad; some single mother about to give up her very own infant for adoption. I can see why you wanted to reform that world."

"I don't want to reform anything, and I'm simply an answering service for Matchmakers, sir."

"Yeah, well, and Bill, he came back from the war sort of broken up about it, I guess. He could've gone back to school, GI Bill. I guess you took care of him, with a regular nursing check, right?"

"He's devoting his life to helping veterans, sir. That's more than you can say about your life."

"Oh, what does he do?"

"He provides office services for veterans, Mr. Silva. That's what we do. And we're proud to do that."

"Tell me about that, Mrs. Henderson."

"Oh, you're just harassing us again. He already told you everything there is to say, and he's shown you the entire place, and if you keep on, we're going to file a complaint."

"I'm sorry, ma'am. We're just looking for information, and not trying to stir up anything. Could you tell me about Bill? He came out of the war with some sort of depression, we take it."

"Why do you say that?"

"Guesswork, ma'am. He didn't finish up school. The war got to him, I guess. I can understand that. It'd get to me, especially as a corpsman in a field hospital. I'd see a lot of things I would never forget, and always hate."

"I nursed him back; I took care of him when he had the shakes and when he cried in the night. I sat with him and helped him lose the war and find a life."

"Yeah, and now he helps veterans in pain?"

"There's hardly a veteran who's not in pain, Mr. Silva. Physical, from wounds, emotional, from what he's seen and heard and felt. Yes, my husband is devoted to ending the suffering of these people, I mean curing them of the things that have tormented them ever since they were discharged and pushed back into a society in which the world pretends to be normal."

"Yeah, that's good. He gets veterans on pain medicine?"

"It's more complicated than that."

"He gets them counseling?"

"How do you counsel a man who has no hands, one leg, one eye, and can't hear?"

"Sort of like that fellow down near the Wood Veterans Home. We found him dead, his uniform on, his leg and arm pinned up. He sure was glad to find a way out, ma'am."

"I don't know what you're talking about."

"He found a supply of sedatives, and put them to use."

"You know, you were going to talk about nursing, and I've told you what I know. I've helped a lot of people and I'm proud of it, and now I'm going to hang up. All you do is harass us."

The line clicked dead.

Silva pushed a thumb upward. Elvira and Bill Henderson had become visible people at last.

Sonntag had the usual bad feeling. It sure was easier to crack down on thugs and crooks, burglars and con men, wife-beaters and pickpockets. He began to think of the Hendersons as radicals. Such people have a vision and pursue it, without regard to the settled views of the society that embraces them. Sometimes radicalized people would do what they were driven to do, no matter the consequences. Maybe these two fit into that mold.

But maybe not. Maybe these two had set up some night medicine and were skimming all the cash they could off of it. The problem was, they were hard to catch. He thought of all the times he knew who was guilty of something, but had no way to nail the person.

"Frank, you want to come up with a theory?" Sonntag asked.

"Hendersons tie together a lot of illegal medicine, but I don't know how or why. There's those women out at Camp Ravenswood, with their vision of female life, who may be using the camp as a recruiting ground for pregnant girls. There's Pendergast, probably pushing hundred milligram Seconal out the door, to contacts made by the Hendersons. As well as making the stuff available to his in-house patients at a nice profit. Then there's someone performing abortions, and it may be less for cash than for what they think of as compassion. Who's that, and how is she tied to the Ranger Girls, if at all? And you know what? I'm changing my view of the Hendersons. I'd thought of them as the hustlers, the pill-runners, the deal-makers, all for forty or fifty percent. But now I'm wondering if they're idealists too—oh, don't give me that look when I call them idealists. Idealists can break laws faster and harder than crooks. But ideals may be what's driving them. Maybe Bill Henderson is another war-ruined man, trying to ease the torment of other war-ruined men."

"Yeah, it's bugging me, too. Is there a money-grubbing crook in all this?"

"Let's head over to the Burleigh Rest Home and have another visit with him," Silva said.

"Follow the pills, follow the money," Sonntag said, reaching for his hat.

"We're thinking like cops again," Frank said. "Maybe we should be following the ideals."

When they reached the Burleigh Rest Home, out on 60th Street, they headed straight for the Wellness Center, and pushed in. A young woman in wire-rimmed glasses barred the way. "This is off-limits, sirs."

"We're Milwaukee police," Sonntag said, pulling his badge. "I'm Lieutenant Sonntag, and this is Detective Silva."

"Well, this is unusual," she said.

"We're trying to learn how prescription drugs are put in the hands of patients. Maybe you could help us, Miss? Miss—"

"Laboeuf, sir, Madeline."

"Good, good," Sonntag said.

"You order most of your drugs from Wisconsin Pharmaceutical?"

"Yes, sir. I do the ordering."

"How about Seconal?"

"A lot of that, sir. We usually order four lots—that's five hundred a lot—of the hundred milligram, and various amounts of the other dosages."

"Two thousand? You're passing out a lot of pills."

"Actually, no. We use between one and two lots a month."

"What about the rest?"

"Mr. Pendergast has a hospice service for the gravely ill, so they go out with his visiting people. They're such a blessing, you know. People in agony, they take one and peace creeps up on them, and their suffering is something they can endure."

"Are these prescribed?"

"We have a visiting geriatric doctor here, two hours on Thursdays, and he makes those decisions. Mostly he prescribes as needed. That gives us some flexibility. As needed is the key to everything."

"What's his name, miss?"

"Doctor Oxnard, sirs."

"And he just lets your people adjust the dose?"

"Sometimes he doesn't want someone on a sedative, and that goes on the record for that person. But mostly we have the authority to adjust doses."

"Could we see some of his prescriptions?"

"Oh, there's a whole pad here, all stamped."

She handed Silva an RX pad, with Oxnard's signature stamped on each one.

"Mind of I keep one of these?"

"Is he doing something wrong?"

"Maybe, maybe not. We need to find out, miss."

Silva pulled a form off the pad.

"Who runs the home care service, miss?" Sonntag asked.

"Oh, Mr. Pendergast owns it, sir, but it's managed by Bill Henderson. He comes here frequently, and picks up the lots that are reserved for him."

"He's licensed to do that?"

"Oh, it's all part of Mr. Pendergast's Burleigh Rest Home license."

"So this fellow comes by and picks up the Seconal, and what does he do with it?"

"You'd have to ask them, sir. I know little about all that."

"Where does he take it, do you know?"

"Their offices are out on Bluemound Road."

"Now, miss, what do you do here?"

"Mostly I fill these little paper cups with pills, so the orderlies can take them to the patients. Most everyone in the Terminal Wing gets two a day, and they can take them any time."

"And Dr. Oxnard okays that?"

She shrugged. "You'd have to ask about that, sirs. I'm a

pharmaceutical tech."

"Do you keep records—such and such got three Seconal on such and such a day?"

"Monthly is all, sir. Usually, I just write the patient's name, and sixty-two of the hundred milligram Seconal, and the month."

"I guess that saves a lot of hassle," Silva said.

"It's not how we were taught, but it does save time."

"Does Dr. Oxnard ever change the amount?"

"Yes, if someone is really hurting, he'll increase the dosage. I have twelve four-pill patients just now. And one six-pill, a woman named Ardith Frobusher. Every four hours."

"Six pills?"

"Feel sorry for her, I really do. I don't think even six Seconal gives her the release she needs. She has pancreatic cancer."

"Is she near death?"

"That's the problem. The rest of her is vital. She's still a month or six weeks from death, they say."

"I'll remember the name," Silva said.

"Who bills who? Does Pendergast send an invoice to Henderson?" Sonntag asked.

"I've never seen an invoice, sirs. I've been here seventeen months, and I've never seen a financial document. Am I supposed to?"

"I guess not, miss. Are there receipts for the prescription drugs? I mean, when Henderson picks up his two lots, does he sign for them?"

She shrugged. "It's all the same company, I think."

"Why is the amount constant? Two lots, a thousand capsules, each month going to Henderson's hospice home care?" Silva asked.

"I've never asked. You'd think some months he'd want more, sometimes less."

"Yeah, that's got me wondering too," Silva said.

"I'm sure Mr. Pendergast could explain all that," she said. "He's always got about six businesses going at once. He's a wonderful man."

"He sure is amazing, miss. I guess that's it. You through, Frank?"

"I'm through."

In the hallway, they hesitated. "You want to go talk to pendergast while we're here?"

"No, he wiggles too much. And he's got his guard up now. Let's go try Henderson again. I sure want to know where a thousand capsules of Seconal vanish to each month."

"Down Eden Stumpf's throat, I guess," Silva said.

Chapter Thirty

It didn't take long to get to the farm. Bluemound Road had little traffic on a sleepy October afternoon. Sonntag turned the unmarked Plymouth into the gravel drive, and parked in front of the old farmhouse. The place seemed somnolent in the weak sunlight. They got out, banged on the door, and got no answer. They saw no cars anywhere, not in the drive, or the barn aisle, or behind any outbuildings.

Sonntag peered into the parlor window, the one with the office services store in it, and found it empty. Nothing there. Not a stick of furniture. The telephone console and phones had vanished. Silva circled the house, and headed for the barn.

Sonntag checked the mailbox, and found nothing in it. He tried the bell a few more times, but no one responded. He tried the front door, but it was locked. He was heading for the rear door when Silva returned from the barn.

"The loft—it's unlocked and there's not a stick of furniture in it," he said.

"Flew the coop," Sonntag said, as he tried the rear door. It opened.

They stared at each other. "We could get into trouble," Silva said.

"We have enough," Sonntag replied. "Flight of suspects."

There was enough against the Hendersons to warrant the entry.

They headed into the old stone house, which remained oddly cold even in the afternoon warmth. Silva drew his automatic; there was no sense of walking into surprises. But there was nothing there. Nothing downstairs, nothing but naked rooms upstairs. Nothing left behind. The house echoed hollowly at their every step. Silva restored the weapon to its breast-holster.

"Are we going to do a search?" Silva asked.

"You mean, like buried treasure, or bodies down the cistern? Not for now, unless you've got something in mind."

"Put out an all-points bulletin?"

"Can we work up some charges that'd stick?"

They couldn't. So far, whenever they had reached for something, it seemed to dissolve in their hands.

"Any guess?" Sonntag asked.

"They're both from around here. I don't think they're heading for a Nevada dude ranch."

"They could be rich."

"Do you know what the black market rate for Seconal is?"

"Not that rich," Sonntag said. "Do you think they turned in their keys to the owner? Needham?"

"Guess that's our next stop," Silva said.

"Have we missed anything here?"

They walked the place, they tried one loop out in the cornfields, they studied the barn. Nothing. Not even trash.

"I always figure that when they run, that says something," Sonntag said.

"You're a regular Torquemada," Silva said.

Sonntag didn't know what that was, but damned if he'd admit it.

They drove back to the station, each mulling theories. Without a detailed knowledge of Elvira and Bill Henderson's pasts and tastes, not even guesswork would help.

"We could put out an APB and the license number," Silva said. "Not that we've charged them with anything."

"I'm thinking they didn't go far. Their markets for their medical portfolio are all right here. What have we got now? Abortion mill, assisted suicide, peddling narcotics, operating an illegal adoption service, and maybe operating a hospice or home-care deal if that gal's right."

"Whoever knew that so much body comfort is illegal?" Silva said.

"When we get back, call that doc, Needham. It's his place. There's an off chance they left the keys and a forwarding address. Oh, yes, what's the post office out there?"

"If I can," Silva said.

When they walked in to the station Sonntag found a message. Call Doctor Stoppl. Well, okay.

"Stoppl here, and yes, I want something from you. You told me that Sandy Millbank's mother said she had a rare blood disease. Do you know what it was?"

"'Fraid not, doctor."

"Could you find out?"

"Maybe the half brother or sister might know. I'll call."

"I have a new theory."

"I'll get back to you as soon as I find out."

Theories. Oh, well, cops tried them out too. He dug into his Millbank folder and found some numbers. Half-sister, Marge Wald in New York, half-brother, Darren, in California. He tried the sister, who'd probably had her baby by then.

Operators clicked on through some infinitude of wire, and got her.

"This is Lieutenant Sonntag, ma'am, Milwaukee police. Have you a moment?"

"Is something wrong? Is this about Sandy?"

"Yes it is, ma'am, just a question the medical examiner wanted me to ask. With your folks in Peru, you're the best hope I have of an answer."

"I'm not sure I know much of anything, sir. Are you sure this is all right?"

"It's all right, ma'am. Do I understand you have a new baby?"

"Oh, yes, a girl, and we're naming her Sandy."

"I'm glad of that, ma'am. Now this is a simple question. Did Sandy have some sort of rare blood disease?"

"She didn't, but my stepmother did."

"Sandy's mother?"

"Yes. Sandy's mother."

"Something she might transmit to Sandy?"

"I don't know if I should be telling this. But yes, sir, Linda, her mother, came from a family of hemophiliacs. And she's a carrier. That's why they wanted a girl so badly, and not a boy."

"It's a male disease, right?"

"Yes, most hemophilia boys die after just a few years, bleeding all the time. But Sandy was the girl they wanted. Everyone was so relieved."

"Girls are carriers but don't get the disease, right?"

"That's what I was told."

"And Linda, she must have been overjoyed when Sandy came along."

"Yes, but they didn't dare try again, sir. It was a gamble they won, and anything more would be just plain heartache."

"You've really helped me. That's all I need to know. I'll tell the doctor. He's been a little puzzled about...about Sandy."

"About her death?"

"Yes, it doesn't quite add up for him."

"Please tell me what you find out. Please call me at once."

"I promise, ma'am. My name is Lieutenant Sonntag, if you should think of anything more."

"If you only knew what a healthy baby means," she said.

"I do know. Polio took one of mine, ma'am."

"I guess you do know," she said. "I'm sorry."

Sonntag made a few notes. Hemophilia. He sighed, dialed Stoppl, and was rewarded with an immediate response.

"Have your answer, Doctor. Sandy's mother is a carrier of hemophilia. They prayed for a girl, and got her."

There was only silence.

"Doctor?"

"It all fits," he said. "It's possible that Sandy Millbank never had an abortion."

"No abortion? Really?"

"Well, let me step back a bit. I'm ahead of myself. Tell me this, if you can, Lieutenant. Had Miss Millbank been intimate, shall we say, a little earlier—for the first time? That's important."

"Yes, we determined that."

"Ah, it fits, it fits. So, then. It's little understood, but females who carry the flawed chromosome that causes hemophilia can also suffer mild manifestations of the disorder. It's the male X chromosome that yields blood that can't coagulate. The male victim has the damaged X and another X, while the woman carrier has an X and a Y, and usually isn't affected because the Y is what keeps her safe.

"Sandy Millbank had a fifty-fifty chance of receiving the damaged X from her mother, and that happened. It's rare and unlikely for a woman to get full-blown hemophilia, but it's not rare for a woman to have mild forms that don't impair her life. She might simply find that hematomas don't soon disappear, but there is one symptom, hematologists see it now and then in women with hemophilia in their lines and that is, heavy menses."

Sonntag's mind was filled with images.

"Are you there, sir?"

"Yes, I was just imagining what might have happened at the girls' camp."

"The natural termination of the period depends on coagulation, sir. Initial congress with a male might also have opened small veins in the hymen, sir, or abraded delicate cervical areas. And an early miscarriage might have opened some placental bleeding. Do you follow me?"

"I do, sir, but I'm better at sorting out the Cubs' batting averages."

"You may wish to inquire who found Sandy Millbank and perhaps jumped to the wrong conclusions. It would very likely be someone with medical skills. There was no blood in her or on her, not a bit. So that suggests some very determined manipulation of the evidence. Just why she was carried to the zoo is quite beyond my competence."

"Is there any possibility that you're wrong?"

"In medicine, there is the known and unknown, as well as misinterpretation. Yes, certainly. I might have been more positive about this had I known from the start that she was a carrier of hemophilia."

"Could you write me a report, sir?"

"It will be in tomorrow's mail."

"Say, one last thing. What's the probability of this?"

"So low it doesn't really exist."

"But it happened."

"Medicine is full of things that simply happen."

"Doctor, thank you."

Sonntag put the earpiece back on its hook and stared into space. This whole thing had started with what seemed obviously a botched abortion. But now it all changed. The abortion probably never happened. But he had uncovered a major abortion ring, and a whole medical underground, all based on supplying what doctors and pharmacists were prohibited by law from doing. It was the strangest case he had ever worked on.

Someone out there at Ravenswood had found Sandy, probably lying in her own blood. And there had been some swift decisions. Someone who wanted to avoid scandal wanted Sandy out of there, and didn't care about Sandy or her family or truth or what the law required. Get her out! Get her as far from Camp Ravenswood as possible. Get her as far from Ranger Girls as possible. Who was that, and who had she enlisted?

He headed for Captain Ackerman's warren, and braved the wall of cigar fumes.

"So tell me. I saw you deflating out there, the telephone in your dying hand."

"Sandy Millbank probably never had an abortion."

Ackerman's cigar bobbled up and down. "So she died of leprosy?"

"No, she died of a mild form of hemophilia."

"Wrong gender, Joe."

"Here's what I got from Sandy's half-sister Marge Wald, and what the pathologist makes of it."

He laid it out to Ackerman, whose dogturd cigar bobbed

dangerously. "Stoppl's been paid off by the abortionist," Ackerman said. "Go after him."

"I'd be willing to get another opinion from another pathologist, for starters. But that doesn't break the ring. We've got a medical moonlight ring. I don't know what else to call it. And the Hendersons, who're the spiders, have flown the coop."

Sonntag told about the Bluemound Road farmhouse.

"Guilty as hell," Ackerman said.

"We'll find them. I don't think they went far. Not with all their business right here."

Ackerman was yawning, which was his favorite insult.

Sonntag fled, knowing Lizbeth would send his cheap suit off to the dry cleaners if he stayed in there much longer. He found Eddy Walsh and Frank Silva in the bullpen. A nod of the head brought them over.

"Something came up," Sonntag said.

"I'm too old for that, and full of envy," Walsh said.

"Maybe no abortion," Sonntag said, and told them the whole line he had pursued, and where it ended in Doctor Stoppl's reconstruction of events.

Walsh thought it was comic. "Let's go tell Dorothea Blue," he said. "That's society news."

"That reminds me, I have a call to make," Sonntag said.

He found Marge Wald's number and put the call through, Spring Valley, New York, station to station, hoping she'd be there.

She was. "It's Detective Sonntag," he said. "I promised I'd call with the news."

"Oh, how good of you."

"Your sister, ma'am. I, ah, she probably died of natural causes."

There was a pregnant pause.

"I, ah, am not good at explaining this, but I'll try. It turns out, at least the pathologist says, that on rare occasions a woman who is a hemophilia carrier can be somewhat affected by it. And Sandy, ah, was."

"She didn't die of an abortion?"

"The doctor believes she never had one."

"Could you explain this, please?"

"Ah, I could have you talk to the pathologist, Doctor Stoppl."

"It's hard for you, I guess. Be brave, kiddo. Tell me. I'm a big girl."

"Well, ma'am, it's like this," he said. "The most common problem in female carriers of hemophilia is, ah, a heavy period."

She helped him through the rest of it, and sounded oddly cheerful.

"I guess that explains it," he said when he was finished.

"It's sure going to rock those people, the movement," she said.

"What movement?"

"They're naming it the Sandy Millbank Movement. It's a new feminist group. Legal abortion and birth control are the goals. Free love and ending legal marriage are the other goals. They were going to make Sandy their martyr, and make her death at the hands of an illegal abortionist their cause célèbre. Over our dead body, detective! We absolutely hate the very idea. I don't want my sister celebrated as a martyr, period. The family's just appalled. But this, this! This changes everything!"

Sonntag soon had the story. Sandy Millbank's death by back-alley abortion made her a martyr to unjust and oppressive laws that kept women from controlling their own bodies. And that was the flashpoint, the event that was now galvanizing a new political movement. But now their martyr to oppressive law turned out to be simply the victim of an inherited disease.

"Who, ma'am, who's running this show?"

"Those people in Ranger Girls."

"Who's in charge, do you know?"

"The athletic director, Wendy Vestal. Let's see, Amanda Winthrop. Those are the ones who've told me what's going on." She laughed. "They sure are going to be unhappy."

"And you'll be happy?"

"My sister will rest in peace," she said. "That means everything to us."

Chapter Thirty-One

Sonntag got hold of Maxine Andrews at Wisconsin Telephone Company

"This is your old fan, Joe," he said. "What're you warbling today?"

"Beer barrel polka, Joe."

"Makes me thirsty," he said.

"It's more about my waist," she said. "What can I do for the PD?"

"You steered me to the Hendersons on Bluemound Road last time. They bailed out of there. Did they leave any forwarding, or a place to mail a final bill?"

"Missing in action, eh? It's William Henderson? And Speedy Secretarial, and a few other numbers?"

"That's it. We want to know where they went."

He waited a couple of minutes, and then she returned. "They paid their bill at our office before they left, so there's no forwarding. But the phones, yes. They want all calls forwarded to a service in town here, The Phone Maidens. I guess that's an answering service. That's all I can tell you."

"Did they start a new account somewhere in Wisconsin?"

That took another five to ten minutes.

"Yeah, sweetheart, there's a new number for Compassionate Care, Elvira Henderson, Hartland, Wisconsin."

"I know where that is. Little sleepy town twenty-five miles west. It has a good cheese factory."

She gave him the address and the number. "If that's the abortion mill, Joe, knock 'em dead."

"Are you referring to the mothers or the unborn?"

"Jeeze, Joe, I think I should report you to the cops."

He dug up the number of Phone Maidens, which was located on Water Street, and got the head maiden. "This is Sonntag, Milwaukee PD, ma'am. I understand you forward calls to a Hartland number."

"That's confidential, sir."

"Don't impede an investigation, ma'am. If you're receiving calls to these numbers, I want to know what you do with them." He read her numbers off the cards.

"Well, all I will say is that we take messages, and the owners call in and take the messages, and return the calls if they wish, sir."

"You just collect the messages, right? You don't forward the calls, or give the callers the Hartland number?"

"We follow our instructions, sir."

"How are you paid?"

"Cashiers check, sir, in advance."

"Okay, you've been helpful, ma'am. We may be back to you soon."

"I don't want to be in trouble, sir."

"That's good," he said.

So the Hendersons hadn't gone far, and were still doing business. They should have quit when they could, and gone to Australia or some place. He headed for Frank Silva.

"Want to take a ride out in the country?"

"As long as I can stay in the car."

"Good idea. There's pythons where we're going."

Silva eyed him nervously.

"We might stop at a cheese factory along the way," Sonntag said.

"I don't want to walk into one and think about what all those microbes are doing in there."

"We're going to Hartland, over twenty miles out. Sleepy little town. The Hendersons moved there."

"Your friend at WTC?"

"Yep, she slides me what I need."

"You sure you need me? I'm trying to get a line on Pendergast's background. He ran a VA hospital until he left abruptly. I'm trying to find out why."

"You're stuck, Frank. Get your mosquito netting and rubber waders and we'll head out."

"I have a date with Wanda Wisniewski," he said.

"We'll be back in time."

They clambered into an unmarked PD car and took off. "I'm going to stop in Elm Grove and talk to the postmaster," Sonntag said.

"What's there."

"Nearest post office to the Bluemound Road farmhouse. They must have done something with a thousand capsules of Seconal a month."

"Are there any spiders around there?"

"Daddy longlegs," Sonntag said. "They're little tarantulas, you know."

Sonntag liked Elm Grove, a bright, tree-lined town, becoming an enclave of people who lived comfortably. He always thought it would be a good place for mobsters to settle in, maybe next to the big convent there.

The post office turned out to be a tiny street-front affair, with an elderly postmaster holding the fort.

"We're Milwaukee PD investigators, sir," Sonntag said, showing a badge. "You have a moment?"

"I have more moments than I know what to do with," the old duffer said.

"You send a lot of little packages out of here, at least until recently?"

"How little?"

"Real small."

"Oh, yes, the Wisconsin Bead Works. They sell wooden beads to people who make necklaces, lots of styles and types. They showed me some, bright enameled ones, some of them oval or long. Nice folks."

"They stop sending them recently?"

"Yes, it's puzzled me, but suddenly they stopped."

"Sent all over the place?"

"Mostly out of state, sir. I couldn't say where."

"Paid cash for postage?"

"Nice couple, seemed to have plenty of money."

"If they start sending more of those, could you give me a call, sir? Here's my card."

"Nice couple," he said.

They headed out country roads for Hartland. "Guess we've got a line on another Henderson business," Sonntag said. "I wonder how much he marks up the price, how he gets paid, and how much goes back to the Burleigh Rest Home."

The leaves were mostly down, but a few trees lingered bronze in a cloudless day.

"I think we can start with a visit to the post office," Sonntag said, cruising the little jumble of commercial businesses. An American flag steered them.

"This town's too small. What if a skunk wandered in?"

"There's badgers lurking out there, Frank. They're nature's Mafiosi."

"I like my desk at the station house. It's the only safe place anywhere."

The postmaster this time turned out to be a postmistress, with wire-rimmed glasses and blue-tinted gray hair.

"Got a moment, ma'am?"

She eyed them skeptically. "If you're trying to sell me a bill of goods, no."

"We're from the Milwaukee police department, and perhaps you can help us."

"That's a new one," she said.

They both pulled their badges, encased in leather folders.

"How do I know this is the real metal? You probably got

these out of a Wheaties box. My grandson has a Dick Tracy wristwatch that cost a dollar fifty."

"Okay, you nailed us, we're crooks, ma'am," Silva said. "You been shipping out a lot of little packages lately? Maybe a bead company?"

"A bead company? Are you addled?"

"Okay, just little packages."

"The new people have a Quick-Lax business."

"Like what people swallow to help nature along?"

"That's it. I've sent out a few packages."

"I've never tried it. Is it good stuff?" Silva asked.

She smiled. "They gave me a package. I won't tell you the results. But I'm tempted to join the Radio City Rockettes."

"Okay, are they selling lots of the stuff?"

"I wouldn't know, sir."

"Do you have the power to inspect contents?"

"Sometimes. Like letters going as printed matter."

"Who are the people mailing the Quick-Lax?"

"That's not public information, sir."

"Okay, we need to have you withhold these boxes and turn them over to a postal inspector. Here's my card. Have him contact me," Sonntag said.

"Not on your life. What happens in the post office stays in the post office."

She glared, formidable behind her counter.

"Okay, ma'am. Do us one favor. Not a word to these people."

"That, sir, is an invitation. The next time they walk in, I shall tell them about this plain abuse of them."

"How do we get over there, ma'am?"

"Please don't address me as ma'am. I am not a cow."

"Yeah, well, could you direct us?"

"You go that way, that road there, until you see a big country inn with a veranda around the front and side. It's white with green trim."

"That's it?"

"That's more than you deserve."

"I guess you showed some Milwaukee cops a thing or two," Frank said.

"Are there any skunks around here?" Sonntag said.

"You don't want to insult me," she said.

Back in the black sedan, they enjoyed some relief from the withering glare.

"I told you I don't like small towns," Silva said.

They found the big inn easily enough. Its windows opened on bucolic woods and meadows. It was enormous, with the grandeur of an earlier time, when the countryside was well populated.

"You want to go in?" Silva asked.

"I'm thinking we might. They'll know about our visit soon enough, if that postal lady makes good her threats."

"They'll fly the coop again."

"We could look for the Seconal."

"Without a search warrant? In this county?"

"Let's see if they squeal," Sonntag said.

So they crossed the deep shade of the veranda, and rang the bell.

Henderson opened, took one look, and started to close the door.

Sonntag's shoe prevented it.

"I'd make a good vacuum cleaner salesman," he said to Henderson.

"You have no business here."

"Bill, my friend, we have business wherever you are. Do you want to let us in for a little palaver?"

"You can tell me right here."

"Okay, Bill, we know your game. Or should I say games? If you cooperate with us, help us nail down all the loose ends, it'll go a lot easier for you."

"I don't know what you're talking about."

"Nice old country hotel here," Sonntag said. Lots of rooms upstairs. Nice pill-room, ideal for packing up the Seconal and shipping it off to lots of people who want it under the counter, sent from a little country town, Quick-Lax by mail. That's a good one, Bill, Quick-Lax. Nice rooms for little surgeries, good place for a girl to recover. Nice place for a little baby traffic, line up the new parents, nice hideaway for the girls. Lots of little rooms for lots of little deals. Good place to pack up a blue bottle and deliver it to some old vet who's awful tired of his war wounds, right? I mean, lots of little rooms, each room worth about five years in Waupun, and maybe some of those rooms worth life, right?"

"I haven't the faintest idea what you're talking about,"

"Well, invite us in, and we'll go over the deal, okay?"

"Where's Elvira?" Silva said.

"I wouldn't know," Henderson said. "Not here."

"We were wondering who the lady is who does the little procedures, and now we know," Sonntag said. "This is too far out of town. Elvira's a nurse, right? We were looking at another gal, one connected to Camp Ravenswood, but she's not going to drive this far every time she needs to do a little cutting and scraping, right?"

"Bill, I think you're itching to cut and run," Silva said. "But there's no way. We've got the big eye on you. The only chance you've got is to cooperate. Hop in the car, and we'll go have a nice visit, okay? This is a big deal, and we don't know how it all comes together. But I'll tell you this: the more you sing, the more we'll try to lighten up the load."

"This is nothing but a fishing trip," Henderson said. "Sorry."

"We've got things pretty well nailed down," Sonntag said. "We've got a gal who was aborted in your barn on Bluemound Road. She might be able to pick Elvira out of a lineup. We've got what we need on Pendergast. We got a dead veteran, the hundred milligram Seconal provided by you in a blue bottle. We're still working on odds and ends, Bill, but it's all coming together. We've got your new answering service, Phone Maidens, wanting to do right by us. We've got the Elm Grove postmaster, and I think we'll have a postal inspector on it pretty fast. Quick-Lax, Bill. You enjoy your game. You want to help out or not?"

Henderson was looking twitchy.

"Nice set-up you have here," Sonntag said. "I sure like these country inns, lots of private rooms. Sleepy country road. Little barn in back to hide a car or two. You want to give us the tour?"

Henderson was white. "I'm going to slam this door, and if your foot's in the way, it's your problem."

He pulled the door wide, and swung it hard, and Sonntag yanked his foot back just in time. The door slammed hard, and they heard the bolt fall into place.

"You were almost a one-legged cop," Silva said.

"Good odds that he'll drive in for a talk," Sonntag said.

"Where next?"

"Waukesha. The county seat here. A little talk with the sheriff about Hartland's new citizens. He'll keep an eye on things."

Chapter Thirty-Two

Amanda Winthrop was not thrilled to see them. Sonntag didn't expect her to be. He and Frank Silva waited in the teachers lounge while she finished a social studies class. She stormed in, looking ready to flunk the cops and send nasty notes home to their parents.

"Good news, Mrs. Winthrop," Frank said.

That startled her. Sonntag let Silva carry the ball, because he was so good at it.

"I mean, your new outfit, the Sandy Millbank Movement, seems to have lost its martyr."

"I don't know what sort of game you are playing, but please don't waste my time."

"No, really, you're naming your new movement for the wrong gal."

Winthrop simply stared, refusing to be drawn into this.

"I mean, the pathologist doesn't think she ever had an abortion. She didn't die of some back-alley abortion. She never contacted an abortionist. She never attempted anything illegal."

"Are you done, sir?"

"Nope. What you need is a real victim, not Sandy Millbank. I'm all for radical movements myself. I've belonged to a dozen. But this one hasn't got legs."

"Would you get to the point, officer?"

"Sure. Doctor Stoppl lacked certain information, which made his autopsy seem very uncertain. In fact, it haunted him. Things weren't right."

She stood, lips compressed. Sonntag thought that she would be dangerous with a pistol in her hands.

"Here's the lowdown, ma'am. Sandy Millbank's mother came from a family with hemophilia. Her mother's a carrier. Women don't get the disease, right? Only boys, and they die in childhood. But Sandy had a fifty-fifty prospect of inheriting the flawed X chromosome, the one that leads to blood not coagulating. She got it. She didn't get her father's chromosomes."

"You're wasting your time, officer."

"Okay, Dr. Stoppl said that some female carriers are mildly affected by the disease. It shows up in various ways, especially periods that don't end."

"So it's all women's fault," she said.

"Nope, nature's fault. Three things happened. Sandy had her first intimacy shortly before she died. That probably produced some bleeding. She may well have had an early miscarriage, which may have produced more bleeding. She then had a period that wouldn't quit, and this cascade eventually overwhelmed her. How do we know? It was much too early for her to suppose she was pregnant. Much too early. All of this happened in a time frame of three or four weeks. Dr. Stoppl isn't positive how all this played out, but that's his best hypothesis. We know from phone records that Sandy Millbank never contacted the one going abortion mill in the area, not from the camp, or from her parents' home, and we also know that from the record of all incoming calls to the abortion mill. So mark this up as a probable tragedy, and forget the idea that Sandy Millbank is any sort of martyr to oppressive laws."

She sighed. "It doesn't make the slightest difference. The movement is underway, and Sandy Millbank is going to be the one to be remembered, and there isn't a soul who'd believe you. We're going to promote birth control and legal abortion, and won't stop until the laws are changed and male domination of females comes to an abrupt end."

Silva was grinning.

"That's how movements go, ma'am. Good luck."

"And Sandy Millbank's death will continue as our rationale."

"Ma'am," said Sonntag, "now that you know there was no abortion, would you mind telling us what happened? How her body arrived at the zoo?"

"You mean, if there's nothing illegal about her death, what happened?"

"You bet, ma'am. We're curious."

'Oh, me, how to begin? Our athletic director goes out there all the time; the camp's like home to her, and she backed up Sandy in caring for all the things that need attention. She found Sandy in her bed, soaked in blood. It was obvious to her that Sandy had gotten an abortion and it went bad and she died. In a panic she called me. I confess I didn't want a scandal to come upon Camp Ravenswood, or the Ranger Girls, so I was upset, too."

This was going well, Sonntag thought. The floodgates were open.

"Wendy volunteered to remove her. She went beyond the call of duty, and, well, prepared Sandy for discovery. It was all her idea, I mean, carrying her to a place of honor and arranging her tenderly. I just couldn't manage any of that myself, but Wendy did it. She's slight, but she had no trouble at all, and carried her, and arranged her there, and called me to say it was taken care of, and you know the rest."

"Well, ma'am, you've run about ten red lights," Sonntag said. "There'll be a reopened coroner's inquiry, and you and Wendy Vestal will testify, and it will be up to those people to decide what happens after that."

"Red lights?"

"This is so complicated I'd have to discuss it with the county attorney," Sonntag said. "There's a few laws that got stepped on, and I'm a little rusty on remembering them all. But it would have been best if you had just called for help, the sheriff, I guess that's Waukesha County. Called them and let them handle it."

She stiffened. "Well, I'll sacrifice myself for the cause."

"I don't know what it'll come to, ma'am."

"I wouldn't have done anything differently," she said.

"Ma'am, I hope this goes well for you. You're a good woman. I'm glad you believe in these things. Believe me, if there were any way I could relieve you of the burdens you face, I'd try to do it," Sonntag said.

"That goes for me, too," Silva said.

She stared, disbelieving.

"We'll drive down to talk with Miss Vestal now," Sonntag said. "Call her if you want. It might make things easier for her if she knows what you've told us. We should be there in half an hour, all right?"

The teacher nodded, so distracted she hardly heard Sonntag.

"During the war we were all Rosie the Riveter. Now we're back to being little mommies. We're the prisoners of our bodies," she said.

They left Amanda Winthrop in the lounge, looking lost, and headed quietly down the terrazzo steps and into their patrol cruiser.

"You know, Joe, I'm mostly on their side," Frank said.

Sonntag wondered what would make Lizbeth happiest; what sort of world, what sort of rules, what sort of arrangements. Women carried life, and fiercely loved and protected that life. Somehow, Amanda Winthrop and her friends were upsetting the balance.

"I don't know where I am on it; I'm just a flatfoot trying to enforce the law," Sonntag said, by way of escape.

"Yeah, the laws protect life, such as it is," Silva said, something metallic in his tone.

Sonntag knew Frank was thinking about Eden Stumpf, the man with two limbs, hearing, and other senses missing, who only wanted to be free of life.

They drove quietly through an overcast November day, to pulaski High School. They found Wendy Vestal waiting for them, dressed as she usually did, in a short athletic skirt, a knitted top, and tennis shoes.

"I'll add my story, and you can do what you will," she said.

"I'm glad you cared so deeply about Sandy Millbank," Sonntag said. "There she was, surrounded by ferns, composed,

straightened out, her arms folded. That was an act of honor
and care, wasn't it?"

Wendy Vestal didn't snap at him; instead tears welled up. "I
was very fond of her," she said.

"We noticed you had placed her next to the lioness."

"I didn't know anything more I could do."

"She must have been heavy for you to carry."

"She was so light, she was so floating in my arms, I never
thought of her weight."

"You cleaned her up?"

"All the rivers that flowed out of her, yes. With a syringe,
with soap and water, with a washcloth. She was so pale. She had
lost so much. She was waxen in the lamplight. I washed her as one
would wash an empress, as one would wash Cleopatra, or Queen
Elizabeth, or any other great woman. I washed carefully, and
dressed her with fresh clothing, and then carried her to my car,
and laid her across the back seat, and drove through the night, my
mind still uncertain about where to take her until I remembered the
walkway of the lions at the zoo, and so I drove there, when no
one was around, and the dark was deep and safe, and there I gave
her to the world."

"And the sheets?" Frank Silva asked.

"The sheets no longer exist. They're ash. And the mattress
cover."

"And Amanda Winthrop was worried about the camp? Its
reputation? A scandal?"

"She was. I was worried about Sandy. Her reputation. Her
honor. We differ, you know."

"But in the end, it would come back to Camp Ravenswood,
no matter what?"

"Amanda hoped it would somehow slide by. I knew it
wouldn't."

"You've founded a movement," Silva said.

"We don't have our female who died of oppressive abortion
laws. Amanda told me about the pathologist's theories. I suppose
they're the best explanation. But it'll still be the Sandy Millbank
Movement, and we'll still try to make life a little better for those of

us who don't want to be the second sex." She stared. "All right, what are you going to do with me?"

"It'll be up to the coroner's jury, Miss Vestal. As I told Amanda Winthrop, there were regulations that got stepped on. I think they might be open to your explanation, but that's not for me to say. You'll need to tell them your story as completely as you can."

"And then go to jail."

"I can't say what will happen, Miss."

"All right. Do you think there's a heaven for women, sir? Or is it all males, with St. Peter at the Pearly Gates?"

"Well, Miss Vestal, if it's just a male place, I'm going to start a movement of my own, and picket the place," Frank said.

"Too bad we can't strike," Wendy Vestal said, a faint smile building.

There was some odd connection between Silva and Vestal, one that made Sonntag feel left out.

"If you think of anything more, give me a call," he told her.

"I have a headache," she said, and laughed.

Sonntag liked her, too. He and Frank headed back to the station house to write up notes and begin a report to the coroner. They had gotten one corner of this odd puzzle figured out. He wondered just where the law stood on half of what happened. Cleaning Sandy, burning sheets, moving her, not calling officers of the law, not even a doctor, taking the body elsewhere—it'd take the county attorneys a few days to figure all that out.

About the time that Sonntag got the stuff written up, his two-finger typing rough, slow, but serviceable, Matt Dugan of the *Journal* showed up. Sonntag was annoyed. Two minutes later he would have been out of there, catching a Wells car, on his way to a well-deserved drink with Lizbeth. But here Dugan was, his porkpie hat perched recklessly on his balding head.

"Hey, Lieutenant, what's with the Sandy Millbank case?" he asked.

"We're getting there," Sonntag said, vaguely.

"I got word that she was aborted out at a mill on Bluemound Road, and that it went bad and she died of a botched job."

"Where'd you hear that?"

Dugan shoved his hat even farther back. "Phone Maidens. Man, do they open up for me. They love to gossip. So I go out there, and the place is empty. And I go to the county offices, and find it's owned by a busted doc named Arnold Needham, and I say, A hah! And man, I got the goods on him, and how he got his ass into trouble a few times. So here's my favor. I just gave you the name of the abortionist, and you can take it from there."

Dugan was beaming. That was the game. Throw out some stuff, and see how the cops respond to it. Sonntag smiled.

"I've got one for you," Sonntag said. "Space aliens in flying saucers started that place out on Bluemound, so they can get genetic material and turn themselves into earth-walkers."

"May I quote you?"

"Go right ahead, Dugan."

"Why don't you arrest Needham?"

"He interested us for a while."

"But not now. I guess you're saying you've got your cyclops eye on someone else."

"We do, and we expect to wind things up pretty quickly."

"You've got a line on who did some surgery on Sandy Millbank?"

"I didn't say that. I'm saying we're going to bust up an abortion mill—and you'll discover it had a few other operations going too."

"So that's my other question. The Seconal Suicides, as we're calling them now. How many? Who'd delivering the pills?"

"We're closing in on that too."

"That guy at Wisconsin Pharmaceutical Supply says there's a couple of big-time buyers of Seconal, hundred milligram. The Wood Veterans Home, and Burleigh Rest Home. You want to fill me in on that?"

"Nope."

"So what's this big deal about the Sandy Millbank Movement?"

"Some women believe she's a martyr to laws that are unbearable for women."

"That ain't gonna float in Lutheran and Catholic Milwaukee."

"I guess you're right, and you're going to have trouble writing a story that the paper will publish."

Dugan grinned. "Hey, I hear the guy who's got all the goods is Doctor Stoppl, the pathologist. I called him a few times, and he's not talking, which means he's got something hot for you. What's he telling you?"

Sonntag debated it a little, and took a flyer. "He's saying that Sandy Millbank never had an abortion."

Dugan whistled. "Goddammit, Sonntag, quit playing games. She died of a hemorrhage, and that's on the coroner's report."

"She probably died of a complicated series of events, all of them operating on a hereditary disease in a peculiar way."

"Hey, Lieutenant, are you full of it?"

"I'm glad you phrased that as a question, Dugan."

"How'm I supposed to print that?" Dugan asked.

"Just wear a smile and a Jantzen, Dugan."

"Hey, Sonntag, I'll drive you to the other side of the Wells Streetcar Viaduct, and you can catch it the rest of the way home without the usual sweat."

"I have no secrets," Sonntag said.

"The hell you don't," Dugan said. "I'll see if I can get any of this past my editors."

Chapter Thirty-Three

Sonntag knew from the crackle that the call was long distance. "Lieutenant? This is William Henderson, sir."

Sonntag immediately motioned to Frank Silva, who ran to another phone to get the phone company to do a call trace.

"Yes, sir, what can I do for you?"

"Well, it's like this. I've been thinking about what you said. I mean, I've heard a few things, and maybe that would help you a little. And you said that would give me immunity, right?"

"Ah, not exactly. Mr. Henderson. If you cooperate with us, it would mean that we'd tell the district attorney about it, and he'd recommend clemency to the judge, right?"

"Well, I don't know about that. If I were to drive in from Hartland, just for a little preliminary talk, what would be a good time?"

"Can you get here in an hour, sir?"

"Maybe a couple hours. We could drive in. Just for a talk, right?"

"Or we could come out there, sir. Would you like us to drive out to Hartland?"

"No, but maybe we could meet half way. Maybe we could talk at the Bluemound Road farmhouse."

"Is there a reason?"

"That was our home."

"You want to tell me what we're going to talk about, sir?" Sonntag asked.

"I mostly wanted to talk about Pendergast. He's sort of the leader of a ring, I guess you'd say. He's not like the others. He's all for the money. The others, me and Elvira, we have ideals. But Pendergast, he saw how to get rich on night medicine, that's what it's called, night medicine, the stuff that never happens in daylight."

"Never heard of it, sir. Maybe you could tell me a bit more, if you don't mind running up your long distance tab."

"Well, I do mind. But night medicine's the word for what doctors aren't allowed to do. Me, I came out of the war wounded and hurting all the time, and around me, there are these ruined human beings, just ruined, blind, deaf, lacking limbs, big wounds that won't close or heal, not even fingers to hold a spoon to eat, and some of them wanted just to be freed of it, sir, just to let go, just to end their misery, but the law says no, and medical ethics say no, and so the misery goes on and on, sir, and that's where I come from. It's just how life turned for me. So that's me, but not Pendergast. He's got a mind like an adding machine. He gets capsules for a nickel and can sell them for five dollars apiece. He gets inmates there, and they have GI life insurance, and he gets it all when they die. That's him, not me."

"Yeah, well, it'd be good if you came on in and talked to us, sir."

"You really need to talk to Elvira," Henderson said. "She's the one with the story."

"Well, it's worth a few nickels of long distance, right?"

"Elvira's the best nurse anywhere. How'd she get that way? When she was in her teens, she was abused. Someone real close did it. She got pregnant. Someone else in her family, a person with a lot of training, got her fixed up. That changed her life. Instead of a life of torment, she was free, and she moved away from where she was, and became a nurse, and learned all she could about women's things, and knew more than doctors knew. She never forgot, and always knew that what's forbidden in most places was what rescued her. We met, and we had things in common, and they were night medicine, medicine by the light of the moon, that's what drew us together. You know what? Desperate women found her and begged for help. Abused women, women with real bad disease who'd been told they couldn't live through another childbirth. Desperate, desperate women, sir, and she never failed. She was so good she got each one through. So that's her story."

"I'm glad you're telling me, sir. I think if you drive in, you can help us."

"A couple hours, all right? I just needed to blab at you a little."

Silva stuck a note in front of Sonntag with the word, Trace? Sonntag nodded.

"You're in Hartland?"

"We'll come in. We don't need to meet at the farmhouse. Look, I gotta go. This is expensive."

The phone clicked dead.

Silva was talking to Wisconsin Telephone. Sonntag put in a call to the sheriff out there, and finally got a dispatcher. "Sonntag, Milwaukee PD here, sir. I need you to get over to Hartland, and see about a car."

He gave an address and a license number, and asked for an immediate report.

Henderson had at least done some tacit confessing. It was not so much a confession as a justification of them both—and a general accusation. Sonntag waited impatiently, and decided to fill the time with notes about Henderson's call. There were two listeners, enough to stand up in court. But the phone company was a long time tracing that call.

When at last Silva got the news, it wasn't good.

"That call didn't come from Hartland. It came from Chicago...from a pay phone in the arcade that runs at street level through the Palmer House on State Street."

"Down in Illinois? Trains west, south, east and north, flights out, interurbans connecting to other cities, good paved roads to California, Louisiana, Florida, New York..."

"All points bulletin?"

"What descriptions?"

"Gorilla has some photos of Henderson."

"Okay, they're close to Union Station, LaSalle Street Station, and the Chicago Northwestern station. Get a description together and have them start with those."

"What charges?"

"Anything that can stick."

It took a while. The sheriff finally phoned in to say the Hendersons' car was still there, the house filled with furniture, lights on in some rooms, but no one visible.

They'd made an adroit exit.

"I'll get a search warrant and have you go in and look around. We're looking for contraband pills, medical equipment, money or securities, pharmacy bottles, any ledgers or records, okay? Someone helped them out of there. Look into that, okay?"

That would take a while, too.

He corralled Frank. "Did Henderson ever talk about relatives?"

"No, and they're both from around here."

"Is there a car ferry out of Chicago, across the lake?"

"I'll find out."

"Have we got a description?"

Silva was grinning. "Five-ten, forties, brown hair, medium build, clean-shaven."

"Jaysas, what about her?"

"Five six or seven, medium light hair, somewhat stocky..."

"Eye color?"

Silva was grinning again.

"Any birthmarks, wounds, scars?"

"Henderson was wounded in the war, he said."

"Any limp?"

Silva shook his head.

It wasn't going to be easy, stopping two nondescript, anonymous people without photo identification, without a prior record, without known relatives outside of Milwaukee.

"Travelers checks?" asked Silva.

"Call the banks on the west side, and out in the Waukesha area. And ask about big bills."

Captain Ackerman materialized out of nowhere. He had a mysterious instinct for showing up at critical moments, as if he had bugs hidden in every desk in the bullpen. "You're too late," he said. "It takes Chicago five to seven hours to put a watch in place if it comes from outside, like here."

"The Hendersons will still be on some train," Sonntag said.

"Flew the coop," Ackerman said. "Start collecting relatives. They'll be in touch with relatives sooner or later." He licked his gummy lips. "How many illegal operations did she do?"

"You heard some of it?" Sonntag asked.

"No, but I've listened to a lot of confessional calls, and I spotted it. That was a confessional one. Henderson was justifying himself, explaining why he broke the law, and why that was good. So he probably included Elvira, too, and you probably were fishing for all you're worth."

"I was. He didn't say. Instead, he claimed she had never done a bad one. Maybe he was saying they had nothing to do with Sandy Millbank."

"No bad one by his standards, anyway. You know what the odds are for back-alley abortions? Thirty percent go bad. A lot of girls die or end up in hospitals. Thirty percent bad. And a lot of those women can never have a baby after that. It's over for them. Their life is changed."

"He said she was better fitted to do it than a doctor. I don't know how she got that way."

"I believe him. She had a lot of practice around here. Every one's a felony. We'll run her into her little cell for the rest of this life and the next two or three."

"We'll catch 'em. They're people with a mission, and those are a lot easier to get than people whose mission is money."

"Henderson's pretty smart."

"They're all pretty smart, and that's why we nail them. Too smart. You heard him recite, and that means they'll go into business somewhere, and soon, and we'll get them when they open shop. They can't quit. Henderson, he's going to help veterans bump themselves off, and she'll get out the instruments and start scraping away. I'll make a bet on it. Here's what you do. You keep an eye on FBI data, and any time there's an abortion case, you inquire, all right?"

Sonntag wanted him out of there. The cigar was ruining the environment, so he just nodded.

Ackerman grinned, knocked ash on Sonntag's battered desk, and wandered off.

Sonntag took a collect call from the Waukesha sheriff, Garth Hoffmeister. "Yeah, Sonntag, we got in pretty fast with a fugitive warrant we got out of district court and looked around. They sure didn't take much with them. Clothes here, furniture, bedding. Lights going. Their car outside. Just sitting there. No keys, either. They got a little printing deal in one room upstairs, right? Hand-printing, silk screen, little hand press, paper cutter, right? That interested one of my deputies, and he poked around in there."

"They used it to print up cards," Sonntag said. "Like, Need Help? In Pain? That's how they got their customers, that and word of mouth. You can't run a business without advertising, and they didn't want to use a print shop. So it was do it yourself."

"Well, yeah, my deputy found some photography stock in a wastebasket, and it had two little rectangles cut out of it, like with one of those hobby knives. So he pulled out his drivers license and it dropped exactly into the holes in that stock, and he's thinking the Hendersons maybe made themselves some new drivers licenses, new names, and he found more stock, like Social Security stock, and more rectangular holes cut into it, and he tried his social security card in the holes, and it was a match, and there's blue and red ink around here, so what we're saying at this end is, they're not Henderson any more, they're brand new babies, born in the last few days, right?"

Sonntag absorbed that bleakly.

"You and your deputy have done some excellent work, sheriff. You have our thanks."

"Well, we're just started here, and before we're done, we'll know what there's to know around Hartland."

"Call me any time, sir, day or night."

"There's always something worthwhile," the sheriff said. "I can tell the kind of people just by seeing what magazines they read."

Ackerman was gumming up his cigar again. "He's a lucky man, Sonntag. He's got a deputy with an IQ over a hundred."

It took a while more before they had enough together to teletype out into the rest of the world. It named the Hendersons, added that they might be traveling under other names and papers, gave some general descriptions, and the reasons they were wanted. Wire-photo of Henderson would follow.

Sonntag watched it go out, sensing that it would sail into an uncaring world, and that he'd probably never see or hear of the Hendersons again.

He collected his black lunch bucket, climbed into his old trench coat, caught the Wells car home, barely aware of the chill of the November day, and dragged himself into his house at dusk, now that the days were shortening fast. He had stories to tell her: how Sandy Millbank probably died. What happened to the abortion suspects.

Lizbeth took one look at him, said nothing, and waited.

"Flew the coop," he said. "Went to Chicago."

"It's not like catching mobsters," she said.

"They killed a lot more babies than mobsters ever did."

"Future babies, yes. But saved a lot of lives, too. You know what? I like the idea of saving mothers, the ones too sick to carry a child."

He nodded. There were women alive in Milwaukee who wouldn't be if they had not taken desperate measures to save their lives because no one would help them do it.

"You want a drink? You want to take me to the Chinese place for chop suey? You want a Greek dinner?"

"How about Mexican?" he asked.

"I'm your enchilada," she said.

Chapter Thirty-Four

Nailing Artie Pendergast wasn't going to be easy. The man op
erated behind layers of staff, and was a public figure, a leading proponent of nursing home innovation. Still, there might be chinks
in the armor. He had made his pile with uncommon speed, and had
recently purchased a lake shore home.

Lieutenant Sonntag collected his two best man, Eddy Walsh
and Frank Silva, for a little planning. They poured some day-old
coffee, scooped some dried up donuts, and hashed it out.

"What have we got? Mostly a lot of unproven suspicions,"
he said. "And it's going to lead to the dullest stuff we do, mostly
digging through records, looking for the telltale item."

"Yeah, whenever someone in the rest home died, a lot of
insurance went into his pockets. And it's hard to make anything
stick," Silva said.

"We've got profiteering from prescription-only drugs—the
big purchases from the wholesaler, and the much smaller use of
them in the rest home. We need to know what went into the
distributers' hands, the Hendersons probably, and where the money
went. Henderson said something about Pendergast getting the
Seconal for a nickel and selling it for five bucks."

"There'd be some middlemen, maybe the Hendersons, getting a cut," Walsh said.

"Okay, we've got the whole induced suicide business, and that's where we have to do some real digging. How many deaths in that place, and was that normal, and how many benefits got turned over to the home, like GI life insurance, social security death benefits, privately held insurance. How did the home become the beneficiary of all these policies? And we still have to prove that suicides were assisted; whether leaving some Seconal lying around for a hurting old person, or a wounded vet, is a felony. We're into tough, shady, and hard to prove turf, I think."

"We're going to need witnesses. We're going to have to interview a lot of the nursing staff, and maybe the housekeeping staff. We need to know how those capsules got placed on bedside tables, an invitation if ever there was one. And maybe some of the nursing staff was in on it, maybe getting a cut to give old people a little push."

"This just gets bigger and bigger," Walsh said.

"And we need to see whether Pendergast's place was tied in any way to Elvira Henderson's abortion mills. There are whole wings in that rest home and convalescent center that catered to younger people. It wasn't all old folks."

"So how do we do this?" Walsh asked.

"We'll each specialize. Eddy, you like to talk to people, and you sure have a way of disarming them, so I'm putting you onto the staff there. You're looking for evidence of assisted suicide, abuse of prescriptions, bonuses or payoffs that Pendergast might be sliding to some of them, odd stories about sudden death, whether death certificates were properly issued, whether there were autopsies—you get the idea.

"Frank, I'll put you on the money end of things, and that includes the whole drug distribution end of it. Like, what shows up in the nursing home records, and whether it stacks up with services. Where do government death benefits come in?"

"Am I an accountant? Shouldn't we get a good accounting firm? Am I gonna see what a good CPA's gonna see?"

Sonntag saw the reality of it. "We'll need some help. But

before we bring in the accountants, I'd like you to look at the files for each death, especially GIs, over the past year or so. Let's get a warrant, we have probable cause, and dig in."

"If Pendergast's a socialist, I'll be mad at him," Frank said.

They drove out to 60th Street that afternoon, after obtaining the papers. The modern, clean, utilitarian Burleigh center spread its wings in three directions, with the administration in the core area where they joined. It looked to be a model of postwar simplicity. Sonntag wondered why he hated the place, and sensed that it was not built for the comfort of its residents. It was as if the architects had set up their own criteria: how small can we make the rooms? How can we improve efficiency? How can we eliminate things that wear out, like carpets? How can we heat it cheaply? How small can we make the windows? How can we reduce staff?

They headed into the central complex, asked to see Pendergast, and finally were ushered into his office, as modern as the rest, with Scandinavian-style furnishings.

"Well, we're pleased to see you," the man said. "We welcome the opportunity to show Milwaukee's finest how we operate. In fact, this is our window on the world. I'll invite the press to come in, and I'll tell my people to cooperate with you in every respect. Now, the files are scattered. The medical files are in the Wellness Center; administrative files right here, and if there's anything I can steer you toward, or any questions you want me to answer, I'll be right here.. I'm not quite sure why you're here, but if you'll give me some idea, maybe I can be of further assistance."

He sure looked confident, standing behind his modern desk, his suit coat off, the desk naked except for a shiny black phone.

"We're looking for some problems with the prescriptions," Sonntag said.

"Oh, that's state and federal law, my friends. That's not really the province of the Milwaukee police, but have a look. You'd need a real task force to work through it. We handle hundreds of prescriptions every day, and order large quantities weekly."

"Well, yes, but we'll have a look," Sonntag said. "I'm going to put Detective Silva on those, and Detective Walsh here'd like to visit a little with your staff, and I'm going to have a look at how this is administered. What I want, sir, is the closed files. The ones in which a patient has died, been buried, and the accounts are closed."

Now, at last, a tiny flicker caught in Pendergast's face. His welcoming seemed to freeze on his face. "We'll cooperate as much as possible, sir. Those patient files are really over in the Wellness Center. That's where you'll see the medical records."

"Not medical records, sir. The arrangements."

"Well, you're dealing in confidential matters between the families of the deceased and the center, sir. But I can show you a sample or two, so you see how it's done. Usually, the departed is in deep debt to the center, and the center has a lien against his assets, which sometimes are insurance, sometimes death benefits, such as Social Security, or sometimes assets in the hands of his family. And of course we are owed for the treatment we've provided for weeks and months and years, payment for which has been deferred. So, that's what usually happens, and I'd be entirely pleased to show you how this proceeds. In fact, we have a fellow, died this morning, a World War One vet, and it looks like we may not recover what we've expended. They didn't have any benefits to speak of, so it's probably going to be a loss for us."

"What did he die of, sir?"

"Well, I wouldn't know. He was in his sixties. He was brought to us a few months ago. Poor fellow was in a lot of pain, you know. We pride ourselves on helping those who suffer."

"We'll want an autopsy."

"Autopsy? But the family—"

"We're going to have one," Sonntag said. "I want his name, and where the remains are, and we'll send for personnel."

"This is a scandal, invading the privacy of a veteran and his family."

"We'll want the records. What's his name?"

"I'm not sure. I'll of course find out."

"You're not sure of his name but you're saying this place may not recover what it expended? And you say he had no benefits?"

"I couldn't pull up the name, off hand, gents. Why, we'll have these files for you promptly." He headed for the receptionist. "Walter Miller, the files, please."

"Oh, sir, they're gone," she said. "The accountants have them."

He turned to Sonntag. "There, you see? We'll get them back shortly, after everything's totted up."

"What's the accounting firm? And why isn't that being done here" Why outside accountants? You mind if I inquire at your accounting office?"

"That's highly unusual, officer."

"I think we will," Sonntag said. "Eddy, would you phone the coroner? We want an autopsy at once. Frank, would you find the accounting office here and see what's available on Miller?"

"I certainly wish to cooperate in any legitimate inquiry, but you seem to be pursuing some thing here that smacks of abuse, sirs, and you're forcing me to defend our company. Now, please show me by what authority you're here, and why you're suddenly interested in an old veteran. And if you have purposes hidden from me, sirs, place your cards on the table. I will not tolerate an abusive fishing expedition."

"What's the name of your outside accounting firm, Mr. Pendergast?"

"Well, we have two, one for the Burleigh Foundation, which is entirely separate from the Burleigh Rest Home Corporation."

"And where's the deceased?"

"Arrangements are being made by...I'll have to check."

It went round and round, and not until late in the afternoon did Sonntag manage to have Walter Miller's remains removed to the morgue. But even then it was too late for some aspects of the autopsy, because Smithson and Smithson Mortuary had begun to embalm the body. But the examining doctor would find out what he could, which wouldn't be much.

As for the rest, the files dealing with Mr. Miller's health and prescriptions, and his financial agreement with the rest home, were not to be found. Sonntag, Walsh and Silva spent the entire afternoon trying to find out how things were done. They hadn't even begun to examine the medical and financial records of those who had died there. They spent their time trying to figure out where medical records were, why prescriptions were in some other place, why the rest home's finances were broken into several accounts, why the payroll accounts were done outside the center, and why there was no single file for each patient or resident in the center.

At quitting time, they clambered into the black sedan and headed downtown, a sense not so much of defeat as of dread pervading them. This was the Gordian knot of all knots, and if anything was clear, the gifted and slippery Art Pendergast had devised it that way, knowing that layer upon layer, obstacle upon obstacle, stood between himself and any investigator who might probe the place.

But that wasn't the worst of it. When they walked into the bullpen, there was Captain Ackerman, looking amused. That was a bad sign. When he looked amused, there was grave trouble for the police.

"Yeah," he said, "we've been hearing from the mayor. Did you know that your pal Artie Pendergast is a pal of Mayor Horvath? Not only that, but Mayor Horvath has officially declared a special Day of Appreciation next Friday, in which the honorable mayor's gonna hand out a Mayor's Roll of Honor Award, at a luncheon at the Pfister, and will proclaim your boy the Milwaukee Citizen of the Year for outstanding and innovative progress in the field of convalescent and senior care. How's that for big apples?"

Sonntag stared. Silva stared. Walsh grinned.

"There's gonna be big coverage in both papers and on radio. There's gonna be a dinner that evening hosted by the mayor," Ackerman continued, relentlessly.

"So?" asked Sonntag.

"So I'm not saying to shut things down, and the mayor didn't say we should put the lid on, and his office didn't threaten us with budget cuts or review, and no one has said that Artie shouldn't be looked at, and I'm not telling you to quit, and you're not entitled to think that I'm telling you to quit, and the press shouldn't assume that Mayor Horvath's friendship with Artie Pendergast has anything to do with the police department's decision to set aside the investigation into pill-running and assorted crimes, because that is obviously untrue, and the department has never said that it is influenced in the slightest by the administration of this or any other mayor, now or in the past or in the future."

Ackerman was just smiling like that, just smiling away, just mouthing one of his dogturd cigars, even as Lieutenant Sonntag nodded.

That's how it was, some times. Sonntag knew that he was going to nail Artie Pendergast. Maybe not today or tomorrow, but the next day. He would keep an eye on that rest home, and every dead person issuing from that rest home, and one of these days he'd get in an autopsy before the Pendergast machine got the old veteran buried and forgotten, and then it would all come out, but little by little because it was all so complicated. To hell with Mayor Horvath. Let the man elevate his pal Pendergast to Milwaukee Citizen of the Year. The following year, Art Pendergast would be wearing stripes and pounding rock as Waupun's citizen of the year.

"Enjoy the evening, captain," he said.

"They've invited me to the ceremony and the dinner that night," Ackerman said.

"You'll have a fine old time."

"If I don't resign first," Captain Ackerman said.

"For me, it's unfinished business," Sonntag said.

"Nah, we'll do a Capone."

"A Capone?"

"If we can't touch him, the feds can. We'll call in the Treasury men. They got Al Capone on tax evasion."

"What's their number?" Sonntag asked.

>> | <<

About the Author

Axel Brand is the foremost practitioner of eye-level fiction. He is the pseudonym of a novelist whose surname comes at the end of the alphabet (who grew up in Milwaukee), and whose books are displayed where almost no one sees or buys them—at toe level. So Axel Brand was born to meet the eye and be first in line at the upper left in any bookstore or library shelf. He is happy there and does not plan to relinquish his catbird seat to anyone.

Visit his website, AxelBrand.blogspot.com, and contact him at BrandMysteries@gmail.com

Made in the USA
Charleston, SC
20 September 2015